Cast o

Phyllis La Fond. A vivacious bl   d admits she'd do almost anything to mak

Ralph O. Tate. A Hollywood director who's shooting a movie on Catalina.

Tony Morgan and George Weir. Mr. Tate's young assistants.

T. Girard Tompkins. A distributor of Catalina pottery, made on the island.

Thorwald Narveson. A Norwegian whaling ship captain.

Marvin and Kay Deving. Newlyweds honeymooning in Catalina.

Lewis French and Chick Madden. Pilots of the *Dragonfly,* a flying boat.

Miss Hildegarde Withers. An angular, inquisitive schoolteacher with a talent for detecting.

Amos Britt. The jovial chief of police on Catalina Island.

Ruggles. His octogenarian assistant.

Dr. James Michael O'Rourke. The island's no-nonsense doctor.

Olive Smith. His pretty, capable nurse.

Roswell T. Forrest. There's a $15,000 price tag on his head.

Barney Kelsey. Forrest's bodyguard.

Roscoe. The hotel's elderly bellhop.

Rogers. The hotel handyman.

Dan Higgins. A night watchman.

Mister Jones. A black and white wirehaired terrier.

Harry L. Hellen. A very determined process server.

Patrick Mack. A self-described businessman from Bayonne, New Jersey.

Inspector Oscar Piper. A New York City police detective and longtime friend of Hildy's.

Books by Stuart Palmer

Novels featuring Hildegarde Withers:
The Penguin Pool Murder (1931)*
Murder on Wheels (1932)
Murder on the Blackboard (1932)
The Puzzle of the Pepper Tree (1933)*
The Puzzle of the Silver Persian (1934)
The Puzzle of the Red Stallion (1936)
The Puzzle of the Blue Banderilla (1937)*
The Puzzle of the Happy Hooligan (1941)
Miss Withers Regrets (1947)*
Four Lost Ladies (1949)
The Green Ace (1950)
Nipped in the Bud (1951)*
Cold Poison (1954)
Hildegarde Withers Makes the Scene (1969)
(completed by Fletcher Flora)

*Reprinted by The Rue Morgue Press

Short story collections featuring Hildegarde Withers:
The Riddles of Hildegarde Withers (1947)
The Monkey Murder (1950)
People Vs. Withers and Malone (1963)
(with Craig Rice)
Hildegarde Withers: Uncollected Riddles (2003)

Howie Rook mysteries:
Unhappy Hooligan (1956)
Rook Takes Knight (1968)

Other mystery novels:
Ace of Jades (1931)
Omit Flowers (1937)
Before It's Too Late (1950)
(as by Jay Stewart)

Sherlock Holmes pastiches:
The Adventure of the Marked Man and One Other

The Puzzle
of the Pepper Tree

A Miss Withers Mystery
by Stuart Palmer

The Rue Morgue Press
Lyons / Boulder

The Puzzle of the Pepper Tree

Copyright © 1933, 1971

New Material Copyright © 2008 by The Rue Morgue Press

ISBN: 978-1-60187-030-8

Rue Morgue Press

87 Lone Tree Lane

Lyons CO 80540

Printed by Johnson Printing

Boulder, Colorado

Restoration work on the original
dust jacket art by
Mark Terry of
Facsimile Dustjackets
www.facsimiledustjackets.com

PRINTED IN THE UNITED STATES OF AMERICA

About Stuart Palmer

Stuart Palmer (1905-1968) referred to Hildegarde Withers as that "meddlesome old battleaxe" but he was as fond of her as were the readers and moviegoers of the 1930s. She debuted in 1931 in *The Penguin Pool Murder*, where she met Inspector Oscar Piper of the New York Homicide Squad. Set in 1929 shortly after the collapse of the stock market, *The Penguin Pool Murder* was filmed a year later with Edna May Oliver as Miss Withers and James Gleason as Oscar Piper. The lighthearted movie became one RKO's biggest hits of the year. Oliver was perfect in the role, perhaps because Palmer was inspired to create Miss Withers after seeing Oliver on stage during the first run of Jerome Kern's *Showboat*, although he also used other people from his past to round off her character. They included a librarian from his home town of Baraboo, Wisconsin, who disapproved of his literary tastes, and a "horse-faced English teacher" from his high school days. He credited his father as the inspiration for Miss Withers' Yankee sense of humor.

Miss Withers appeared in eight novels between 1931 and 1941 and then went on sabbatical for six years while her creator labored in Hollywood, where he eventually wrote 37 scripts, including several in the Falcon and Bulldog Drummond series. In 1944 at nearly the age of 40 he enlisted in the army and was sent to Oklahoma, where he produced training films on field artillery. In 1947, Palmer revisited Miss Withers in *Miss Withers Regrets* and went on to produce four more books in the series during the early 1950s. The last Withers novel, *Hildegarde Withers Makes the Scene*, was completed by Fletcher Flora after Palmer's death in 1968. Jennifer Venola, Palmer's fifth wife, whom he married when he was 60 and she just 21, called his death a "rational suicide" following a diagnosis of terminal laryngeal cancer. At his wish, his body was donated to the Loma Linda Medical School for study.

For more information on Stuart Palmer see Tom and Enid Schantz' introduction to The Rue Morgue Press edition of *The Puzzle of the Blue Banderilla*.

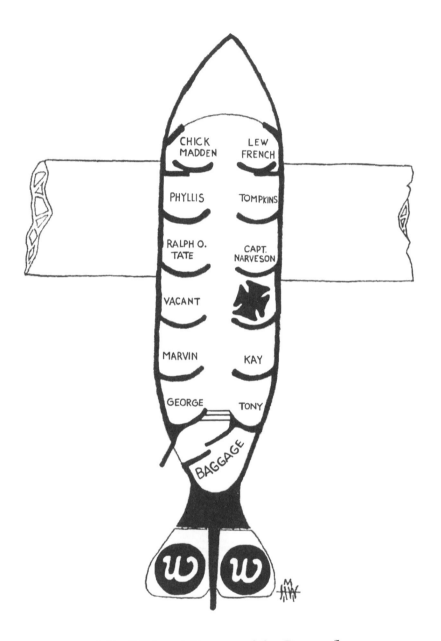

Miss Withers' diagram of the *Dragonfly*

CHAPTER I

THAT morning saw the mighty Pacific, in the guise of a chill and luminous fog, sweep in upon the arid valley of Los Angeles. It drifted up the slope of cactus-clad hills, obscuring alike the clean, serrated ridge of the northern mountains and the nearer gaunt skeletons of the oil derricks, and left only a greasy black ribbon of highway down which a Ford roadster flung itself headlong into the mist.

The lone driver shivered as the fog seeped through his light sport jacket. His plumply handsome face, over-soft from frequent massage, was gray with cold.

He glanced at a white-gold strap watch on his wrist and saw that it indicated fourteen minutes before ten. That left him plenty of time, unless somewhere he had taken the wrong turning.

No—he was all right. He jammed on the brakes as the mists ahead of him lifted a little to disclose the outlines of a mammoth excursion steamer, bearing at masthead and stack a blue flag with a large white "W" in its center.

The man in the cocoa-colored sport outfit knew this apparition almost at once for what it was—a tall billboard standing dead ahead at a V in the road. Above the exceedingly lifelike painting of the white excursion steamer stood forth a legend in scarlet—"Catalina Terminal—one-quarter mile—turn right," and beneath it was the assurance, "In All the World No Trip Like This!"

With a screech of tires on wet pavement the little roadster swung to the right and was immediately swallowed up in the mist.

Ten minutes later the man in brown scrambled out of his car to stand a little foolishly upon a barren and deserted wharf. For the second time that morning he was seeing the outlines of a gay white excursion steamer through a curtain of fog.

On masthead and stack were the familiar blue flags with the big white "W"—but this time a wisp of steam followed by a tantalizing farewell blast from her siren assured him that here was no billboard, but the pleasure steamer *Avalon* herself, departing without him.

For some reason never explained satisfactorily by science, there is nothing more thoroughly ludicrous than the sight of a man missing a train or a boat, except, perhaps, a man losing his hat.

As if determined to afford his audience—limited as it was to idlers and a few longshoremen—the highest possible gratification, the man in the brown sport outfit whipped off his modish straw and deposited it before him on the dock, where he proceeded to leap upon it with both heels. His lips moved, as if in silent prayer.

A young man in blue coveralls detached himself from a sheltered spot in the lee of a cluster of piles and approached briskly.

"Park your car, mister? All day for fifty cents."

The stranger removed his tan suede shoes from the wreckage of his hat, rammed both fists into the pockets of his razor-edged trousers of pinstriped creamy flannel, and finally found words.

He wanted to know what kind of a so-and-so steamship company this was to send out its so-and-so ships ahead of schedule. With unnecessary unction he displayed his watch, which still hovered a little before the hour of ten.

The man in the blue coveralls grinned widely. Then he raised his eyes to the big clock which was visible over the open doors of the garage end of the terminal. Here the time was represented as fourteen minutes past the hour.

"You're not the only one to miss this boat," he confided. "Lots of them get on the wrong boulevard coming down from L.A. or else set their watches by those screwy time signals that come over the radio."

"I haven't needed to set this watch since—in the last month," insisted the man in brown. He pronounced it "wartch."

He went on, his voice rising. "I'd like you to tell me why I should pay you to park my car *now!*" he demanded. "I ain't going anywhere."

"You can still hop on the *Dragonfly,*" he was told. A greasy thumb was extended toward the wharf at the right, where for the first time since his arrival the man in brown noticed a thick-winged flying boat rocking lazily at the foot of a slip.

"They always hold back a few minutes so as to pick up them as miss the boat," went on the garage helper. "It's only three-fifty fare—and you'll be on the island two hours before the *Avalon.*"

The man in brown looked down at the varnished newness of the red-and-gilt Douglass amphibian without visible enthusiasm. He shook his head. "You don't get me on one of those box kites again," he decided. "I'll wait for the next boat—when is it?"

"Same as always, ten o'clock." The man in the blue coveralls reached tentatively toward the handle of the car door.

"What? No boat till tonight?"

"Ten tomorrow morning," he was laconically corrected. "Plane's your only chance. Here's your parking ticket."

The Ford rolled smoothly in through the gaping doors of the Terminal Garage, while he who had driven it here pocketed his parking slip mechanically. Down beside the waiting cabin plane a young man in a white uniform surveyed him speculatively and swung a pair of goggles. Out in the harbor the mist was beginning to give way before the sea wind and the sun. There the man in brown saw the steamer, three decks loaded with pleasure-bent humanity, as she derisively swung toward him her high fat buttocks.

Be it marked down upon the Everlasting Record that at this crucial moment the belated traveler was seen to hesitate. Whether it was the sound of merry laughter mingled with dance music which drifted back from the departing *S.S. Avalon* or the crisp "All aboard!" from the pilot in the white uniform which impelled him to take the leap, no one will ever be able to say with authority. At any rate, the man in brown quietly and fervently kicked the remains of his straw hat off the dock and then hurried down the steep-slanting gangplank onto the slip.

Here he paused before a miniature ticket office and information booth, manned at the moment by a white-clad duplicate of the first pilot. This young man was somewhat officiously making entries in a ledger. His name, as attested by an "on duty" card beside him, was Lewis French, and the silver wings on his lapel had not yet dulled.

"It won't be rough up there, will it?" the would-be passenger wanted to know, as he put down a five-dollar bill and waited for change. "I was sick as a dog coming out on the Transcontinental."

"Fog's clearing," French told him. "Air hadn't ought to be rough. Anyway, the trip takes less than twenty minutes. We'll have you in Avalon before you have time to be sick." He proffered an official release-from-damages form. "Sign this, please."

With practiced fingers he tore off the stub bearing the illegible scrawl of a signature and put it with a sheaf of others in the tin cash box beside him. The rest of the ticket, together with a small envelope containing two wads of ear-cotton and three pellets of sugarcoated chewing gum, he handed to the man in brown.

"You can tickle her, Chick!" he called toward the plane. The pilot with the goggles waved his hand and popped through a narrow door near the tail fins.

French closed and locked the little office, handed up the cash box to an office boy who appeared suddenly behind the piling of the wharf, and then herded the last passenger across the slip and into the gently rocking plane. They stooped to pass through the door, though the man in brown was not by any means tall.

On their right was a cubicle for baggage, now well filled with overnight bags, cameras, and various impedimenta. From one of the cases, through a wire window, there sounded an appealing whine as they passed down three steps into the cabin itself.

Here were ten deeply upholstered seats of blue leather, five on each side, with only the narrowest of aisle between. Eight of the seats were filled. There was a strong smell of leather, burned gasoline, and gardenia scent, for the heavy plate-glass windows were hermetically sealed, and the pilot French had already slammed and made fast the single door behind him.

The man in brown made a quick survey of the situation in which he found himself. There were only two girls aboard the plane. The blonde in plaid, who was responsible for the scent of gardenia, interested him most. But she was sitting in the front seat on the left, with a bored, baldish man in riding breeches close behind her, and a dull, middle-aged person lurking behind a paunch and an elk's tooth across the aisle. She would, he decided, have to come under the head of "unfinished business."

With the decisiveness of an old campaigner, the man in brown chose the third seat from the front on the right, placing himself thus directly in front of the girl with the red curls. The usual pair of dark sun glasses obscured her eyes, but her mouth was pleasantly tinted in an orange that matched her hair and contrasted well with the blue of her corduroy trousers. The seat across the aisle was likewise vacant, but since it would only have placed him between the riding breeches and the slick young man with whom the redhead was sharing a package of chewing gum, he never considered it for a moment.

It was not that his intentions were dishonorable, or even that he had any intentions, but just that, as he had often remarked philosophically, "You never can tell what'll happen." In this case he was quite right.

Pilot French made his way up the aisle, greeted a paunchy person in a front seat with, "Morning, Mr. Tompkins," and paused in the doorway of the control room where the young man he had called "Chick" was already tickling the motor.

"All right, folks," he said cheerily, his eyes paying a passing compliment to the blonde in the front seat. "In four minutes we'll be looking down on Uncle Sam's Fleet. And—you know what the paper containers are for."

Phyllis La Fond moved her slim hips to a more comfortable position in the blue leather seat and arranged the skirt of her plaid suit so that her crossed ankles got the ace display position in the aisle to which nature and her last pair of four-dollar stockings entitled them.

She magnificently failed to notice the flare of interest in the handsome, bronzed face of Lew French, for all the glory of his new white uniform with the crossed wings. Phyllis had outgrown uniforms these many moons. Now she gave herself to a survey of her fellow passengers, her wide gray-green eyes staring insolently, lazily, beneath their heavy lashes.

There was something of the grace of a hunting panther in the poise of her body, something feline, mysterious, and beautifully sinister. What was in her mind we shall not inquire. It is enough to say that her worldly goods and chattels consisted at the moment of a five-dollar bill, a gold vanity case, a suitcase full of dresses and underwear, and a small black and white terrier.

She was intensely aware of the bored man in riding breeches and a turtleneck sweater immediately behind her, but she wasted no time on him. Across the aisle was Tompkins, the middle-aged, paunchy personage with the elk's tooth. His hands were overmanicured, and his face a little spotty and choleric, but Phyllis mentally rated him eighty-five and passed on. Behind him was a massive man with so many freckles that they even dotted forehead and ears. His eyes, which were a bright innocent China blue, were fixed on some notations on the back of an envelope. Now and again he added painfully a few more figures. He looked prosperous, in spite of his well-worn suit of dark blue serge, but all the same Phyllis only gave him a seventy.

Behind Freckles was the newcomer for whom they had all been kept waiting—the man in the brown symphony of color. He was at the moment busily engaged in strapping himself in his seat, and Phyllis in spite of herself smiled widely. He saw her, realized that he was the only one in the plane to take this precaution, and looked vaguely uncomfortable.

"Damn," said Phyllis to herself. "I've done it again—and he's the best bet on this plane."

His rating would be in the nineties, certainly, for there was an aroma of the easy spender about him, an air of good living. Any man who takes the trouble to match handkerchief to socks, and tie to suit, is apt to interest himself in the other niceties of life, Phyllis had discovered.

Behind him was the redhead in the corduroy trousers. Phyllis never gave her a glance, except to note that at least the girl had sense enough not to use scarlet rouge with that shade of henna.

In the two rear seats of the plane were two young men in turtleneck sweaters and flannel trousers, at the moment busily matching dimes. In ordinary times Phyllis would have rated them at around seventy-five, but since she knew that they were satellites of the man who sat behind her, she gave them an even ninety apiece.

An absolute zero was chalked up for the slick youngster who was leaning across the aisle to talk to the girl in the corduroys. Phyllis had no time for petty larceny, and the redhead had quite evidently taken up her option on him.

That left an even hundred percent for the bored man behind her, but Phyllis wasted no ammunition on him this early in the game.

Slowly Chick swung the stick hard over, and the red-and-gilt flying boat slid away from its mooring. They taxied easily along the water-way, past barges and anchored windjammers, slowly picking up speed. Then the *Dragonfly* swung sharply to port, and the roar of the twin motors became a scream in Phyllis's ears.

A wall of white water rose against the windows on either side, shut-ting out the busy harbor world and leaving only these eleven human beings in the darkened box which they optimistically hoped would take them aloft and down again. The *Dragonfly* was skimming the surface like a flung pebble now. Her tail wagged like a salmon's attempting to leap the falls. Once she rose in the air, only to fall back with a sickening crash on the crest of the next roller.

The pilot cut his motor down and turned to murmur something un-mentionable to French. "Air's goofy again today," he added.

The white wall of water fell momentarily away from the windows and then rose again higher than ever as the motors screamed their loud-est. The tail wagged, and Chick rammed the stick into his chest.

"Climb, you damn mud scow!" he implored.

The damn mud scow climbed, skimming above the smooth surface of the next roller and slanting up steeply as the offshore wind lifted beneath her wings. All sense of motion was gone, and the harbor seemed to be lazily pushing its way past beneath them.

"Passing over the battleship *Texas,*" French called back into the cabin. The man in brown had his nose pressed against the window. Phyllis, who had no interest in battleships or sailors, seized the opportunity to touch up her lips.

Three hundred feet beneath them a stone-gray battleship rocked at anchor, her decks crawling with busy blue-jackets. One moment all was serene and calm, and then—

Suddenly the battleship *Texas,* together with the blue-jackets on her decks and the motor tenders lined alongside to transport them to the delights of the San Pedro waterfront, all leaped madly toward the plane for a delirious moment, and then fell away to one side with difficulty.

Blonde hair tumbled across Phyllis's eyes, and the lipstick pencil drew a crimson gash across her face. The man with the freckled ears dropped his envelope and forgot that he had ever had it, while the girl in the blue corduroy trousers let out a shrill yip and clutched wildly at the shoulders of the cocoa-colored sport jacket in front of her.

As was the obvious duty of the copilot, Lewis French turned with a somewhat mechanical smile. "Just an air pocket," he began to recite glibly. "Caused by running through a column of cool and descending air."

He swallowed the last of his sentence as the plane suddenly bucked her tail high in the air and regained in one fell swoop all the altitude that she had lost.

From that moment the nine passengers on board the *Dragonfly* lost all traces of dignity, even of individuality. They were peas, shaken in the same pod. Most of them were too busy affixing around themselves the straps that they had scorned, to notice the white steamer *Avalon,* bound to the city of the same name, when she tooted in salute beneath them as they rocketed past.

"Bumpier every damn trip," complained French.

Chick showed a mouthful of strong white teeth. Five years with the air mail had burned the seriousness from his hot brown eyes. "It'll all be nice and smooth when we get Technocracy," he promised. "They say—"

Whatever it was that they said was forgotten as he braced both feet against the kicking rudder in an effort to keep the *Dragonfly* from going completely crazy. The floor beneath their feet fell away and then rose shudderingly, fitfully swaying from side to side.

The nine passengers in the cabin likewise swayed from side to side, much to their discomfort. Ships plying the sky are capable of inducing in their passengers a *mal de ciel* as much more intense than ordinary seasickness as their speed is greater than that of vessels briny-bound. The *Dragonfly* was making nearly two hundred miles an hour.

Queasiness gripped Phyllis immediately beneath the silver buckle of her plaid jacket, even as it gripped each of the nine. But none of them was hit harder than the man in the brown sport outfit. He began to moan softly, in abject wretchedness.

Jarred out of their shells, the others began to forget their own lesser misery in the sight of his. Phyllis, with the resiliency of her sex, recovered first. From the cellophane bag which had accompanied her ticket she proffered a last remaining pellet of sugarcoated mint.

"Hold everything," she called, above the din of the motors. "Chew this and see if it helps."

The man in brown shook his head. He was already chewing gum, his jaws moving mechanically. Drops of sweat were beginning to break out on his forehead.

Phyllis replaced the gum in her handbag and surveyed the sufferer with a sympathetic but critical eye. She was a good judge of types, and she noted instantly the circles beneath his slightly bloodshot eyes, the liver-like tone of his overmassaged skin.

But she hadn't given up playing Good Samaritan yet. "Always hits you worst when you've got a hangover, doesn't it?" she observed conversationally to the bored man behind her. He had swung his round, baldish head above the rolled wool of his high-necked sweater to stare with her at the man across the aisle.

The man with the freckled ears likewise had turned, and showed a face mildly apprehensive. He could have been any age from forty to seventy, Phyllis thought, and she noted again the childish blue of his eyes.

He spoke over his shoulder, which he had swung as far forward out of range as was possible, and admonished the man in brown.

"If yu going to be sick, yust use the container." His deep Scandinavian bass was kind, yet it held an accustomed note of command.

The man in brown uttered another moan. Phyllis turned suddenly and addressed the man behind her.

"How about it, Mr. Tate? What he needs is a *hair of the dog* ... " The plane made another series of breathtaking dips, and when it was on an even keel again, the man she had addressed nodded.

He felt no surprise that this personable young lady with the bright hair happened to know who he was. There was not a blonde in Hollywood who did not know Ralph O. Tate, Paradox Pictures director, by name and by sight—and if there had been a brunette in Hollywood, she too would have known him.

Tate pulled from the hip pocket of his white riding breeches a gleaming silver flask and fumbled for a moment with its complicated cap and mouthpiece. Then he leaned back across the aisle, proffering it to the sufferer in brown.

It was eagerly accepted. Tate held it to the other's mouth for as long as one might have counted ten, and then took a long pull at it himself.

Phyllis eyed him hopefully, but Ralph O. Tate was used to being eyed hopefully by blondes. He reached to replace it in his pocket.

A hail came from the rear seats, where the two young men, likewise in turtleneck sweaters, had recently been matching dimes. They held out beseeching hands.

"How about it, chief?"

Tate glared back at them. "You know my rule," he barked. "No assistant of mine does any drinking on location."

The flask disappeared, and the *Dragonfly* fluttered on through a gusty sky scorned even by self-respecting sea gulls. In spite of all her bouncing, the twin motors on either wing never missed a beat. Steadily the fog-mantled coast line grew smaller behind them, and as steadily a gray-green mountain rose out of the sea far ahead. They were alone above a dappled ocean with only a grotesque and wide-winged shadow dancing across the waves to keep them company.

Phyllis rested her chin on the back of her seat and turned both of her gray-green eyes full on Mr. Ralph O. Tate. Even if she had missed on sharing a drink with him, she had succeeded in breaking the ice, and she was resolved not to let it close over again.

"Oh, Mr. Tate," she broke in upon his reverie in a voice a little desperately bright and pleasant—"Oh, Mr. Tate, it seems to be getting quieter now, don't you think?"

"It *was!*" Tate grunted inhospitably.

Phyllis blinked at that one, but before she had decided upon which retort *not* to voice, there sounded another plaintive wail from behind them.

The man in the brown sport outfit croaked something, in a voice half-way between a choke and a gasp. All of the well-fed, massaged plumpness had been drained from his face, leaving only wide-open eyes and mouth. Whatever temporary respite he had gained through a gulp of Tate's liquor was gone, and in spite of the fact that the plane had subsided to a gentle rocking, he fought to rise against his straps.

"I'm dying!" he gasped. Above the roar of the twin motors his voice came clear and frightened. "I'm dying—I don't want to die!"

The other passengers were all turning toward him again, feeling the real chill of the panic which possessed him. Fear can be as contagious as smallpox, and it moves more quickly.

"I'm dying—get me down!"

There is an ironclad rule on every airline that in cases of real or imagined danger the spare pilot takes a seat with the passengers, to reassure them with his own calm acceptance of whatever the situation may be. French didn't need to have Chick motion him back into the cabin before this whining nuisance got the women hysterical.

He brushed past Phyllis and dropped into the vacant seat. Leaning across the aisle, he placed his hand on the shoulder of the man who thought he was dying.

"You're all right," said French cheerily. "Just quiet down now. Why, I've been flying ten years, and never died yet."

The other passengers were smiling now, all tension gone. The frightened man murmured something, lost in the roar of the motors.

"We're coming up to the landing," French assured him. "Have you down in a jiffy, and you'll forget that we struck this bumpy air. Just lean back and relax."

The other leaned back, but he did not relax. He still seemed to have something to say. French drowned him out with good-natured reassurances.

"Want the container? No? Chew some gum, it helps."

The man in brown was already chewing gum. His hands moved waveringly toward his face and then dropped to the arms of the leather seat. Phyllis saw that his lips and mouth were almost white. But he was quiet now, staring at the freckled ears of the man in front of him.

"It won't be long now," French told him comfortingly.

The plane coasted down on so sharp an angle that Phyllis felt her vanity case slide from her lap. Suddenly the starboard windows showed that they were dropping along the steep slope of a bright green mountain. As if to make up for her bronco-like antics in the air, the *Dragonfly* came to rest on the water in the lee of the cliff softly as a tired sea gull.

A little ahead of them Phyllis saw a half-moon of beach, bisected by a concrete runway that led up to a cheerful little yellow building, bright with colored tiles and landscaped gardens. Beyond the gardens waited an open bus, a bright red bus with a sprinkling of brightly dressed people aboard.

Even the green-blue water through which the *Dragonfly* nosed her way was several shades more brilliant than other water, and the fish which darted away on either side were a bright yellow gold in color.

French brushed past Phyllis again and knelt to spin the crank which dropped two gray rubber doughnuts of landing gear. With a precision that was beautiful to watch, Chick rolled the dripping amphibian up the runway and out upon a concrete turntable. He roared the motors once and then cut them dead.

French ran swiftly back along the aisle and unlocked the door in the rear. Then he looked at his watch.

"Sixteen minutes running time," he announced. "One at a time please, going out."

Obediently the passengers filed out, singly. Forgotten was their common discomfort, their common sympathy and terror. French, standing on the cement, helped them to alight, and saw that each took his own baggage.

Phyllis was last, and she came down the step with a bag in one hand and a black case in the other which showed a frantic muzzle behind its wire window.

She put both bags into the hands of the waiting bus driver, turning a deaf ear to the eager whines for freedom. She was looking back, over her well-rounded shoulder, and her eyes were filled with a vague alarm as they met those of the young pilot.

"The man—the man who said he didn't want to die! He doesn't get up!" Her voice was puzzled.

French stared at her and then went slowly up and into the cabin, just as Chick appeared in the doorway of the pilots' room, pulling off his gloves. Together they bent over the man in the brown sport outfit, who had ceased to strain against his bonds.

He hadn't wanted to die, but he was dead.

CHAPTER II

Up a sloping walk of varicolored tile moved the passengers of the *Dragonfly,* through the landscaped formal garden with its fountain, stone benches, and gay sun-brellas, toward the waiting red bus at the gate. Their transient unity was gone—the kaleidoscope had shaken, and this scattered design of humanity had rearranged itself.

Leading the way, a stained canvas sea bag at his side, was the freckled man with the bright blue eyes. He walked with a swing, glanced neither at the looming mountains nor at the picturesque Spanish villa which served as an office, and spoke to nobody.

Behind him, hand in hand, was the young couple—the girl with the red curls and the youth with the rapt expression and the slickened hair. They were gazing at the dark hump of mighty Mount Orizaba to the west, but they did not see it.

Fourth, fifth, and sixth in the scattered procession came the three men in turtleneck sweaters—the great Ralph O. Tate ahead, carrying a cigarette, and his henchmen close behind, carrying suitcases, brief cases, and still cameras. The seventh was the paunchy T. Girard Tompkins, whose elk's tooth swung wildly as he strode along.

Last came Phyllis La Fond, plaid skirt whipping in the wind. She was still looking back over her shoulder—looking down to the smooth slope of concrete where the *Dragonfly* was poised on its turntable.

As she watched, the white-uniformed figure of Lew French appeared in the door of the plane. His mouth was open. He dropped to the ground, and then set out for the yellow villa at a ludicrous trot. Almost immediately he reappeared and trotted back to the plane, with an older man in a blue uniform and carpet slippers in tow.

As she stood there, halfway between plane and bus, Phyllis sensed rather than saw that up the slope the others were already engaged in a scramble over baggage and seats, sweeping over against the farther rail the three or four sightseers who had ridden out from town to witness the arrival of the *Dragonfly.*

The driver, a round young man whose few and lazy movements threatened constantly to burst the seams of the tight blue overalls which contained him, was already racing his motor as a gentle hint to hurry her along.

But Phyllis still stared at the *Dragonfly*. In a moment, the blue-clad official half fell out of the plane and came laboring up the walk.

"I'm sorry, ladies and gentlemen," he announced as soon as he could get his breath. "But you'll have to get off."

There was a moment of silence. Then Director Ralph O. Tate passionately inquired as to why the hell must they get off and who the hell said so?

"My name is Hinch," explained the man in blue. "I'm manager of the airline, and we've—we've had an accident. A man has been taken sick, and we'll have to use the bus to rush him over to the town."

There was a note of intensity, almost of desperation, in the voice of Mr. Hinch. But even more compelling than his command was the sight of the man in brown who was being carried swiftly up the walk between the two pilots, his new brown-and-white oxfords scraping on the tile.

"We'll try to get the bus back for you folks just as soon as we can," Hinch promised. "Or—it's just a short walk to the town."

Phyllis looked at her fragile sandals. "Say!" she said. "I'm not going to hike, and I'm not going to stand here in the hot sun—"

She was interrupted by a defiant, decisive voice from the front seat of the bus, where a tall and angular lady had up to now held against all comers the place of honor next the driver.

"Young man!"

Hinch turned from his shepherding of the other passengers, baggage and all, to see a pair of somewhat glittering eyes turned full upon him. "Young man, that girl is right. I paid my fifty cents for a round-trip ride, and I have no intention of waiting here in this blistering sun, or of walking back either, at my age!"

The age of Miss Hildegarde Withers has been classed as "indeterminate." If so, it was the only undetermined thing about that sharp-tongued but amiable schoolma'am. Her long and slightly equine visage bore traces of recent sunburn, and her temper was as ruffled as the silken scarf of blinding green which fluttered from her neck. In her hand was a sketchbook, with which she gestured, and over her shoulder was an open umbrella of black cotton.

"I came to Catalina for my first vacation in five years—and not to take a walking tour," she continued. "I have no objection to riding with a sick man, and I'm sure he is too ill to object to a fellow passenger.

Besides, I've had some experience with first aid, and I might be of some—"

She stopped short as she got her first good look at the man who had been sick. The two pilots were engaged in easing him up onto the rear seat of the bus. Miss Withers got to her feet and gripped the back of her seat with both her chamoisette gloves.

"What's wrong with him?" she demanded. The timbre of her voice had subtly changed.

Chick looked at French, and French looked at Chick. Then they both looked at Hinch.

"Why—I think it's a heart attack," that worthy explained. "We've got to rush him to the infirmary at Avalon. It's quicker than sending for Dr. O'Rourke. Now we've got to hurry, will you please—"

Miss Hildegarde Withers folded her umbrella and closed it with a snap. Then she edged her way out on the footboard of the bus and stalked back to where the man in brown was lying, face to the sky, along the rear seat.

With a circle of wide, startled eyes upon her, Miss Withers bent over the man who lay staring at the sky. If she flinched inwardly, the bearing of her angular frame did not show it as she stripped off her gloves.

She touched the hand of the man in brown, and then she pressed her fingers to his temple.

"There is no need to hurry," she said calmly, as she faced them all. "This man is not sick. He is dead."

There was an audible, frightened gasp from the girl in the blue corduroys. But Manager Hinch protested.

"We can't be sure ..."

The grizzled man with the sea bag and the freckled ears was standing close beside Miss Withers. His blue eyes were open very wide. "Ay have been forty year at sea," he said softly. "Ay have seen men die. He was dead on the plane—Ay knew it."

The pilot Chick ventured a halting question.

"Ay am a faller who minds his own business. Anybody who knows Thorwald Narveson will tell you that."

Captain Narveson blinked his innocent, China-blue eyes, and stared all around him.

Pilot Lew French broke the stillness. "It was his heart, all right. He was awful sick when he struck the rough air, and scared besides. Told me when he bought his ticket he couldn't stand the air. Said he'd had a bad time coming out on the Transcontinental." The hot California sun was beating down on the upturned, mildly wondering face of the man who centered their attention. French drew off his uniform coat and covered him. "Well, let's get him to Avalon."

The fat youth in the overalls, his hands trembling with excitement, jingled the starter for a long minute before he discovered that his ignition switch was off.

"Seems strange to me that a man who lived through a plane ride across the continent would die of fright on a twenty-minute jaunt like this," Miss Withers cut in. She saw the blue eyes of Captain Narveson upon her, speculatively.

Miss Withers had a strong impulse to mind her own business, following his undoubtedly excellent example. "—if you ask my opinion," she amended a little tardily. After all, this was not her absolute domain in the third grade of Jefferson School back on a side street in Manhattan. She was some three thousand miles from her old friend and onetime fiancé, doughty Inspector Oscar Piper of the New York City Homicide Squad, on whom she had leaned so heavily on the previous occasions when she had been faced with death in its more sudden forms.

To these harried men in uniform she was no more than a meddlesome old maid, and they wasted little effort in concealing this feeling.

"Come on, ma'am," insisted Hinch. "You'll have to get down."

The Withers dander began to rise, and her umbrella appeared, tightly clenched in one hand.

"This man is dead," she repeated softly. "No one knows whether or not it was a natural death. He should never have been moved from the flying machine at all. The best thing you can do is to send for the coroner and the police at once, and let them take charge."

But the others showed no sign of listening to her. Hinch made the mistake of advancing to put his hand on her arm. "Come on, ma'am, get down!"

He stepped back suddenly at the expression in her face.

"Young man," she told him firmly, "I'm sitting right here. Unless you want to put me off?"

Nobody, it developed, wanted to do that. But Miss Withers wasn't through. "I also advise you to send in on this bus all of these people who were on the flying machine. The police will want to question them, and perhaps hold them."

There sounded a shrill squeal from the girl in the blue corduroy trousers, as she seized her young man firmly around the neck. The note of terror in her young voice was very real.

"Marvin! They can't take us to jail on our *honeymoon!*" Her voice hung on the last word, thin and reedy. Luscious brown eyes, behind the sun goggles, were welling with tears. Miss Withers noticed the band of white gold which glittered, brand-new, on the third finger of the girl's left hand, and the schoolteacher's face for a brief second held an expression which might have been either envy or pity, or both.

The young man appeared naturally ill at ease. He tried to reassure the girl who clung to him. "There, there, Kay, honey. Nobody is going to take us to jail."

"Or anywhere else," Phyllis found time to interject. All the same, there was a silver lining. Ralph O. Tate, who was making it clear that he considered the man in brown had chosen to die at this time in a definite plot to hold up his plans, was strolling off moodily toward the shore. Phyllis sensed that the movie director's defenses were temporarily down, and she unhesitatingly moved after him.

Captain Narveson placed his sea bag on the ground, seated himself upon it, and took out and lit a blackened corncob pipe. But Miss Withers still held the fort.

"Somebody has to go along and see to things," she insisted. "This is a case for the police."

Hinch, shaken out of the ingrained politeness which marks every employee of the millionaire who purchased Catalina Island and made it what it is today, drew his breath angrily. And then:

"Madam, you are absolutely right," broke in a calm, dispassionate voice. The man with the elk's tooth, who had kept himself and his paunch well in the background up until now, pressed forward to the side of the bus.

"Bad business, this," he observed to Hinch. The manager looked as if he agreed.

"Hello, Mr. Tompkins. Sorry this happened with you on board to mar your trip."

T. Girard Tompkins waved his pudgy hand. He spoke with all the confidence that a regular weekly commutation ticket on the airline could give him. Regularly during the summer season he came to inspect the island pottery works, which gave him the status of an insider instead of tourist.

"The lady is right," he decided, nodding toward the belligerent figure of Miss Hildegarde Withers. "This is a matter for the authorities. In fact, I believe that I shall myself accompany her to the office of my friend Chief of Police Britt. If you have no objection—"

Mr. Hinch objected very strenuously. "This has got to be hushed up," he insisted. "It'll drive the tourists away. Sorry, Mr. Tompkins, but you can't go. I don't care if your company does buy up all the pretty pink flowerpots they make down to Pebbly Beach. I'm sending this—this accident case in alone." He swung on Miss Withers. "Come on, get off that bus. That's final!"

So it was that Hildegarde Withers went rolling through the hills to Avalon village in an improvised hearse. For company she had a frightened, fat chauffeur, a brace of white-uniformed and disgusted pilots, a paunchy distributor of pottery, and a stiffening corpse in a sport outfit of cocoa brown.

CHAPTER III

FROM the airport landing at White's Beach to the town of Avalon itself is only a matter of two miles of winding macadam road, which skirts the slope of Mount Orizaba itself, swings east toward the shore cliffs again, and finally descends in a long slope to the valley where the new Hotel St. Lena spreads its palm-shadowed balconies.

When the piled grandeur of the hotel and its beaches and tennis courts and promenades is past, there still remains half a mile of shore road, which curves out around a promontory, ducks between a cliff and the tremendous marble pillbox which is Mr. Wrigley's new Casino, and finally loses itself somewhere on Avalon's half-mile of Main Street.

Everywhere, on that bright August morning, a strange and varied assortment of humanity was enjoying itself after its own preferences. Brown-faced gentlemen moved shoreward, bearing the heavy rods and tackle that spell menace to swordfish and leaping tuna. Red-faced gentlemen bore large and shiny golf bags. Little boys swung bright tin pails. Old ladies beamed from wheelchairs—and young ladies beamed from everywhere.

There were girls, girls—thousands of girls. Girls in furs and girls in cotton pajamas. Girls in riding habits, girls in Paris models, girls in homemade frocks—but mostly girls in very little of anything. Young, tanned bodies in the briefest of shorts, with a wisp of silk haphazardly bound across their breasts … the essence of Catalina.

Discordantly, jarringly, through this swarming hive of humming, workless bees moved the red bus, bearing the body of the man who hadn't wanted to die. Strangely, no other motor vehicle was in sight. The pleasure seekers drew aside to let the bus pass, and then closed in behind it, intent upon their own plans for the holiday. Nobody saw the stiffening figure half covered on the rear seat of the bus, for the simple reason that nobody expected to see such an apparition there. It was as out of place as a ghost in a kindergarten.

Down Main Street, with its clusters of curio stores facing the two high piers, rolled the red bus, and finally came to rest before a small building on a side street, a modest frame building which flew above its doorway a flag consisting of a white cross on a red field.

Through the door into the infirmary the two pilots swiftly carried their passenger, like a sack of meal. Behind them, on the bus, T. Girard Tompkins turned nervously to the schoolteacher at his side.

"Perhaps it would be better ..." he began.

"It most certainly would," Hildegarde Withers told him decisively. She faced the driver. "Young man, you go find the chief of police. Go on—scat!"

Reluctantly, the fat youth detached himself from his seat behind the wheel and set off down the sidewalk.

Miss Withers took her parasol in a firmer grip and bustled through the door of the infirmary. At the same moment a stiffly starched nurse appeared, concealing a yawn, from an inner room. She seemed a very businesslike young woman, as she stood in the doorway and rocked back and forth on her low and sensible heels.

"Dr. O'Rourke isn't here," she was saying. "If it's absolutely necessary I can get him—"

She caught sight of the limp figure which the pilots had stretched out on the high iron table. "Another sunstroke case? Because if it is, I can take care—"

"You cannot," cut in Miss Withers. "Call the doctor."

The nurse went calmly over to the table, lifted the covering and replaced it. Then she nodded. "I'll call the doctor," she agreed.

She went to the door, stepped outside, and felt above her head for the lanyard. Then she lowered the flag with the white cross to half-mast.

"A quaint local custom?" Miss Withers inquired with raised eyebrows, when the starched young lady had returned.

"Not at all," the nurse informed her. "Dr. O'Rourke can see it from where he is. He'll be here in a minute."

As a matter of fact, it was something more than three minutes by Miss Withers's ancient timepiece before a lean and hairy little man, attired in sneakers and a dripping red bathing suit, burst open the door and entered from the street. He ignored the rest of them and faced the nurse, who had retired to a stool in the corner.

"What's this? Can't a man have his swim without—" The doctor caught sight of the covered figure on his operating table.

"So?" He removed the covering and surveyed the body of the man in the brown suit.

He held the dangling wrist for a moment and then bent as if to press his head against the dead man's heart. His lips formed a silent whistle. "Gone, eh?" He replaced the wrist. "Within the last half-hour, I'd say. Looks like a mild alcoholic case, too." With his fingers he forced the staring eyes wider and scrutinized the pupils. He frowned and then shrugged his shoulders and stepped back.

"You might as well have let me finish my swim," he complained. "I'm no miracle man; there's nothing I can do here."

"You can tell us how he happened to meet his end," Miss Withers suggested hopefully.

"Maybe I can," hedged Dr. O'Rourke. He extended a thumb toward the two pilots, who still lingered by the door. "This happen aboard your *Dragonfly?*"

"Half a mile up," agreed Chick. "He was making a big fuss about being sick to his stummick, and then he went into a howling funk. Yelled something about not wanting to die, and then he was quiet. I figured he'd got under control, and when we landed, we found out that all that'd been holding him up was the straps."

"There you are," said Dr. O'Rourke. "Pump played out on him. Doesn't take much to knock over one of these chronic booze fighters. We can write this down as simple heart failure."

He replaced the covering on the dead face. Then he went over to a sink against the wall and washed his hands thoroughly with blue soap.

Miss Withers found herself vaguely dissatisfied. "But, Doctor—do you know that this man just made a coast-to-coast plane trip without dying of heart failure? Yet you say he died of fright on a short trip like this!"

"Good Lord, woman!" Dr. O'Rourke stared at her impolitely. "There always has to be a first time for everything. Particularly for dying, you know. Why—" he waxed heavily facetious—"Why, that's one thing even you have never accomplished!"

Hildegarde Withers stared at the hairy little man. There came a look into her eyes which he could not understand. She was remembering a quarter of an hour that she had spent once upon the witness stand in the case of the People of the State of New York *versus* Gwen Lester, and another moment in the cellar beneath Jefferson School when the murderer of lovely Anise Halloran had crept after her in the darkness.

"Haven't I!" she said softly.

"You a relative?" The doctor wanted to know.

Miss Withers hesitated at that one.

"Naw, she's just a kibitzer," cut in Chick. "Well, that washes this business up as far as we're concerned. Come on, Lew, let's get back to the airport. The stiff is all yours, Doc. We're fed up with him."

The door slammed behind them. Miss Withers came closer to the hairy little doctor, who was still dripping onto the carpet.

"Wouldn't a postmortem be likely to show—"

"Postmortem?" He cut her short, irascibly. "Why in the name of the blessed Saint Vitus should there be a postmortem? Just because a stew passes out in a plane instead of in his bed or against a brass rail—"

"All the same, I sent for the chief of police," Miss Withers told him tartly.

The doctor was fast losing patience. "Look here, are you trying to teach me to run my business?"

Hildegarde Withers sniffed, audibly. She turned and looked out into the street, above a ruffled curtain which covered the lower half of both door and windows. The bus was still there, the two pilots climbing aboard, but there was no sign as yet of the fat youth who drove it, or of the official he had been sent to fetch. T. Girard Tompkins had also taken himself off, presumably to join in the search for his friend the chief.

"Chief Britt will certainly be grateful to you for dragging him away from his store at the noon rush hour," observed O'Rourke in an edged voice. "The chief just loves to close up his curio shop and trot around on wild-goose chases."

"Wild geese my Aunt Hannah," said Miss Withers. She sniffed again. "Young man, I have had the good or bad fortune to have been in contact with several notorious and unsavory cases of homicide during the past two years. Perhaps that poor fellow over there looks like just another case of heart failure to you, but I'm getting so I can detect the very smell of murder."

A lean forefinger wagged in O'Rourke's face, and Miss Withers pronounced solemnly, "I can smell murder now!"

At that moment the door opened, and a large nickel-plated shield entered. Pinned to the shield was a large, jolly person whose smallish eyes welled from between rolls of fat, a beaming convivial person who looked like a bartender rather than a limb of John Law.

Behind this dignitary followed a little procession of tourists, sprinkled here and there with natives. As the infirmary door was closed firmly in their faces, they began to billow against the windows, their muffled and excited voices filtering through onto the scene like an offstage-crowd noise. The big man cast at them no backward glance.

"Hello, Doc! How'ya, ma'am?" He nodded cordially in the direction of Miss Withers. "Now what seems to be the trouble here?"

"Trouble enough," Miss Withers told him. "If you ask me, I'm of the opinion—"

"Of course," agreed Chief Britt consolingly. "Certainly." He peered around the room and finally discovered Exhibit A. "Dear, dear! What is it, Doc?"

"Tourist croaked while the *Dragonfly* was coming out," said the doctor. "This lady thinks it's assassination." He snorted and began drying himself with a convenient towel. "Simple case of heart failure."

"Naturally," agreed the chief. He approached the white-covered figure. "Naturally," he echoed himself.

Miss Withers had the impression that his thoughts were very far away, perhaps back in the curio shop which was losing its noon tourist trade. Then the chief suddenly surprised her.

He leaned both pudgy hands on the back of a chair, and blinked. "Who did?"

"Who did? *what?*" The doctor snapped.

"Who died?" Britt inclined his head toward the body.

Miss Withers looked at the doctor, and he looked back at her. "I don't think anybody inquired into that," admitted O'Rourke.

"May make a difference," beamed the chief. "Shouldn't wonder."

He rubbed his hands together and moved ponderously toward the body. "Funny he was all alone," Britt offered, as the nurse drew back the covering again. "They usually come over here with friends." He hesitated a moment, as if reluctant to violate the secrecy of the dead. "Got to find out who he is before we can tell his folks," he finished, almost apologetically.

With a certain clumsy system about it, he removed from the pockets of the dead man a heterogeneous collection of odds and ends, which he juggled helplessly in his hands until he sighted a small table against the farther wall of the room, where he dumped them.

"Ought to make a list," he announced. Miss Hildegarde Withers already held sketchbook and pencil in her hands.

"I can take shorthand," she offered, eager to assist. But Chief of Police Britt held out his hands for the book and pencil.

"Thank yuh," he said. Then he began a studious enumeration of the dead man's chattels.

He wrote:

> Blk leather billfold, no calling cards, contents fifty-five dollars in fives and tens, parking ticket Terminal Garage, receipt for plane ticket, two newspaper clippings, one eight-cent airmail stamp.
>
> Two letters addressed R. Roswell, Hotel Senator, Los Angeles, unopened. Postmark New York City. One smelly pink paper, the other letterhead legal firm Fishbein, O'Hara, & Fishbein, Park Place, Manhattan.
>
> Change—twenty-dollar gold piece, Canadian quarter, dollar fifty in silver.
>
> Pair of red dice [the chief rattled these thoughtfully as he wrote], fountain pen with initials R.T.F., expensive make, brown silk handkerchief in breast pocket, unmarked. Key ring with two Yale keys and folding corkscrew.

"That seems to be the story," finished the chief. "Name's Roswell. Lives over to the Senator in Los Angeles."

"If his name is Roswell," pointed out Miss Withers, who was leaning over his shoulder, "then why the initials on his fountain pen?"

The chief of police stared solemnly at the initials R.T.F. "Cuts no ice," he decided, after ponderous thought. "Prob'ly borrowed it off somebody. Never manage to keep one of the things myself."

From the hip pocket of his dingy white linen suit, Britt removed a large blue bandanna handkerchief, in which he dumped the articles which he had listed. Then he tied the corners together.

"Got to notify his hotel," he announced. "Doc, you make out a certificate of death and send it t' my office so it can go in to the mainland with the corpse tonight."

O'Rourke had donned a bathrobe, and he looked up from his slippers in surprise. "Where d'you think I'll get a death certificate? Nobody died here in two years."

"Make one up out o' your own head, then," pronounced the chief. At that moment a hollow siren outside made the windowpanes rattle like castanets. "There's the *Avalon* now—I got to get back and open up the store—"

"Wait," demanded Hildegarde Withers. "There's more to it than that. This man Roswell—or whatever his name is—died suddenly under mysterious circumstances. It isn't exactly any of my business—"

"Hear, hear," offered Dr. O'Rourke.

"But all the same, it is my honest opinion that this is a case for a coroner."

Chief Britt smiled, sleepily. "We ain't got a coroner, ma'am. When there's any need we use the one over to Long Beach, on the mainland. I'll send the corpse over to him and if he wants to, he can have an inquest."

"And by that time it will be everlastingly too late!"

Miss Withers was intense. "All the people who were on that plane when this man died will be scattered."

"Yes, ma'am, but—"

"But nothing! Hasn't this town got a mayor or anything besides you?"

"Yes, ma'am. There's Mayor Peters, and we got a city manager, too, name of Klein. Both of 'em out in Klein's boat after sea bass and won't be back for a couple of days anyway."

Britt stowed his blue bundle away in a pocket of his coat. He began to show that he was impatient to wind up the matter.

"Now listen," he approached Miss Withers. "You keep saying you think this fellow was killed. Do you see any reason why you think so?"

"She doesn't see reasons—she smells 'em," offered Dr. O'Rourke.

Miss Withers sniffed. "Chief Britt, haven't you ever had a flash of intuition—a premonition—a *hunch*, in other words?"

The chief blinked his tiny, cunning eyes at her. "Yes, ma'am. In poker games. And it costs me money every time."

The crowd which lingered outside the little infirmary was increasing steadily, and Miss Withers noticed an admixture of newcomers with suitcases and light coats swung over their arms, as the chief opened the door again.

"G'bye, ma'am, g'bye, Doc," he spoke politely. Then he stopped short and said, "Hello."

Through the open doorway a shaft of noon sunshine poured into the dark little room, spreading a track of gold across the floor and touching the bared face of the dead man with a semblance of life.

Then the shaft of sunlight was blotted out again, blocked by the square shoulders of a man so tall that he had to stoop in order to enter the doorway.

His face, Miss Withers instantly noted, was handsome, almost too handsome, in a soft way. The eyes were the only jarring feature, for they showed momentarily a flickering, evasive look. Then he smiled apologetically, and the eyes were like other eyes.

"Excuse me," he said. His voice had an Eastern tang that was almost harsh among these drawling Californians. "They were saying on the pier that somebody had died, but they didn't know who it was. I expected a friend to meet me here, and he didn't show up. I wondered—"

"Take a look for yourself," said the chief hospitably. "Letters in his pocket identify him as being named R. Roswell. Know him?"

The newcomer removed his Panama and moved toward the body. Immediately he became ten years older than his oddly young face, for his hair was streaked with gray. As yet he had no eyes for the doctor or the two women, but stared at the figure which lay on the operating table as if he expected it to rise and salute him.

For a long minute he stared at the face of the dead man. Then he turned toward the others, his handsome face expressionless.

"I was afraid of that," he said slowly. "It's my friend—and his full name is Roswell T. Forrest."

Miss Withers gasped, audibly. The newcomer turned toward her. "I see you know," he said. "I was his traveling companion—my name is Barney Kelsey." Then he continued, dully: "We were supposed to make this little outing together, but Forrest missed the boat."

"But the letters," protested the chief. "The letters were addressed to him by his first name only?"

"I'll explain all that. But, first, do you know who—what happened to him?"

Dr. O'Rourke started to speak, but Miss Withers, in a voice that kept him silent, interrupted.

"A paralytic stroke is a terrible thing," she observed, commiseratingly.

The newcomer's eyes flickered once as the chief and the doctor stared at each other blankly.

But before they spoke, Barney Kelsey nodded his head.

"Forrest has had trouble like that before," he went on, swiftly. "The doctors warned him that another attack would be fatal."

There was a dead silence.

"Oddly enough," continued Miss Hildegarde Withers, "Dr. O'Rourke here discovered no trace of paralysis past or present in the body. My remark was purely general. The doctor leans toward heart failure, at the present moment. My own ideas lead in quite another direction. I suppose your friend Forrest was *also* subject to heart trouble?"

Kelsey's eyes were those of a trapped animal for a flash, and then they became bland and open.

"On second thought," he said softly, "I agree with you that Roswell Forrest was murdered."

"I thought you would," said Miss Withers.

CHAPTER IV

"This is getting no clearer, fast," admitted Chief of Police Britt, after a long moment of uncomfortable silence. He looked at a massive silver watch and then definitely gave up any hope of getting back to his curio shop that noon. "S'pose you get down to cases and tell us what you mean by all this stuff about murder, and about your friend Roswell named Forrest or vice versa?"

The chief went wearily over and turned a key in the door. Then he faced Barney Kelsey, expectantly. "Don't mind the audience, just go ahead."

The stranger nodded. "I'll try to make it short," he promised. "This lady here"—he indicated Miss Withers—"recognized the name of Roswell T. Forrest. I'm surprised it means nothing to you, Chief."

"Maybe it does," hedged the chief cautiously, "and maybe it doesn't."

"Well, it's been in the newspapers enough, anyway. Forrest has been dodging the Brandstatter Committee investigation, back in New York City, for a couple of months. He was confidential secretary to Welch, the Commissioner of Docks and Harbors, whom they've got on the grill right now. They wanted to make Forrest testify against his boss—"

"In regard to the safety deposit boxes he shared with Welch!" cut in Miss Withers triumphantly. "That's it! The New York papers were full of it when I left, and the clippings in Forrest's billfold are about the same thing!"

Kelsey bowed in agreement. "I've been traveling around the country with Forrest," he continued. "Helping him dodge process servers and the newspaper men. You see—"

"Wait a minute," said the chief. "Let me get this straight. You did all this traveling around for love—or money?"

Kelsey hesitated.

"He means," interrupted Miss Withers, "did you receive a salary from Forrest?"

"I received salary and expenses, yes," admitted Kelsey. "But not from Forrest. He couldn't afford anything like that. Every week he received a money order from a New York lawyer—who, I don't know—and along with his came one for me. You see, it was pretty important to a lot of people that Forrest shouldn't come back to New York by mistake."

"So we see," said Hildegarde Withers. Dr. O'Rourke grunted disagreeably in the background.

"You realize," the chief inquired, "that this makes you an accessory after the fact to anything Forrest may have done?"

Kelsey shrugged his shoulders. "There were no charges against him, Chief. You get me wrong. They only wanted to subpoena him as a witness."

"Then why all the hiding out?"

"Some pretty important people didn't want his testimony brought forward—and besides, Forrest was no squealer."

"Still sounds funny to me," objected Chief Britt. "If there were no criminal charges against Forrest, all he had to do was to stay out of the jurisdiction of the state of New York. They could serve subpoenas on him till the cows came home, and it wouldn't mean a thing."

"Wouldn't it! If they stuck a writ on him, he could be cited for contempt of court and fined."

"Go on," said the chief.

"We've been in Los Angeles about two weeks," continued Kelsey. "Adjoining rooms at the Senator. We've been laying pretty low, and Forrest kept in communication with New York only through his first name, under which he was registered. But nothing happened and nobody seemed to be on our trail, so lately we've been moving around a little more freely. We decided to take this little outing together, partly to keep his mind off other things. Forrest went out alone Thursday—yesterday afternoon—and stayed out. Phoned me he would meet me at the boat this morning, because I had the tickets. But he didn't show up."

"Know where he spent the night?" In spite of himself, the chief was growing interested. Dr. O'Rourke was puffing impatiently at a cigarette, and Miss Withers seemed engrossed in a cameo brooch which she wore.

Kelsey hesitated at the question. "He visited a friend—a Miss Frances Lee, out on Sunset Boulevard in Hollywood. He phoned me from there."

The chief rubbed his chin. "Frances Lee? Frances Lee …"

Here Dr. O'Rourke interrupted. "You wouldn't know, Britt. The madame runs a deluxe—er—bagnio."

"A *what?*" Miss Withers was bewildered.

"A home for falling women," O'Rourke enlightened her, wickedly.

Chief Britt nodded and turned again toward Kelsey. "D'you know anybody who might have a reason to kill Forrest?"

Kelsey didn't.

"Know if Forrest had any relations?"

"He had a wife in Yonkers," was the reply. "If you call that a relation. I can give you the address."

The chief laboriously made a note of it. Then he turned toward O'Rourke.

"Well, Doc, what d'you think we better do?"

O'Rourke surveyed the corpse with disfavor. "Do? Get him off our hands quick as we can. Send him over to the coroner at Long Beach. I still think it was a natural death. There's not a sign of violence—no wounds, no bullet holes. Why make a big stink about it?"

Hildegarde Withers faced him belligerently. "Young man, no matter what you try to say or do, there's going to be a big—er, smell. Hushing it up won't help."

The chief, torn between opposing forces, scratched his head.

"But I've never had a murder case yet, in all my ten years in office!" he protested dubiously.

"There has always to be a first time for everything," Miss Withers told him. "Dr. O'Rourke reminded me of that but a moment ago."

Barney Kelsey stole a furtive glance at the corpse and then looked quickly away.

The chief was tramping up and down the room. "Things like this don't happen here," he argued with himself. Then he stopped short, facing Miss Withers. "Listen," he offered. "I'll have them bring the passengers off that plane down to my office and see if they noticed anything that wasn't as it should have been. Now that ought to take care of your objections, Miss—what's your name?"

"Hildegarde Martha Withers," that lady reminded him tartly. "Obviously you will have to question the passengers of that plane before they get separated and scattered. You mustn't let this body go over to the mainland, either, until—"

"Easy there, ma'am." The chief was drawing near the end of his patience. "Now I wouldn't walk into your classroom and tell you how to teach your kids their ABC!"

"You're welcome to!" Miss Withers assured him. "Any time you see me doing my job the way you're doing yours. Can't you see that this is a full-fledged, front-page murder mystery? If you try to hush it up as a natural death, there's bound to be a big—a big smell, and I can well imagine what the newspapers will have to say about you and Dr. O'Rourke!"

With that last broadside, Miss Withers crossed to the door, unlocked it, and closed it gently but firmly behind her. Barney Kelsey hesitated, gave his intended address, and then followed her example, leaving the door ajar.

Chief of Police Amos Britt stared at James Michael O'Rourke, M.D., and the doctor returned his stare, wordlessly.

"And the sad part about it is that she's right," O'Rourke remarked softly, as if anxious not to awaken the dead man in the brown sport outfit.

"Mebbe she is and mebbe she isn't," Chief Britt announced. "Anyway"— his face brightened—"Anyway she's finally taken herself out of it."

At that moment Miss Hildegarde Withers, far from having taken herself out of anything, was doing her best to involve herself deeper into what was to be famous in newspaper annals as "The Red Dragonfly Mystery."

Half a block from the infirmary, on a covered arcade connecting two side streets, is the Avalon post office, and next door to this invaluable institution glows the blue-and-white globe of a telegraph office. Miss Withers pushed aside scornfully the stub of pencil with its inevitable jingling chain, and with her own slim fountain pen set down the following message:

POSTAL TELEGRAPH

AVALON CALIFORNIA 12:45 P

INSPECTOR OSCAR PIPER,
CENTRE STREET
POLICE HEADQUARTERS
NEW YORK CITY

CURIOUS TO KNOW PLEASE RUSH DESCRIPTION AND WHAT INFORMATION
YOU HAVE ON FILE REGARDING ROSWELL T FORREST AND BARNEY KELSEY
REGARDS

HILDEGARDE

When this telegram was safely on the wire, Miss Withers took from a pocket of her coat a small, limp, modern-library edition of *The Meditations of Marcus Aurelius*. Making her angular body as comfortable as possible on one of the wooden benches near the telegraph desk, she proceeded to put completely from her mind all thought of the dead man and the officials who were at the moment so embarrassed by his presence.

That lady's remarkable patience and calmness, however, were not shared by the seven marooned individuals who were still waiting at the airport for a bus to transport them on to the village of Avalon.

The great Ralph O. Tate took it hardest. With a small and brittle twig which he had torn from a nearby bush he whipped viciously at the sleek black leather of his riding boots. Before him stretched a blue ocean, with a haze that was California in the far distance. Behind him were the yellow villa and the barrier of mountains. Out of the corner of his eye he could see Tony and George, his two satellites, busily matching coins. They had run through dimes to quarters by this time.

Beside him, her well-rounded body resting upon well-rounded heels, Phyllis La Fond chatted companionably—inevitably. Now and again Tate flung a stone at the water, but most of his missiles refused to skip. That, too, was in key with the rest of his morning—for at the other end of Catalina, Tate knew all too well, there was a moving-picture company on location. Waiting since sunrise this morning—waiting for him. At something like two hundred dollars an hour.

"Someday," Phyllis was saying—"Someday I'll get my chance in pictures. Somebody will look at me and realize that there's something hidden in me, something that everybody doesn't see—"

Tate surveyed her form-fitting plaid suit impartially. "I don't know where you'd hide it," he remarked.

At that moment a siren sounded from the gateway beside the village—a raucous yet welcome blast from the red bus which had just coasted down the slope to a skidding stop.

"It's about time," emitted the great Ralph O. Tate. "All right, boys!" He rose to his feet, replaced the blue beret upon his shining poll, and made off up the beach.

Phyllis picked up a small oval stone, looked longingly at the back of his skull, and then spat daintily upon the pebble and sent it skipping across the water, to her deep inward satisfaction.

Then she, too, followed the procession.

"It's all right, folks," Manager Hinch was announcing. "The bus finally got here. Step lively, please!" Phyllis needed no invitation to step lively.

Hinch had had a bad hour and had finally locked himself in the office where no one could get at him. But now he was himself again, distributing smiles.

Captain Thorwald Narveson tapped out his corncob pipe against the stones and rose to his feet. Around him was a little circle of dottle and match stubs, but he was otherwise just as he had been left an hour or more ago. The innocent blue eyes still twinkled, and the freckles on his ears and forehead stood out even darker than before. The captain tossed his duffle bag on the bus and then placed himself heavily and firmly in the rear seat.

Ralph O. Tate was the next on board, followed by his two assistants and the baggage. He took his seat between them, effectually preventing Phyllis from any further promotion of her fortunes. Philosophically, she joined the captain on the rear seat, defeated but not dismayed.

Last to come were the newlyweds. Desperate shouts from Hinch and a series of earsplitting blasts upon the horn beneath the thumb of the fat youth in overalls finally brought them forth from the shadows of a eucalyptus clump. The redhaired girl was still cool and comfortable in sweater and blue trousers, and in her hand she gripped tightly a wilted bouquet of nondescript flowers. The young man was busily combing his hair. Without further mishap they scrambled aboard, and the girl hastily set about wiping orange lipstick from her young husband's nose.

"All aboard!" shouted Hinch cheerily. He seemed to be washing his hands. "All aboard!"

The motor bus roared, and then Phyllis suddenly rose to her feet, shrieking.

"Wait—wait!" Her hands waved, wildly. "I forgot my baggage. It's —it's in the office!"

"It'll be safe there until you come after it," Hinch shouted above the roar of the moving bus.

He waved the driver on. After all, he had received his instructions, and if Chief Britt wanted these people to question, he could have them on the double-quick. The sooner the better, said Hinch.

The bus lunged forward as the plump youth noisily shifted into second gear, and then roared up the slope. Phyllis sat down, hard, and only the thick hand of Captain Narveson kept her from rolling off sidewise.

Phyllis murmured something impolite. The captain nodded in hearty agreement. "Yas, indeed," he said. His blue eyes twinkled more than ever.

Phyllis grinned in spite of herself and then calmly took his arm and clung to it through the rest of the ride.

They were deposited before a doorway marked "Curios—Pottery—Postcards—Chief of Police," just as the town carillon located on the hill above Mr. Zane Grey's summer residence sounded the first hour of the afternoon.

Everywhere around them, from the open counters of the little restaurants, rose the aroma of hot dogs, hamburgers, and abalone steaks, but the hungry passengers of the *Dragonfly* were herded briskly through the doors of the curio store and on toward a rear room. Their shepherd was a gaunt and slightly doddering person who announced himself, in a thin cracked voice, as "Chief Britt's deppity." His name, it later developed, was Ruggles, and this was his crowded hour. He made the most of it.

"Jist a little formality," he promised them. Director Tate's impassioned objections met only with an "I'm a mite deef ..."

Through a maze of mother-of-pearl boxes, framed photographs, embalmed swordfish, and the like, went the passengers of the *Dragonfly*, coming at last to the chief's office, where that worthy awaited them in the only chair. Dr. O'Rourke stood by the door, still in dressing gown and slippers over his bathing suit.

"Not going to take long," Chief Britt promised them. He cleared his throat. "None of you saw anything out of the ordinary on that trip out here, did you?"

Nobody ventured a reply.

The chief nodded. Then he took a deep breath. "None of you noticed anything that'd make you think Mr. Forrest, the sick man, was anything worse than just sick?"

"Not until he died," Phyllis offered.

"Exactly. Couldn't have anybody—harmed him, so to speak, without the rest of you seeing, could there?"

There was a general chorus of "No."

The chief turned triumphantly to Dr. O'Rourke. "There you are! It's just like we figured. Now there ain't a reason in the world why we shouldn't put this case down as a natural death and let these people go about their business."

Captain Narveson fidgeted a little. "Ay never saw a faller die from being seasick before," he put in. The blue eyes turned toward Ralph O.

Tate. "Maybe that drink you give him to make him feel better was bad liquor?"

Tate took off his beret and mopped his bald dome. The others were all staring at him. "Please," he said. "You all know who I am. Why should I— I mean, I buy the best liquor that can be got. It's smuggled in every week from a ship that comes twice a year from Scotland and lies off shore until it's unloaded. No rotgut for me. Anyway—I took a drink after the sick man did. You all saw me!" He did not offer to display his flask.

"That's true," burst in the girl with red curls. She had removed the sun goggles, and her lashes were long and curling.

"Sure it's true," said Phyllis La Fond. But all the same she stared very hard and very thoughtfully at the great director, Mr. Ralph O. Tate.

The young man with slick hair settled that problem at once. "No matter if somebody gave a man a swig of the worst wood alcohol, death wouldn't follow in less than a couple of hours at the quickest. I know— I used to work in a drug store. So it doesn't matter what kind of liquor was in the flask, it couldn't have been the cause of Forrest's death."

Chief Britt nodded and waved his hand. "All right, folks. Sorry to've kept yuh from your dinner. Mac's place down the street has pretty good food. Tell him I sent you. ..."

They made a concerted rush for the door, but it was barred by a tall, spare figure.

"Excuse me," said Miss Hildegarde Withers, "but the party isn't over."

As the others pushed past her with varying expressions of annoyance upon their faces, the schoolteacher drew from its envelope a blue-and-white square of paper.

"Read this," she told Chief of Police Amos Britt. "Read this—and then tell me again that you think Roswell Forrest died a natural death."

Britt looked at the message, and his lips moved slowly:

POSTAL TELEGRAPH

NEW YORK CITY NY 5:15 P

HILDEGARDE WITHERS
AVALON CALIFORNIA

THOUGHT YOU WERE ON A VACATION WHY ARE YOU INTERESTED IN FORREST HIS DESCRIPTION FOLLOWS BORN AUSTRALIA AMERICAN PARENTS AGE THIRTYFIVE BROWN EYES DARK BROWN HAIR MEDIUM BUILD

DRESSES VERY WELL NO PHOTO AVAILABLE BARNEY KELSEY FORMER
BARTENDER NO POLICE RECORD SUPPOSED TO BE WITH FORREST AS
BODYGUARD UNDERSTAND CERTAIN PARTIES HAVE OFFERED SPEND FIF-
TEEN GRAND IF FORREST UNABLE TESTIFY BEFORE BRANDSTATTER COM-
MITTEE WHATS UP

OSCAR PIPER

Chief Britt put down the message and whistled. "Musta cost two-three dollars to say all that," he hazarded.

"But don't you understand?" Miss Withers stared at him, searchingly. "Don't you see what it means?"

"Mebbe I do, and again mebbe I don't," Chief Britt said. He turned toward O'Rourke, who was reading the message.

"If you ask me," said the doctor thoughtfully, "it means that somebody earned fifteen thousand dollars this morning."

"Hear, hear!" came from Hildegarde Withers, triumphantly.

Chief Britt looked from one to the other. Then he went swiftly to the door. "Hey, Ruggles!"

The aged deputy appeared, grinning toothlessly.

"Ruggles, you better round up the people that just left here and tell'em not to leave the island just yet," ordered the chief. "Tell'em to stick around the hotel in case I want to ask a few more questions."

"Okay, Amos." The deputy disappeared.

"I suggest that you give the same order to Mr. Barney Kelsey," Miss Withers put in.

"Him? Oh, he ain't going away. Offered to stick around as long as we wanted him to. Nice feller."

The chief relaxed in his chair again. "You showed me your telegram, ma'am," he offered. "I sent one myself, and I got an answer, too. I may as well let you see what Mrs. Roswell Forrest had to say when she got the news." He presented a blue-and-white slip of his own, which Miss Withers eagerly seized:

POSTAL TELEGRAPH

YONKERS NEW YORK COLLECT 5:35 P
CHIEF AMOS BRITT
AVALON CALIFORNIA

IF ABSOLUTELY NECESSARY WILL GUARANTEE MINIMUM FUNERAL EX-

PENSES FOR BURIAL THERE

MAE TIMMONS FORREST

"That word 'absolutely' cost me an extra sixty cents," the chief told her ruefully.

"It certainly seems that his wife was crazy about him, doesn't it?" Miss Withers handed back the message. "She wants him put under ground as cheaply and quickly as possible—and if absolutely necessary she'll pay for the coffin!"

"Handsome of her, I calls it," said Dr. O'Rourke. "Now if you will excuse me, I think my invaluable assistant will have a pan of chili on the oil stove over at the infirmary. The company is none too appetizing right now, but—" The little doctor turned toward Miss Withers. "I don't suppose you'd care to make it a foursome?"

"Another time," said that lady calmly. "I have things to do—and so has the chief here."

Chief Britt nodded. "So I have. Only I'll be dad-blessed if I know what they are!"

"I'm going to send another telegram," said Hildegarde Withers. "And wait for another answer."

POSTAL TELEGRAPH

AVALON CALIFORNIA 1:35 P

INSPECTOR OSCAR PIPER
CENTER STREET POLICE HEADQUARTERS
NEW YORK CITY

SUSPECT MURDER LOCAL POLICE BEWILDERED HAVING FINE TIME WISH YOU WERE HERE

HILDEGARDE

The answer was not long in coming, and it was to the point:

POSTAL TELEGRAPH

NEW YORK CITY NY 6:20 P

HILDEGARDE WITHERS

AVALON CALIFORNIA

I WILL BE

OSCAR

Chief Britt, though he did not send another message, received an answer all the same. A messenger delivered it into his hands as he bent over a steak at Mac's Place:

POSTAL TELEGRAPH

NEW YORK CITY NY 6:25 P

CHIEF OF POLICE

AVALON CALIFORNIA

FORREST CASE HIGHEST IMPORTANCE POLITICALLY CONSIDER IT EXTREME FAVOR IF YOU HOLD EVERYTHING UNTIL I ARRIVE WEDNESDAY

OSCAR PIPER INSPECTOR NYC POLICE

The chief read it through three times and then folded it and put it away in a pocket of his soiled white linen jacket. He turned to Ruggles, the ancient deputy, who was mumbling away at a plate of milk toast beside him.

"You better go down to the carpenter shop," he pronounced judicially, "and tell 'em not to make that pine box, after all."

Ruggles let his mouth hang open.

"Y' mean you ain't going to send the remains over to the mainland on the steamer, Amos?"

Britt shook his head. "We're going to hold everything till Wednesday," he said.

But as Miss Withers could have told him, he was more than optimistic.

CHAPTER V

A ROUND red sun beat down upon a city seemingly deserted. The swarms of natives, tourists, and summer people had wisely distributed themselves between the beaches, the glass-bottomed boats, the Aviary, and their hotel rooms, leaving only a blistering Main Street, a solitary red bus, and an angular and determined lady who engaged the driver of that bus in animated argument.

"Two dollars is the price for a trip to the airport, lady," insisted the plump driver. "Unless you want to wait until four-thirty for the regular run."

Miss Hildegarde Withers was most emphatically opposed to waiting. Neither did she want to pay two dollars for a two-mile trip for which a taxicab in her own Manhattan would have charged fifty cents. But there were only half a dozen motor vehicles in all Catalina, and this was the only one for hire.

"I'll give you a dollar," bargained that canny lady. But the plump young man in blue overalls shook his head and returned to his studious perusal of yesterday's newspaper. It was evident that he would just as soon stay where he was.

Miss Withers was at the point of weakening when a vibrant young voice beside her cut in.

"Two dollars it is," said Phyllis La Fond. "Dollar apiece, sister—are you on?"

"I'm—er, on," agreed Miss Withers. She surveyed her prospective bus companion carefully. "What's this, another amateur detective in our midst?"

"God forbid," Phyllis told her cheerily. "My baggage is still up at the airport, and I figure that the best way to make sure of getting it is to go after it. So we'll kill a couple of birds with one stone, eh?" They were climbing aboard.

"Let's not speak of killing," requested the schoolteacher, as they sped

43

away. "But I get the drift of your remark. You're the pretty girl who was on the plane this morning, aren't you?"

Phyllis took this as it was meant. "Uh huh. Unless you mean the red-head, and she's a little thin if you ask me."

"No figure at all, from what I saw of her," Miss Withers agreed. She was not one to waste an opportunity. "I've already heard one version of that trip," she remarked with the proper amount of casualness. "Mr. T. Girard Tompkins gave me his outline as he rode in with the body. But I'd like to hear your impressions. It must have been very exciting."

"Exciting?" Phyllis held on tight as they rounded a curve at forty miles an hour. "It was about as exciting as riding an electric hobby-horse. You can have my share, thanks." All the same, Phyllis found herself giving a reasonably accurate story of the ride on the *Dragonfly,* with one important omission.

"And at the end, when we were all saying 'Thank God that's over,' why, the man in the brown suit didn't get up. You know the rest," she finished.

"I'm not sure that anybody knows the rest," Miss Withers told her. "Or that anybody ever will, though I'm going to try."

"Here's luck," Phyllis said. They rode over the crest of the last hill in silence and finally after a toboggan-like descent were deposited beside the gate which led down to the villa and the airport landing.

The plump chauffeur slid out of his seat. He looked at the dollar watch which hung on a knotted shoestring from a buttonhole of his overalls. "I'll get your bags, miss. Starting back in five minutes."

"But—you'll have to wait for me!" Miss Withers was indignant. "I won't be ready to go back in five minutes."

"Then you'll walk," said the man in the blue overalls. He went down the hill toward the office.

"Fresh guy," said Phyllis comfortingly.

"I suppose you'll be ready to go then," said Miss Withers. "For my part, I came to have a look at the plane down there, and a look I'm going to have."

"All I want is my bags," Phyllis admitted. "But I'm in no hurry. Suppose I go down to the plane with you?—I can show you where each of us was sitting."

"And you'll walk back to town?"

"Walk—me? Never!" Phyllis proudly displayed a bit of twisted metal. "Let that fresh hayseed try to start his bus without us now. I've got his ignition key!"

Miss Withers's eyes flashed. "Stout fella," she said. "Come on."

They moved down toward where the big red-and-gilt plane was standing, but as they passed the villa a voice called from the doorway. The fat youth stood there, with a bag in either hand.

"These the right ones?"

"Those are mine," said Phyllis.

At the sound of her voice one of the bags emitted a doleful whine. "What in heaven's name have you got in there?" Miss Withers wanted to know.

Phyllis snapped her fingers. "If I didn't forget about Mister Jones!"

"Who?"

"Mister Jones—he's a dog." Phyllis crossed swiftly to the container and opened a snap. From the box bounded a small black-and-white terrier, which evidenced delight at seeing the light of day again by a series of shrill yelps.

"Did ums get tired all by himself so long?" asked Phyllis coyly.

Mister Jones's only answer was to cavort wildly about the formal gardens of the airport, pausing to sniff at every shrub and cactus, and finally disappear in the bushes.

"Come to me, you bad boy!" called Phyllis hopefully. Mister Jones stayed.

Phyllis snagged a well-chewed leash from the interior of the container. "Come here, sir!"

Miss Withers coughed and lowered her voice. "I think he's—er—"

"You mean gone to see a dog about a man?" Phyllis grinned.

"Come here, sir," she called again.

Mister Jones trotted out of the bushes, once more a docile and well-behaved citizen. With head and ears cocked to one side, whiskers waving in the breeze, white forepaws wide and sturdy, the little dog approached its mistress with the utmost confidence.

"What kind of a dog is it?" Miss Withers wanted to know. She had always preferred cats, but there was something definitely appealing—something a little hungry and searching—in the roguish eyes that met her own.

"He's a pedigreed wire," Phyllis announced. "Wirehaired terrier to you. Supposed to be worth a lot of money. But you can't prove it by me—I've only had him three days, and I'm no expert." She snapped the leash on the little dog's collar. "I suppose I ought to exercise you, useless," she remarked, as she bent over the wriggling animal. "Mind if he comes along?"

"Of course not." Miss Withers rubbed her fingers across the tight twisted wool. "You're a fine fellow, aren't you, boy? A little fat, I should say. But a fine fellow."

"I named him Mister Jones after the man who gave him to me," confided Phyllis amiably. "He went broke, and the pup was all he could give me when he moved out."

"Miss Withers raised her eyebrows and then nodded. "Sort of a diamond-bracelet dog, eh?"

"Sort of. Only I'd trade him for one, any day." Phyllis laughed and tugged at the leash. The terrier, who had discovered an interesting crackerjack box, trotted obediently after them, dragging the prize. Now and then, Mister Jones was confident, it would be possible to swallow a succulent morsel or two of cardboard on the way.

They approached the red-and-gilt *Dragonfly,* hesitating a moment before the narrow door. But they found it unlocked. Phyllis swung it open, and Mister Jones leaped gayly up the steps.

Hildegarde Withers had often read of the psychic sensitiveness of dogs and cats. If she had expected any reaction from the terrier in this narrow cubicle which she was confident still reeked of murder, she was sadly disappointed. The fat little dog strained on the leash, sniffing delightedly at the myriad new odors of the cabin, even discarding the treasured crackerjack box in favor of new findings.

Phyllis patiently explained the situation of the seats and their various occupants on that morning's plane trip. "I know what you're thinking," she said. "You've got an idea that somebody killed that fellow Forrest, or whatever his name was. But I don't see how it could have happened."

"Nor do I," said Miss Withers. "That's no proof at all that it didn't happen." She was busily making a diagram of the interior of the cabin. "And you say the dead man sat here?"

Mister Jones, entering into the spirit of the thing with a whole heart, leaped upon the blue leather seat, pressed two dusty paws against the plate-glass window, and then dropped to investigate the floor again, sniffing noisily.

It was at this moment that the exploring party was interrupted by a stern voice from the door.

"Plane doesn't leave for the mainland till four-thirty," said Lew French. "You'll have to wait in the waiting room—nobody allowed aboard here."

They left the *Dragonfly.* "We were through with it anyway," said Miss Withers. The sunlight was blinding after the semidarkness of the plane.

Up the slope, in the red bus, a perspiring young man was searching vainly for his ignition key.

"Oh—is this what you're looking for?" Phyllis inquired innocently. She displayed the key. "I just found it a moment ago."

The driver found himself at a complete loss for words. He inserted the key and raced his engine.

Miss Withers was already seated in the bus. Phyllis handed up Mister Jones and started to follow. Then she stopped.

"What, again?" she asked wearily. The little dog was wriggling uncomfortably.

Miss Withers turned around, jarred from the train of thought which had been taking her nowhere—fast.

"What's the trouble?"

"Mister Jones wants to *go,* " Phyllis informed her. She lifted down the little dog.

"He doesn't look to me as if he wanted to go," Miss Withers observed. Mister Jones had lain down in the dust of the roadway, an abject picture of discomfort.

"Come on, snap out of it," Phyllis commanded. She caught the dog by the scruff of the neck and lifted it to the flat top of the gatepost. "Let's have a look, nuisance. What's troubling you?"

"Dr. O'Rourke is a pretty good vet," offered the driver. "Better take him in town to the doc."

Phyllis nodded. But Hildegarde Withers was climbing out of the bus. "Wait," she insisted. "Look at him."

Mister Jones was shaken by tremor after tremor. Then followed a series of choking coughs.

"If you want to be sick, be sick," Phyllis admonished the dog.

"If he wants to be sick, keep him often the bus," put in the driver.

It was Miss Withers who analyzed the situation first. She did not hesitate. Swiftly she caught up Mister Jones in her arms and ran toward the shore, with Phyllis dazedly following and the bus driver staring at them as if they were all demented.

The animal's heartbeats were like the pounding of a drum. "Poisoned!" gasped Miss Withers, as she ran. "I've seen it happen before, when neighbors get to fighting over their pets in the city."

"What should we do?"

Miss Withers's sensible heels were clattering over the pebbly shore.

"We ought to have salt and warm water. But there's no time for that. Here—you hold him."

Mister Jones was pathetically easy to hold. Phyllis held on as Miss Withers demonstrated, with the whiskery jaw open.

Then the schoolteacher took her two cupped hands and proceeded to dip up portions of the Pacific, at the expense of her shoes, stockings, and dress. Mister Jones gagged and fought weakly as the bitter salt water drenched mouth and stomach. But Miss Withers kept on.

"All right, you can put him down," she said finally. Phyllis found a large and flat-topped stone and laid the unhappy dog on its side.

It was just in the nick of time, as Mister Jones chose that moment to get rid of sea water, breakfast, crackerjack bits, and, as the auction bills say, "other articles too numerous to mention."

"You've just made him all the sicker," Phyllis complained.

"He had to be sicker before he could be—weller," said Miss Withers. "See—he's all through."

Mister Jones gave her the lie by instantly becoming more unwell than ever.

The two women surveyed the sufferer in perplexity. "Maybe we should have taken him to Dr. O'Rourke after all," admitted Miss Withers.

Finally Phyllis picked up the little dog and started back toward the bus, where the plump young man leaned on his horn.

"I hope he doesn't go and die on me before we get him to town," Phyllis murmured as they came up the walk. "Tell me, do you really think he was poisoned?"

"I do." Miss Withers was very definite.

"And you think it was the same—the same as the man on the plane?"

Again Miss Withers was sure.

"Poor little Mister Jones," Phyllis cooed. "Does he feel better now?" The little dog wriggled in her arms. "Oh, Lord! There it goes again!"

Hurriedly she put the dog down. But this time the invalid made no efforts to die, nor was there a single retch. As the two worried women bent over the tottering animal, they saw what it was that had impelled Mister Jones to want down.

With twin sighs of relief, they hurried on toward the bus while Mister Jones trotted soberly behind with the prize.

The bus swung away from the airport, leaving the landing to the motionless red-and-gilt *Dragonfly* with its dark secret. Overhead the gulls were screaming, and their dark shadows swept crazily across the faces of the two women who were riding back toward the city, a sadder but not wiser little dog cuddling between them with a crackerjack box beneath its paws.

CHAPTER VI

THE wind that blows nobody good blew, upon that sunny August after-noon, a gratifying rush of business through the wide-open doors of Catalina's approximation of a grand hotel, the St. Lena.

"You might as well get off here with me," advised Miss Hildegarde Withers, as the red bus which bore Mister Jones, Phyllis La Fond, and herself came down out of the canyon and skirted the hotel grounds. "It's the best and only hotel."

"And I always stay at the best hotels," Phyllis said. "Heaven only knows how." She signaled the plump youth to stop.

"Unless I miss my guess," went on Miss Withers, "We'll have com-pany before long. For Chief of Police Britt has put his foot down upon the idea of anybody leaving the island—anybody who was on the *Drag-onfly* this morning."

"It ought to be a regular old-home week here," Phyllis remarked, as her bags were being carried through the door and up the stone steps. "We'll sleep well, anyway—knowing that one of the party is a murderer."

"Then you agree with me?" Miss Withers was gratified.

Phyllis grinned and enclosed an unwilling Mister Jones in the leath-erette container. "I might as well agree with you," she admitted. "You seem to be a person who is usually right, and I'm wrong nine tenths of the time. All the same, I don't see who could have bumped off that little guy with all of us sitting right there in the plane."

"That's for him to know, and us to find out," Miss Withers concluded. "When you register, young woman, insist that the clerk give you a five-dollar room. He has a few—the one next to mine was vacant this morn-ing—but he'll try to sell you one on the third floor for eight."

"Yeah? Well, listen to me, sister. If that clerk at the desk was ten years younger and if I wasn't so tired from that ride in our fresh friend's wheel-barrow of a bus, I'd show you how to get a room on the third for five, or maybe even three-fifty."

Phyllis held out her hand, with fingernails like dropsical rubies, and Miss Withers shook it gravely.

"I'll probably see you at dinner, Miss—was it La Fond?"

"Among a lot of other things, yes. Born Schultz. My friends call me Phyd, and my enemies call me towhead. Take your pick."

"His intimate friends called him Candle-ends, and his enemies, Toasted-cheese," quoted Miss Withers. "Well, good-bye, Phyd."

Miss Hildegarde Withers had enjoyed her quiet room near the stairs on the second floor for the past week in comparative seclusion. To that seclusion she now said a painless good-bye.

She washed quickly and changed her dress for dinner. In her bathroom she heard sounds of bustle next door which told her that Phyllis had succeeded in obtaining the five-dollar room.

But Miss Withers had a strong hunch that Phyllis La Fond was not the only one of the *Dragonfly's* passengers likely to seek the luxurious shelter of the St. Lena. "Lucky I came here instead of taking a bungalow," she told herself.

She made a survey of her room and discovered that from the vantage point of a chair mounted beneath the open transom above her door, she could obtain an excellent view of the stair—with only two upper floors the St. Lena did not have or need a lift—and of the hallway.

During the hour or two remaining before dinner, Miss Withers at the cost of a stiff neck had the pleasure of watching Roscoe, the octogenarian who acted as bellhop for the St. Lena, as he variously disposed of the *Dragonfly's* passengers.

The first to come was T. Girard Tompkins, who bore, as if in explanation of his disappearance, additional baggage consisting of a pair of very decorative blue glaze bowls. He was given a room across the hall—Number 17.

Mr. Ralph O. Tate, who followed very soon after, was led on up the stairs toward the more expensive suites. Mr. Tate's two sad-eyed henchmen, Tony and George, were placed in Room 18, far down the hall of the second floor. Then came Captain Thorwald Narveson, freckled and blue-eyed, with his corncob pipe going full blast. His was Room 19—like all the odd-numbered rooms, it faced, not the ocean, but the hills in the rear. It was evident that Captain Narveson placed no premium on a sea view.

One by one Miss Withers checked them off—there had been nine passengers aboard the *Dragonfly*. One of them lay in the infirmary with a sheet over his face. That left only the honeymoon couple unaccounted for. They were probably mooning through the curio shops that lined the waterfront, Miss Withers hazarded a guess as she climbed down from her chair.

The schoolteacher shook her head a little sadly as she thought of the sobering effects that the events of the morning must have had upon the young couple. It was not the sort of excitement that honeymooners seek, to have a dead man topple into the midst of their orange blossoms.

But they were young enough to forget it easily, Miss Withers reminded herself. Probably were too full of the future to think of the present anyway.

Miss Withers replaced the chair in its proper place beside the wide windows that opened out on the balcony above the sea and went down to dinner.

On the stairs she passed T. Girard Tompkins, who, if he was glad to see her, managed to hide his delight admirably.

"Fancy meeting you here," said Miss Withers cheerfully.

"Oh, yes," said Tompkins. "I always stay here. Good hotel, don't you think?" He started to move on and then paused.

"I suppose you're wondering what happened to me after our ride into town together?" Miss Withers wasn't wondering anything of the kind, but she put on an interested expression.

"I made an effort to find Chief Britt, who is a personal friend of mine," explained Mr. Tompkins unnecessarily. "When I heard that he was already at the infirmary, I went about my business at the pottery works, which is very urgent. I hope my absence did not inconvenience anybody?"

"On the contrary," said Hildegarde Withers, and went on. She could not have explained why she disliked the man, but there was something in the air when he was near—an aura of Rotary good-fellowship and cheap gin. Besides, when he talked to her his glance turned to the floor, the ceiling, the pictures on the wall—anywhere but at her.

But then, murderers were rarely shifty-eyed and unpleasant, as Miss Withers had learned to her sorrow. She shrugged her shoulders and strode onward, through the wide doorway that led into the palatial dining room of the St. Lena. Outside the thousand windows a sea was fast losing its blue-green color, and the gulls were swinging back and forth with their haunting cry like the creak of a rusty gate. But Miss Withers had no eye for the beauties of the evening. Her glance was turned toward the center of the well-filled dining room.

There, at a large circle of white linen reminiscent of Arthur of England's storied Table Round, were dining a number of persons whom she had never thought to see gathered together again—unless in a courtroom.

Phyllis La Fond was signaling her frantically, and Miss Withers moved in that direction, tacking between the crowded lesser tables like a schooner making way through an island passage.

"The more the merrier," called Phyllis, as Miss Withers came within hailing distance. "The Ancient Order of Dragonflies is having its first banquet!"

There was an empty chair between Tony, the more worried of Tate's two assistants, and Phyllis herself. Miss Withers sank into it.

"If this is the Dragonfly Club, I'm afraid I'm not eligible for membership," she observed.

Phyllis hastened to reassure the newcomer. "This was my idea," she confessed. "So I snagged everyone of the bunch who ventured in here. We might as well stick together and have a couple of laughs."

"But—"

"Don't worry," Phyllis told her. "You belong as much as any of us. Didn't you discover that Mr. Forrest was—well, discover that he was dead? Besides, I've been telling the others about our trip up to the plane this afternoon—"

Miss Withers could have cut her throat for that, cheerfully. But Phyllis rattled on, while the schoolteacher bit her tongue.

"And about how you're interested in the case and everything. So we'll make you an honorary member, won't we, gang?"

The gang evidenced its individual consent by various monosyllabics. However, Miss Withers could not help but notice that Phyllis's good-humored raillery at their predicament, combined with the dinner which was proving itself excellent, had put a different complexion on the group. Even Ralph O. Tate was unbending a little. Captain Narveson twinkled from across the table as if he considered this all part of a theatrical performance put on for his especial benefit. Tony and George forgot to match coins, and the general air was one of festivity.

"Shall we make it by acclamation?" went on Phyllis, still in the role of master of ceremonies. "No—wait, here comes Mr. Tompkins with the bottle. Hurry up, Tommy!"

Phyllis turned to Miss Withers. "I thought a drink might make the newlyweds feel happier, and Tommy said he had some liquor in his suitcase."

Miss Withers nodded. "He wouldn't have a toothbrush, but he'd have liquor," she remarked acidly.

"Well, the liquor probably took out his teeth years ago," Phyllis came back. Tompkins, who had quite evidently halted on the way to tap one of the square bottles which appeared in either pocket of his coat, was approaching the table.

Already the waiter was distributing tall glasses half full of ice, and began pouring ginger ale into them. People at other tables turned enviously.

"A highball with dinner?" inquired Mr. Tate blankly. But he held out his glass all the same.

"None for me, please," Miss Withers said.

"You aren't supposed to drink this," Phyllis informed her. "All right, fellow Dragons—or is it Flies? Anyway, a toast to our new honorary member, Miss Hildegarde Martha Withers—good health to her!"

The others all rose—all except the newlyweds, who had first to be jogged out of their accustomed daze. Ice tinkled in the glasses. ...

Miss Withers sat in her chair, ill at ease and more than a little nervous at the way Phyllis had dragged her out into the limelight.

"One of you is drinking that toast with a wagon tongue in his cheek," thought Miss Withers, but she did not say it.

As she murmured an appropriate sentiment, her eyes, roving through the crowded dining room, fell upon a man who sat, solitary and somber, against the farther window. He had been staring toward the center table, perhaps attracted by Phyllis's spectacular charms. As their eyes met, Miss Withers was sure that he recognized her. Then he turned away.

"It's too bad that Mr. Barney Kelsey is not sitting with us," she said, very softly.

But none of the others had heard of Barney Kelsey, until sometime that morning the bodyguard of Roswell T. Forrest. There was another who might well have joined the party, but not even Miss Withers was as yet aware of his existence.

The dinner continued—aided on its way by Phyllis's high spirits and by the bottled spirits of T. Girard Tompkins, who by now was urging everybody to call him "Tommy." By unspoken consent they avoided the tragedy of the morning as a topic of conversation.

During coffee—which was diluted with gin to make what Phyllis fondly believed was a coffee-royal, that effervescent young lady had another idea. She clapped her hands together, so that two waiters came running and the people at the nearby tables bit their forks.

"Listen," she cried. "I've got a swell idea. We're all in the same boat, and we might as well have some fun. Suppose we stick together this evening? They have dancing in the Casino—it's free, too. What do you say?"

There were vague murmurs. "I don't see how anybody could object to going—unless he wanted to be an old crab," Phyllis added.

She started around the table. T. Girard Tompkins, on her right, evidenced a loud if sodden spirit of camaraderie. He hoped the party would stick together forever. In all his life he'd never met such a fine bunch. He had, he announced, a house in Pasadena. If the sheriff hadn't got it yet, wouldn't they all come and live with him …? His voice ran off in a mumble.

"He'll go, he says," translated Phyllis. "If he's able." She pointed at Ralph O. Tate. "How about you?"

Mr. Tate was dubious. "I've got to long-distance some of the studio executives and explain why I've lost a day's shooting," he said. "But maybe I'll drop in at the Casino afterwards."

Phyllis leaned toward Captain Narveson, who still twinkled in comfortable silence. "How about you?"

"A boat from my whaling ship meets me about midnight," he told her. "Ay have to be down on the wharf and explain to my son Axel why Ay don't go till tomorrow. But maybe Ay yust stop in to see you dancing with the young fallers here, eh?"

The young fellows, in the persons of George and Tony, were of one mind about it. They had no long-distance calls to make and they had no ships to meet and they would just as soon go dancing as anything else.

Phyllis had got round to the newlyweds. "How about it, Mr. and Mrs. Deving? Hey, I mean you!"

Kay Deving opened her large, soft eyes very wide. "Who—me?"

"Haven't used the name long enough to get used to it, huh? Well, are you coming with us, you two? Bright lights, soft music, and the best dancing floor in California!"

"Well—if Marvy wants to—" said Kay.

"Well—if Kay wants to—" said Marvin. They spoke with one breath, and left off, looking rather foolish.

They began again. "I'm afraid—" said Kay.

"I don't think—" said Marvin.

"Perhaps we'd better go some other night," finished Kay. She smiled, a little apologetically. "You see, we—we just got married—"

"And we haven't even registered and got a room yet—"

"So maybe you'll excuse us?"

T. Girard Tompkins began to chuckle, and a broad remark trembled on the tip of his tongue. But Phyllis kicked him savagely in the ankle.

"And we've been dancing a whole lot lately," finished the redheaded girl. Miss Withers noticed again the eyes, which without their dark shading goggles of this afternoon were surprisingly luminous and deep. They were brown, with little flecks of a green in them which was sometimes almost yellow—eyes that were an excellent reason, Miss Withers thought, for the adoration which fairly surged toward her from the slick-haired young husband.

Phyllis was a young woman of some force. "Oh, come on, you kids. You've got all your lifetime to register and get a room. But you've never seen a ballroom like the Casino!"

Kay Deving looked at her Marvin, and they seemed to share a secret joke between them.

"Oh, go on dreaming, then," Phyllis told them. "You'll come, Miss Withers—I know you're a sport!"

The waiter approached with the check, and laid it ostentatiously in the middle of the table, where the men of the party stared at it.

"Let's make it Dutch, of course," said Miss Withers.

T. Girard Tompkins extended a languid hand—demonstrating where it was that motion pictures got the idea of slow-motion photography. But it was Ralph O. Tate who picked up the check and took out his wallet.

"This circus has cost the studio a couple of grand already in wasted time," he said. "They may as well get stuck for eleven bucks more."

"You're very gracious," Miss Withers told him.

Tate nodded warily. But one generous gesture begets another. Before he left the table he drew from the left pocket of his vest four inexpensive cigars. "Here," he offered, and passed them out to the captain, Tompkins, and his two assistants. Marvin Deving was smoking a cigarette.

There was a murmuring of thanks, and then Captain Narveson sniffed his cigar and crammed it into his corncob. There was a short strained silence.

Ralph O. Tate absently drew from the right-hand pocket of his vest a dark mottled Corona Perfecto and lit it with a gold-and-diamond lighter.

"So long, folks," he said. "See you through the bars." Then he was gone—sweater, riding boots, and all.

"Through the bars, eh?" Captain Narveson applied a fourth match to the bowl of his pipe. "From the inside, Ay bat yu!"

The party broke up at that sally. The captain followed his pipe out toward the pier—Tompkins loudly inquired of a waiter as to the whereabouts of the washroom, and Tony and George departed with the avowed purpose of changing into their dancing clothes.

Miss Withers made her way slowly toward the door, going around the room so as to pass by the table where she had seen the lonely figure of Barney Kelsey. But he had departed, and only a coffee cup and a solitary quarter for the waitress showed that he had been there.

In the doorway Phyllis waited. "You know why I did it, don't you?" she said, as Miss Withers came up. "I thought it would give you a chance to look them all over. Don't I make a swell Dr. Watson? Notice any signs of guilt?"

"I did not," Miss Withers confessed. "But I wish you hadn't told them about my going to the plane."

Phyllis grinned. "They knew it anyway. So I kidded them along—but I left out about Mister Jones getting sick."

"Bravo!" said Miss Withers. "You know, I've never dined like this in my life. With a red-handed murderer, perhaps, in our midst, laughing and chatting like the rest of us. I kept thinking of it—and though I ate all my dinner, I couldn't for the life of me tell you what I had."

"Neither can I," Phyllis confessed. She was looking back into the dining room, almost deserted now. "And neither can *they.*"

She indicated the newlyweds, who still sat, amid the wreckage of the feast, staring into each other's eyes, while the glares of the impatient waiters passed over their cloud-wrapped heads.

"It's like a disease with them," said Hildegarde Withers.

Phyllis turned on her. "A disease! Well, maybe you're right. But it's a disease I'd do anything in the world to get—if I could be like they are!"

"Even murder?" inquired Miss Withers softly. But Phyllis La Fond did not hear.

CHAPTER VII

"HELL'S bells ringing in the rafters, Hell's bells beckon ..." Somewhere on the moonlit loggia a clear soprano voice caught up the tune which the orchestra in the grand ballroom was playing, and continued to the end. "All is forsaken—when roll is taken ..." There was a laugh and a scuffle, and the song ended.

Hildegarde Withers, standing alone in one of the arched doorways, shivered a little, although she was wearing a sensible blue-serge suit, and the night was warm.

"All I can say is—the tunes they dance to today aren't much like the ones when I was a girl," she remarked out loud to nobody in particular. "Then it wasn't 'Hell's Bells,' it was 'Daisy Belle.' "

The Casino was crowded tonight, and nearly a thousand young men were propelling the same number of young women back and forth and around upon a floor of inlaid wood floated, at great expense to the late Mr. Wrigley, upon a bed of resilient cork. From time to time, as the tempo of the orchestra changed, the lighting system veered from orange to soft blue, and then deepened to a sensuous purple spot which wavered across the rapt faces of the devotees who whirled, dipped, glided, and then whirled again with a monotonous sameness.

"And they talk about this young generation and its wild orgy of pleasure," Miss Withers went on. "Those young people look about as orgiastic as if they were playing tennis."

She could see now and then the supple figure of Phyllis La Fond, encased in an evening gown of flaming crimson, with puffed sleeves and a flowing skirt that parodied the party dresses that Miss Withers had worn just after the turn of the century.

Phyllis was dancing with no less a person than Mr. T. Girard Tompkins, and as the dance progressed Miss Withers could see that it was with more and more difficulty that the girl held Mr. Tompkins in a vertical position. In spite of her best efforts, he was prone to stumble on the turns and to work his left arm up and down in a pump-handle motion.

"Hey!" Phyllis reminded him sharply.

But Tompkins only closed his eyes ecstatically. "Beautiful," he murmured and stepped with all his two hundred pounds upon the toe of Phyllis's satin slipper. They turned again, and Miss Withers sniffed.

"Before I'd let a man put his hand on my bare back—"

She turned suddenly as she felt herself surrounded. But it was only Tony and George, the two sad young gentlemen who were paying for past and future sins by acting as assistants to Ralph O. Tate.

"We're looking—" said Tony.

"Have you seen her?" said George.

"I didn't know you with neckties on," confessed Miss Withers. "Have I seen whom?"

"Not whom," complained Tony. "Phyllis. Have you seen her?"

Miss Withers indicated the spot, on the crowded floor, where she had last seen Phyllis in the drowning grip of Mr. Tompkins.

"We can cut," said Tony.

"Okay," said George.

"Match you to see which gets her first and which takes Tompkins off the floor."

"Okay," said George.

"Call it," said Tony.

"Heads," said George, listlessly. It was tails; it was always tails. They wormed themselves through the swaying throng, and Miss Withers was alone again.

She began to wonder why she had come. It was already past her usual bedtime—and yet she had the feeling that something was portending, something hanging and ready to fall. There was a tension, an electric charge, in the very air—or else she was getting jumpy.

She turned and walked out across the marble loggia. All of Avalon Bay lay before her, a half-moon strung with lights which made the dark swelling water a setting for ten thousand jeweled points of diamond.

As she walked couples separated, staring after her and slowly coming closer again as she passed. "An old-maid schoolteacher doesn't belong here," said Hildegarde Withers to herself.

She found a stone bench in a vacant corner and seated herself upon it, her foot swinging back and forth to the music which she would have stoutly maintained was no music at all. Her thoughts were again moiling over the mystery of the morning.

Then the orchestra paused, and a stream of dancers came out into the moonlight. Through them, walking swiftly, moved a lithe figure in crimson—and Phyllis La Fond dropped on the bench beside her with a sigh of relief.

"So here you are! May I stay a minute? I don't want that tank of a Tompkins to find me, and Tony and George are almost as much of a nuisance for different reasons." Phyllis placed her red satin slippers on the balustrade, leaned back against the bench with a wasted display of shimmering silk stocking, and lit a cigarette. "Sorry—will you have one?"

"Snooping is my only vice," said Hildegarde Withers. "Besides, I'm afraid of fire as close to me as a cigarette would be."

"Then you ought to chew cut plug," suggested Phyllis amiably. She did a quick repair job with her lipstick.

"You're not dancing?" she inquired blithely. "You should have snagged the Norsky. I'll bet Captain Narveson can do a mean heel-and-toe."

"I might dance, if they'd play a mazurka," confessed Miss Withers. "Or even a good square dance."

Phyllis flicked her cigarette over the balcony, as if it annoyed her. "Well, anyway, I got everybody here except the captain, the newlyweds, and the Great Tate," she said. "I really didn't think the captain would show up. He's probably in his room writing a letter to some wife that he's had for forty years."

"Everyone to his own taste," Miss Withers reminded her. But Phyllis was thinking of something else.

"I didn't say it wasn't right, did I? But it's Tate I wanted to come. He could do a lot for me if he wanted to." Phyllis stared wistfully at the moon. "He's directing *King Passion* for Paradox—it's an epic of life among the pearl divers. They're going to make the location shots up at the Isthmus, at the other end of the island. He could give me a part if he wanted to."

"Will you tell me the difference between an epic and an ordinary motion picture?" Miss Withers was suddenly curious.

"An epic," explained Phyllis La Fond, "is a picture where the hero and heroine die about the third reel and then their grandchildren fall in love. Tate directs nothing but epics, and sometimes he directs a super-epic. But he's hard to make."

"Fancy that!" said Hildegarde Withers. She looked sharply at her companion. "So Mr. Ralph O. Tate doesn't give something for nothing, eh?"

Phyllis was silent. "Except of course, nickel cigars and nips from his flask—"

The girl gave such a start that Miss Withers broke off. "What's the matter?"

"Oh, nothing. I just remembered something." Phyllis laughed.

"Something about—the trip this morning?" pressed Miss Withers.

Phyllis shook her head. "Something about my career, or what might be my career."

Miss Withers dropped the subject. "You're very ambitious to be a motion-picture actress, aren't you? No matter what it costs?"

"Listen," Phyllis told her. "I'm very ambitious to get ahead, in any way. Nowadays a girl has got to use everything she's got or can borrow—before the old chin line begins to sag. It's a tough racket, this, and I love it. I'm made for it, see?"

Phyllis stopped suddenly and clutched Miss Withers's arm. "Look— no, not there—in the doorway. Who is it? He stared at me all through dinner. I love gray hair on a man."

"So you get a whiff of the quarry, do you?" Miss Withers turned from Phyllis's ardent, predatory face toward the indicated doorway. Inside, the orchestra was playing again, but the stranger showed no interest in the various hopeful and unattached young women who lurked here and there, swaying their lithe bodies to the music.

"Barney Kelsey!" said Miss Withers slowly. "That's his name, young woman. And if you never listen to me again as long as you live, take heed now and keep far away from him."

Phyllis laughed, a low, throaty laugh. "Watch me," she challenged. "He looks interesting—and lonesome."

But as she started to rise, Barney Kelsey wandered away from them.

"He's not as lonely as you think," said Miss Withers dryly. "Look behind him."

As Kelsey disappeared around the curve of the building, there appeared from a nearer doorway the gaunt and doddering figure of Chief Britt's "deppity." A wide dark hat covered his face, and he was taking tremendous pains to conceal his presence from the world in general, but there was no mistaking his intentions.

"Hawkshaw Ruggles—and he's shadowing Kelsey!" Miss Withers turned toward her companion. "Now what do you think of—"

She stopped short, for Phyllis was now little more than a red splash against the doorway of the Casino, followed by a lingering trail of a very strong and very good perfume of which Miss Withers would have liked to know the name.

"She must have seen another lonely man," said Miss Withers philosophically. "Or at least another man."

She rose to her feet, preparatory to bidding the festive gathering a farewell. But she had traversed only a few steps of the walk around the loggia when she ran into the half-open arms of Tompkins.

"Well, if it isn't Mizz Wizzers!" The inebriate greeted her like a long-lost brother. "My ol' pal Mizz Wizzers!"

Miss Withers found herself at something of a loss for words. Finally she managed a polite "How do you do?"

"Come on and dansh!" insisted Mr. Tompkins. "Won't take no for an answer. We'll show them something, you and me." Tompkins demonstrated what it was he wished to show by performing a little dance step all his own, accompanied by much quivering of his paunch and embellished by a final stagger or two. "Come on, baby!"

"I'm standing this one out," Miss Withers told him. Mr. Tompkins's face fell like a shot. "Aw, come on," he pleaded. "Listen to that music. 'S my favorite tune, and nobody'll dance with me. That girl in red skips out with the movie director and now you turn me down."

"She did, did she?" Miss Withers bit her lip and then turned on her heel, leaving T. Girard Tompkins telling his troubles to the moon.

Quickly and quietly she made a survey of the ballroom, finding Tony and George promoting their fortunes with some chiffon-clad local talent. Lew French, one of the *Dragonfly's* pilots, was stepping with the prim starched nurse from the infirmary—now neither prim nor starched. But there was no sign of Phyllis.

The loggia, from one end to the other, proved also a blank, although Miss Withers interrupted tête-à-têtes between half a dozen couples whom that lady fondly and innocently believed to be engaged, at least.

At a loss, Miss Withers paused at the outermost edge of the loggia and leaned over the parapet. To her right, a lantern-hung walk led to the town half a mile away, with at least a thousand places where a couple might be having the interview which she was tremendously desirous of overhearing. Or perhaps they had gone back to the hotel—at any rate, she was, as her pupils would have said, "out of luck."

Resignedly, Miss Withers made her way back toward the main staircase, keeping a weather eye out for any signs of the big song-and-dance man, Tompkins. But she was safe—almost too safe, she thought.

She found herself wondering if Oscar Piper, that grizzled and hard-bitten inspector now on a train somewhere between New York and California, had ever learned to dance. "And to think I almost married him once—and never found that out!" Miss Withers shook her head sadly.

Then she stopped short. Without particularly noticing where she was going, she had come part way down the main staircase which led from the ballroom floor to the lower level and the theater foyer. She was now standing upon a landing, halfway down the stair—and from somewhere near her she could detect that strong and yet elusive scent which adorned the all-too-evident charms of Miss Phyllis La Fond!

She looked all around, but she had the landing to herself. There were no doorways leading into the theater, which had but lately run the last reel of the last *Mickey Mouse* on the program.

But the foyer below was equipped with benches and smoking stands for the convenience of patrons. By leaning far over the balustrade, Hildegarde Withers could catch a glimpse, not of one of these benches, but only of a pair of men's shoes, well-brushed gray suedes—and of a pair of well-filled sheer stockings beside them ending in red dancing slippers.

Miss Withers could have dropped a pebble on Phyllis and Ralph O. Tate—had she been equipped with such a missile and had she been addicted to such minor practical joking.

The murmur of voices came up to her, a murmur only distinguishable as the tones of a baritone and a contralto voice in a blurred conversational duet. The words were drowned out by Mr. Tompkins's favorite tune—which happened to be "Hustling and Bustling for Baby," if that matters.

But finally the dance drew to its end, and the weary orchestra on the platform of the Casino ballroom put up its instruments and mopped its foreheads. Miss Withers gripped the balustrade with tense hands and strained the ears which could detect a whisper in the last row of her third-grade classroom at Jefferson School.

Slowly and painfully, like a distant station coming in over a balky radio set, the words of the couple beneath her grew clearer.

Phyllis was speaking. "... and you wouldn't want that to happen, would you?"

"No, I wouldn't want that to happen," agreed Tate. "I'll see what I can do."

"You'd better decide right here and now," Phyllis continued. Her voice was strained and a little hard. "If you don't come through I'll go to Chief Britt first thing in the morning and tell him about that flask. Don't think I haven't the nerve. If he knew—"

"All right, all right. I didn't say I wouldn't, did I?" Tate's voice had a worried ring in it. "I'll phone the studio in the morning, and I'm pretty sure they'll do what I say. It isn't much of a part, though—"

"I don't care," Phyllis said. "It's a part. I'm tired of being left out in the cold."

Mr. Tate said something which was lost as Miss Withers found herself forced by the approach of some homeward-bound revelers to leave her post momentarily. When the coast was clear again she heard:

"If it comes right down to that," Phyllis was saying, "blackmail isn't anything nowadays. I've heard stories about how you hold your job because of what you know about some of the Chosen People."

Tate's answer to this was lost.

"All right, so I'm what you say," continued Phyllis. "I'm practically anything you choose to call me. But, just to get confessional, why? Because three years ago a little fat man went hunting San Quentin quail, and I was the quail. My Aunt Emma used to sing a song about the bird with the broken pinion never flying so high again. Well, I was broken and he did the flying. So I'm out to get whatever I can however I can. I'll emote as well as any of the frozen-faced floozies that drip glycerin in front of your cameras—and I can do anything else that they can do, too."

There was a long and significant pause, and then the great director of epics and super-epics spoke with a new note in his voice. Unfortunately his choice of vocabulary was such that Miss Withers was quite at a loss to comprehend his meaning.

"Then it's in the bag, baby," he was saying. "You know, you've got a lot of what it takes. I like little girls with nerve, and I can do a lot for you as long as we're friends—"

Phyllis laughed, a little hysterically. "A Hollywood engagement, huh? Why not?" A white, unhealthy hand moved across the silken leg, and Miss Withers's eyebrows lifted another inch. But Phyllis La Fond was rising.

"Have I got to pay the price right here in public?" she bantered.

"Later, then," said Ralph O. Tate confidently. They were coming toward the stair, and Miss Withers drew hastily back out of sight. She had heard all, or almost all, that she had wanted to hear. But she had an odd feeling of letdown. It was not because she had played the ignoble role of eavesdropper. The end justified the means, she considered. But tonight she had seen or rather heard a new Phyllis—a hard, designing, blackmailing Phyllis. And Miss Withers had almost grown to like the girl.

Well, for that matter she had been rather fond of two of the three murderers she had been privileged to know in the past. She had learned to her cost that the descendants of Cain wear no mark upon their brows.

Phyllis and the director were coming up the staircase, so Miss Withers was forced to make a hasty retreat up to the ballroom again. She lost herself amid the throng, coming out at the other end of the room and going immediately to the cool loggia. The stars were somehow dimmer and the moonlight more diffused. A white bank of fog was drifting in from the sea.

"And I'm simply a sentimental old woman," Hildegarde Withers told herself. "After forty years of this grubby old world I ought to realize that you can't make a silk purse out of a sow's ear." Her intellectual honesty made her pause and smile at herself. "Of course, they do wonderful things with rayon—"

She shook her head and straightened her hat. "It's way past my bedtime," she reminded herself. "I've seen and heard enough for one night."

But Miss Hildegarde Withers was far from seeing and hearing all that the fates held in store for her this night. As she made her way back toward the staircase, again she chanced to run, not into Phyllis and Tate, who had disappeared, but into the ubiquitous T. Girard Tompkins, paunch, elk's tooth, and all.

At that moment he was surrounded by newlyweds. With either arm he gripped a Deving—Kay on his left and Marvin on his right.

"Hurray!" he shouted, as Miss Withers hove into view. "Look who's here! These kids were just sitting around mooning—and it took little Tommy to bring them out to make whoopee-eee!"

Kay Deving smiled faintly. Tompkins continued: "Imagine sitting around a hotel bedroom on their wedding night! Imagine it!"

Miss Withers imagined it, without difficulty. Tompkins turned to the redhaired girl on his left. "Mrs. Deving—they're playing m' favorite tune. May I have th' honor?"

Kay looked at her young husband. "If Marvin—"

Marvin looked at Kay. "Well, if Kay—"

Miss Withers stepped into the breach. "I think they ought to dance the first one together," she said. "Really, Mr. Tompkins!"

Miss Withers was to treasure for some time the memory of the grateful look that flashed from the fiery brown eyes of Kay Deving. As Tompkins loosened his grip, the young couple danced off together—slick dark hair against red curls.

"They dance as if they were one person," Miss Withers observed aloud. "As if they'd been dancing together all their lives."

"This's m' favorite tune," insisted Tompkins. As Miss Withers's support was denied him, he leaned against the doorway. "Swee' Rosie O'Grady—"

The orchestra was, at the moment, rendering its interpretation of that classic of yesterday "How Many Times," but Miss Withers did not pause to enlighten him. At the farther door she caught a glimpse of a gentleman in blue coat and flannel slacks, who was signaling to her.

As she drew closer, she saw that it was Dr. O'Rourke. "I didn't know you with your clothes on," she told him as they met in a secluded byway of the mammoth floor.

"It's about the only thing you didn't know, then," said O'Rourke. "I didn't expect to find you here. Just looked in, as I usually do, to see what's going on in our fair village. But I may as well tell you"—the doctor looked all around cautiously—"I may as well tell you that you win."

"I win what?" Miss Withers wanted to know.

"You win round one. Regarding the corpse, I mean. The body of Forrest, lying over in my infirmary." O'Rourke lowered his voice, and there was a new note of respect in it. "Chief Britt got a wire from a guy named Piper, who is a big shot in the New York Police. This guy Piper heard about the stiff and is on his way out here. He thinks it's murder—and tonight the chief ordered me to make an autopsy the first thing in the morning. We're not sending the body in to Long Beach. If there's going to be a big fuss, it'll be right here. And if Forrest died from anything besides heart failure, I'll know it before lunchtime tomorrow!"

Miss Withers nodded. "This is gratifying, Doctor."

"Well, keep it under your hat, see? The chief doesn't like the looks of this guy Barney Kelsey. He wanted those two letters that Forrest had in his pocket, and the chief wouldn't give 'em to him. Britt thinks maybe Kelsey was mixed up in it, and he's got a man tailing him."

"So I noticed," Miss Withers told him. Dr. O'Rourke saw her face set and her eyes focus on a point over his shoulder.

"Quick, dance with me," she whispered. The doctor took her somewhat awkwardly in his arms.

"I don't—"

"You will," said Hildegarde Withers. "Somebody was listening outside that door."

O'Rourke made a soundless whistle with his lips. They moved across the floor in an old-fashioned two-step, and Miss Withers was oddly light in his arms. "Dance towards the door now," she spoke in his ear. "I want to see who it was."

But to her disappointment the loggia was deserted except for the cheerful, twinkling figure of Captain Thorwald Narveson, who sucked contentedly at his corncob pipe from a perch on the parapet.

"That's that," said Miss Withers sadly.

But Dr. O'Rourke held out his arms again. "We may as well finish the dance, ma'am." And they did.

CHAPTER VIII

"AUTOPSY before breakfast," announced T. Girard Tompkins. "Yessir, they're going to open up this Forrest and find out what made him stop ticking."

"Is that so?" George inquired absently. Then with some difficulty he freed his lapels from the convivial clutch of Mr. Tompkins and cut across the dance floor to the corner where his partner Tony was doing a little personal promotion with several pajama-clad young ladies.

"Come here a minute," said George. "I gotta see you alone."

Tony came, somewhat reluctantly. "Listen," said George excitedly. "Last-minute news flash. I just heard—"

"Never mind what you heard," said Tony. "I'm trying to get us invited out to dinner tomorrow night. With this autopsy coming off in the morning, we're likely to be stuck here all week, and we might as well make hey-hey while the sun shines."

"You know about it?" George was blank. "The autopsy, I mean?"

"Who doesn't?" Tony returned, and went back to his women.

George continued on his way. Then he caught sight of Phyllis and Tate, just completing the dance with a sweeping tango step which brought them almost mouth to mouth and then sent the crimson-clad body of Phyllis in a long whirl, ending with her on one knee before her partner.

Phyllis looked ecstatic and Tate looked bored. "Hey," called George. "Listen, Mr. Tate, I got news. Did you hear what's happening? They're going to have an autopsy on the stiff in the morning!"

Tate was still bored. "So I heard," he said. "I'd like to see it, but I never get up that early."

"Shall I call you or nudge you?" Phyllis quoted the ancient smoking-car story, and then as the music picked up again, they danced away.

George looked after them for a moment and then shambled on, with his hands in his pockets. Somehow nobody seemed to be as interested in the news as he himself was. Then he saw a sober blue-garbed figure out on the loggia and made a last try.

"Hey, Captain," he called. "They're going to have an autopsy!"

Captain Narveson nodded toward him and then turned back toward the light-sprinkled waterfront. It was evident that the captain had something pressing on his mind.

He caught George's elbow. "Yust look," he ordered. His thick brown finger indicated a dark hulk which rose and fell in the moonlight, about halfway between shore and fog. Riding lights shone faintly at the mast-head.

"Young faller," he confided, "there lies my *City of Saunders,* the neatest little whale-killer ship in the Pacific. Out there waits my son Axel, and he's all ready to go a-whaling down in Mexican waters. The whales are moving south toward the Antarctic, and Ay have to send word to Axel he's got to wait another day before we can start. And the whales are going past, big blue whales and hooked finbacks and all—what do you think Ay care about your autopsy?"

"It's not my autopsy," protested George. Then he wandered disconsolately out into the night.

Phyllis and the director finished another dance. "Come on over this way," she pleaded. "The newlyweds are here and I want to say hello."

"Can't you say it from here?" Tate wanted to know. But he followed her.

"So you turned out after all?" inquired Phyllis cheerily as they came upon the rapt young couple. "Swell music, isn't it?"

Young Mr. Deving beamed upon her, and young Mrs. Deving beamed also. His was naturally the warmer beam, but Phyllis was used to that. "Mr. Tompkins wouldn't take no for an answer," explained Marvin Deving.

"So we just came over for a little while," finished Kay, with a flash of her red curls.

"Might as well be gay," said Phyllis philosophically. "You can make anything into a party if you try hard enough." She had an idea.

"Suppose we be really informal and trade this dance?" she asked brightly. "I don't think it's quite decent of you two kids to be so engrossed in each other."

Marvin Deving smoothed back his slick hair with a little red pocket comb. His face wore an expression of eagerness.

"Sure, let's trade—that is if—"

There was a long moment while Tate surveyed Kay from toes to the top of her red head. His glance was as piercing, as penetrating, and as sexless as an X-ray.

"Sure," he offered, finally.

Phyllis held out her arms to Marvin Deving, but his young wife drew him back protectively.

"I'd just love to dance with Mr. Tate," she said. "But it's getting late. We didn't intend to stay so long, did we, Marvy? We want to get up early in the morning—"

"Oh," said Phyllis. She dropped her arms. "I suppose you're going down bright and early to see the autopsy performed on our recent ship-mate?"

Kay Deving's milk-white skin became whiter still.

"You've heard about that, haven't you?" asked Phyllis.

"Oh, yes," Kay answered. "The poor, poor man! But what makes you think I'd want to see a thing like that, even if they'd let us? It makes me sick even to think of it. Marvy, let's go home!"

At once the young bride contrived to lean upon her husband's arm and to drag him away from Phyllis, toward the door.

"I was only being nasty," confessed Phyllis. "I'm sorry I broke the baby's heart."

Ralph O. Tate shrugged his shoulders. "Beautiful and dumb," was his verdict. "Too bad she's married. That carrot-top ought to go well in pictures. She's simple enough for me to make an actress out of, given time."

"I don't think she's so beautiful," Phyllis told him shortly. She paused and stared after the disappearing couple. "And I don't think she's so dumb. She's found her man and she's clinging to him like a leech. I think they're both sweet."

Tate was whistling "Hearts and Flowers" softly to himself. Then he broke in upon Phyllis's reverie. "Let's get back to the hotel."

But Phyllis didn't want to go. "I'm for a walk," she said. "In the moonlight."

Walks in the moonlight were nothing to Ralph O. Tate. Nothing but picture hokum.

"See you later?" he asked significantly.

"Why not?" agreed Phyllis La Fond.

At that moment Dr. O'Rourke was depositing Miss Withers in front of the St. Lena. "I still think you're barking up the wrong tree," he was saying. "But the chief is worried all the same. He's not even going to wait for the county coroner, but got the order over the telephone. Pleasant as our dances this evening have been, you've let me in for a very unpleasant chore tomorrow morning. And the sum total of my discoveries will be *nothing.*"

"Quite possibly," said Hildegarde Withers tartly. "But there's something to be found if you're capable of finding it. Good-night, Doctor, and good luck."

Dr. O'Rourke took off his Panama. "I'll phone you in the morning to report that I was right and that Forrest died from natural causes."

"Hmph!" snorted Hildegarde Withers and went abruptly into the hotel, past the drowsing desk clerk, and up the stairway. Safe in her room at the head of the stairs, she picked up her antique watch from the bureau and stared at it.

"Quarter of one! And a fine time for a quiet old maid to be getting to sleep!" she scolded herself. But it was to be a later hour than that before she touched her waiting pillow.

She was sitting before her mirror, sending a brush vigorously through her brown tresses in which very little gray as yet revealed itself, and while she counted the strokes her mind was busily exercising itself with such problems as why a bodyguard should take a boat when his endangered ward was aboard a plane, and why Tate was worried about his flask, and why a little dog named Mister Jones had become violently ill aboard the *Dragonfly.*

"Eighty-seven," said Miss Withers determinedly. "Eighty-eight, eighty-nine." It was at that moment that she became aware of a faint noise in the adjoining room. Her brush went on, but she stopped counting.

Everything was still—and then she heard it again. It was a soft, a furtive noise—evidently a noise that no one was meant to hear. But those were the noises for which this canny lady had learned to listen.

She rose to her feet and put down the brush. Then she gathered her flannel bathrobe more closely around her bony frame and went to the hall door.

She stopped short at the sound of voices outside. She could make out the irrepressible Tompkins, singing "Dixie" considerably off key.

Someone hushed him, and he apologized even more loudly. "Tha's my favorite tune," he confided.

Miss Withers shook her head. Then she crossed the room to the large window which led onto the balcony and flung it open. The night was thick and misty, and already the moon was hidden. There was no one to see her on the balcony, and she slipped swiftly out. Phyllis's window was dark, but she rapped sharply on the open pane.

For a moment there was no answer, and then—"Who is it?"

Miss Withers announced herself and then without further ceremony climbed through into the room. A warm tongue caressed her bare ankles—Mister Jones remembered her. As her eyes became accustomed to the darkness she could make out Phyllis La Fond lying face downward across her bed, still dressed in the crimson gown.

Her shoulders were shaking with the soft, choking sobs that Miss Withers had heard from the next room.

The uninvited guest hesitated for a moment, then produced a fresh handkerchief from the pocket of her flannel robe and offered it.

As Phyllis dabbed at her eyes, Miss Withers went into the bathroom, found a washcloth, and wrung it out under the cold-water faucet.

"Here," she advised. "Wipe your eyes."

Phyllis started to sit up and then buried her face in the pillow.

"Come, come," said Miss Withers. "It isn't as bad as all that, is it? I'll go if you want to be alone, but I couldn't help hearing."

"S-sorry I'm such a ba-baby," sobbed the girl into Miss Withers's handkerchief. "Don't go—I'll snap out of it in a minute."

Miss Withers sat down on the bed. In the darkened room the body of Phyllis looked oddly young and helpless.

"What's the trouble?" she asked after a while. "Did Mr. Tate turn you down?"

Phyllis shook her head. "Tate! No, it's nothing to do with him. I stopped crying over his kind years ago. No, it's—"

"Remember, I'm playing detective, and anything you say will be used against you," said Hildegarde Withers cheerfully.

"Well, it's not remorse over killing this mysterious Forrest, either," said Phyllis. She sat up straight and did something to her tangled blonde hair. "Listen," she suggested hopefully. "I'm over it now, but I'd like to talk to somebody. Wait while I get into something comfortable, will you?"

Miss Withers waited. As the carillon rang out the hour of one, Phyllis La Fond came out of the bathroom dressed in a black lace negligee and purple mules. In either hand she held a tall glass.

"Here, be a sport," she invited. "I need a drink, and I'm no solitary drinker. When you can do that you're beyond the pale, they say. Take it and listen." Miss Withers took it, a little gingerly.

Phyllis drew up a little table beside the bed and curled up near Miss Withers.

"I suppose you think I'm an awful fool," she began.

"Most of us are, at one time or another," the schoolteacher told her.

"Yeah. Well, I'll tell you what I was bawling about, and you'll know how big a one I am." Phyllis put down her drink on the table and leaned closer.

"It was seeing those kids—the newlyweds." Her voice was still a little choky beneath the cheerful, forced tones.

"I should think they'd make you laugh, not cry," said Miss Withers.

Phyllis shook her head. "They're in love," she said softly. "And they've got each other. Maybe they're fools, but it's a great foolishness. And every time I look at them, I think that maybe if I—if things had been different, I might—"

"Yes?"

"Well, I might have been like Kay Deving. Instead of a tramp." Phyllis hugged her knees. "Funny, isn't it? You see, what I said to you today—it wasn't true. I'm in this racket, but I don't like it, even if I belong in it. You know what I mean. Chiseling around, playing men for coffee-and-cake money—I'm just a bum, and I'll keep on going down till I land in a Mexican hook-joint or jump off the Arroyo Seco bridge. I say I don't care, I tell myself this is the deal I got and I might as well play it out. But once in a while I get this way—and it seems as if I just can't go on."

"Must you?" said Hildegarde Withers. "Go on, I mean."

"Of course I must! What else is there to do? Men notice me, but they notice just one thing. They talk to me, but they talk about one thing. It's all I'm good for, but I don't have to like it, do I?"

"How old are you?" Miss Withers wanted to know.

"Guess," said Phyllis.

"Twenty-five?" hazarded that lady.

"Thanks," said Phyllis. "I look twenty-five with the right lights, and thirty in the daytime. I won't say how old I am now. But three years ago, when a fat man picked me up in a Rolls and put me down in the gutter, I was seventeen, anyway."

She lit a cigarette and crunched it out in the tray. "I don't pour the sad story of my life as a true confession into the ear of everybody, you know. But you're the first nice woman who's been nice to me in a long time." Phyllis slid off the bed and stood up. "Thanks for listening. I'm sorry I've bellyached."

Miss Withers did not rise. "You listen to me, young woman." Phyllis sat down again. "This isn't 1900. I'm old-fashioned enough about some things, but I can see pretty clearly, all the same. And remember, nobody has to be anything he—or she—doesn't want to be."

"Doesn't she, though!" put in Phyllis. "Do you think I'm a bum from choice?"

"Somebody—I think it was Henry James—once said that no one ever was a slave but thinking made him so. It isn't what one does, it's what he thinks. And you, if you really wanted to, could drop your past, whatever it is, like a hot cake."

There was a long pause, during which Mister Jones leaped upon the bed beside the two women and fell to chewing Phyllis's crimson dancing slipper with a hearty good will.

"Let the dead past bury its dead," Miss Withers went on. "I'm what you call an old maid. Sometimes I think it's just as bad a mistake to have too few men as to have too many. But I'll give you a piece of advice, and you can do what you like with it. If I were you, with your youth and your looks, I'd pick out the nearest and the nicest unattached man and marry him!"

"And after that—"

"After that I'd play fair," Miss Withers concluded. "And that's more than most men have any right to expect."

She was interrupted by a banging on the door. Mister Jones burst into a fusillade of barks.

"Hurray!" came the thick voice of T. Girard Tompkins. "Come on out, baby, the party's young. They're playing m' favorite tune."

"Don't say anything and he'll go away," counseled Miss Withers. It was a matter of some moments, and then they heard the call repeated next door.

"Come on out, Miss Wizzers," demanded Tompkins. "Come out and look at the stars with me."

Undaunted, Tompkins proceeded down the hall. The two women heard profane sounds from the room shared by George and Tony, telling Mr. Tompkins where he could go to hear his favorite tune, and what he could do with it. Captain Narveson was also aroused, and his sleepy voice barked out a command to be off that was louder than Tompkins's maudlin shout.

Miss Withers and Phyllis were at the door, which was open a crack. "Somebody ought to call the night clerk," suggested Miss Withers.

"The night clerk is probably safe in bed," Phyllis told her. "If only that drunken fool doesn't burst in on the newlyweds!"

Which was just what he was doing. There was a rattle of heavy fists upon the door of the farthest room across the hall. "Come on out, you two," shouted Tompkins. "Can't go to sleep on your wedding night. Come on—it's a chivaree! Come on, le's paint the town red. Le's dance, thish m' favorite tune."

Through the crack in the door Miss Withers and Phyllis could see the other door open and catch a glimpse of Kay Deving, white and frightened, in a frilly nightdress.

"Please go away," she implored. "Don't make any more noise—Marvy is asleep!"

Miss Withers was about to go to the rescue when Kay closed the door again, and Tompkins started back down the hall, weaving from side to side and talking to himself. Finally, to the relief of the aroused guests who were showing themselves in almost every doorway, he happened upon the door of his own room, hammered on it imploring himself to come out for a look at the stars, and finally lurched inside. There was the crash of a chair, and silence.

Phyllis and Miss Withers looked at each other and smiled. Phyllis shut the door and switched on the light.

Their two glasses stood, untouched, on the bedside table. "We didn't do much drinking, did we?" remarked Phyllis.

"I'm going to bed and to sleep," Miss Withers said, still an optimist. "I've done a lot of preaching and I'm not used to it. Good-night—and think over what I've said."

"Sure," said Phyllis.

Miss Withers disappeared through the window, from which Mister Jones watched her out of sight.

Phyllis picked up her drink, downed it, and then took up Miss Withers's. She was laughing, but she took pains to laugh silently.

"And I forgot to ask her about the flask!" Miss Withers remembered, when she was back in her own room again.

She picked up her brush and went to work. Just to make sure that she hadn't missed any strokes, she began at seventy-five again, and went up to a hundred. Then she braided her hair into two tight braids and switched off the light.

But sleep still eluded her. As she lay in her lonely bed, staring at the ceiling above her, she heard someone coming down the deserted hallway outside. It was not, as she at first feared, the heavy tread of Tompkins. Someone was coming with the ponderous secrecy of the half-drunk.

The footsteps stopped outside of Phyllis's door. There was a rattle of fingernails on the panel.

"Open up, baby," came the thick whisper. "It's me!"

Mister Jones vented a few woofs, but that was all.

"It's Ralph, honey," came the whisper again.

Still there was no answer. Finally the stealthy footsteps moved away and up the stairs.

"Well, for heaven's sake!" said Hildegarde Withers to herself. "Did my sermon take root?"

It was not until the next day that it occurred to her that Phyllis might not have been there to hear Tate's signal.

CHAPTER IX

THERE was something wrong with the room, something which took the tang from the cigarette which James Michael O'Rourke had lighted as he descended the stairs from the apartment. It was not alone the presence of that rigid figure beneath the sheet on the operating table, or the thought of the unpleasant task which confronted him, but something altogether deeper and more subtle. All the same it was definitely there—some tiny jog in the ordinary and orderly pattern of the infirmary.

Cold gray morning was showing itself outside, and the little doctor could hear the loud voices of workmen in the excavation on the neighboring lot. O'Rourke threw his cigarette through the window in their general direction and then drew the shade.

He turned on both the overhead light and the lamp which illumined the table. "Silly idea," he remarked aloud. "Wild-goose chase if I ever saw one."

At that moment the window curtain flapped noisily, and O'Rourke, as nervous as if again he faced his first laboratory test in dissection, almost dropped the basin he was preparing.

He whirled and saw through the glass of the front doorway a prim and starched young woman. She rattled the knob. "Forgot your key again?" he called.

"Oh, good-morning, Doctor," said Nurse Olive Smith. "I thought you'd be out to breakfast. No—I didn't forget my key. I left it in this door, and it must have walked off yesterday."

"I thought you'd be on time instead of an hour early," O'Rourke grunted. "I planned to get this dirty business over before you got here."

"I thought there might be something I could do," said Nurse Smith.

"There is," said O'Rourke. "You can get me four fingers of spiritus frumenti out of the medicine cabinet, and then get the hell out of here. This is no place for a woman."

"A nurse isn't supposed to be a woman, is she?" inquired the nurse sweetly. She filled the prescription and stood by while O'Rourke administered his own dose.

"Ugh!" grimaced the doctor. His day improved several degrees. He smiled at the earnest and pleasant face of Miss Olive Smith. "You were passing for a woman all right at the Casino last night," he twitted her. "Cheek to cheek with that harum-scarum pilot—and no back to your dress, either. I counted seventeen vertebrae."

"He isn't harum-scarum," Nurse Smith confided dreamily. "Lew French is going to do big things some day. He'll surprise all of you."

"Yeah?" O'Rourke stood aside as the nurse efficiently completed the preparations he had half begun.

"Yes, Doctor. He and Chick are going to buy a plane of their own and make a big nonstop flight—"

O'Rourke was drawing on his rubber gloves. "I know. A nonstop flight between Tijuana and Hollywood, with a load of what Uncle Sam never stuck a revenue stamp on."

"He's going to do it soon," continued Nurse Smith, wrapped in thought. "And when he puts the big deal over and buys his plane, you get a new nurse."

O'Rourke shook his head. "Can't afford a new nurse. I'm still making back payments on your salary. Anyway, if you wait for your boyfriend to save up enough money to buy a plane, you'll be an old woman."

"Maybe I won't wait," said the nurse, who had definite ideas of her own. She pushed an instrument tray alongside the sheet-draped operating table and added a couple of waste pails.

"Go on, get out of here," ordered the doctor. "I don't need you, and I don't want an audience. I'm a little rusty at this sort of thing, anyway, and— Say, what's the matter with you?"

Nurse Smith was staring, wide-eyed, at the sheet-draped figure which waited there for this last and most terrible profanation. She made a little noise in her throat, like the silent scream of a nightmare.

"Well, what is it?" O'Rourke looked at her blankly. "For the love of heaven don't go probationer on me."

"L-l-look," she said. O'Rourke looked where she pointed.

The morning breeze, pushing past the shade of the open window, had drawn the sheet tightly across the thing it was meant to conceal.

"It hasn't any—any face!" whispered the girl.

O'Rourke crossed the room with one stride and tore the sheet away. The nurse was right.

The thing on the operating table had no face. It had no body. Only the barest framework of a body remained where last night Roswell T. Forrest had lain in his rumpled sport outfit of cocoa-brown. Only the crude mechanical structure of bleached calcium phosphate which we call the skeleton—that was all. The movement of the sheet dislodged a bony arm, which slipped from the operating table and swung back and forth. ...

Olive Smith forgot that she was a nurse and began to laugh, hideously. But the doctor took her by the shoulders and shook her until her teeth rattled.

"Look here!" insisted O'Rourke, pointing toward the ghastly relic which lay on the table, forever out of reach of his autopsy knife. "Look at it again."

He let her go and snatched savagely at a loop of wire which projected from the exact center of the cranium of the skull. One jerk, and the articulated skeleton sat upright. Another, and it slid from the table and dangled beneath his outstretched arm.

"Cut out the histrionics," said O'Rourke. "This is nothing but a be-blasted practical joke."

The nurse came closer. "Why—that's right! It's only poor old Jimmy Spareribs!"

O'Rourke crossed the room, still dragging the skeleton, and opened the door of the little closet where his dressing gown had hung. He looped his burden over a projecting hook, and as the dusty rattling of the bones subsided, he slammed the door and turned the key.

Nurse Smith perched on a stool, and the color began to surge back into her face. "So that's all it was!"

O'Rourke stared at her sharply. "Stop grinning, young woman. We've found a skeleton, but we've lost a cadaver. And the chief will be raising merry hell if we don't find his corpus delicti."

They were not destined to find the mortal remains of the little man in the brown sport suit. The infirmary offered no hiding place big enough to dispose of anything larger than a pair of tonsils. O'Rourke even climbed the stairs again to peer into his bureau drawers, behind his kitchenette icebox, and even under his bed, but there was no trace.

"The corpus delicti is a derelict, sure enough," he said. "It's funny, because everything was okay when I came in last night, around one o'clock."

"Did you look under the sheet?" Nurse Smith suggested.

The doctor shook his head. "No, but I did hang up my coat in the closet, and Jimmy Spareribs was where he belonged."

The doctor snapped his fingers. Now he knew what it was that had struck him as being askew in the room half an hour before. He went to the side window of the room and lifted the shade.

"When I went to bed last night I locked this window," he announced. "And this morning I threw a cigarette butt through it. Unless I'm a bloody somnambulist, someone opened this window while I slept!"

Nurse Smith put her head close to his, and they both stared out upon what had been a vacant lot and was now in the early processes of becoming a chain-store grocery. There was a confused muddle of footprints outside the low window—footprints on which were superimposed a flat and wavering track like the trail of a serpent. It led along the entire side of the infirmary, skirting the excavation, from sidewalk to alley.

The little man in the sport outfit of cocoa-brown had been plunged into this placid place by a red-and-gilt *Dragonfly* from out of the sky. Now, even more mysteriously, he had been whisked away.

"I'd better get the chief," said O'Rourke, as he drew his head in through the window. Nurse Smith stared after him, thoughtfully.

It was all of ten minutes before the doctor returned, leading a little procession composed of Chief Amos Britt, Deputy Ruggles, and the inevitable Hildegarde Withers, who had come into the chief's office hoping for an interview before his day's work began. She had not, however, hoped for anything like this.

"The door was locked, and the front windows don't open," explained O'Rourke. "But this window on the side looks as if somebody had monkeyed with it."

"Somebody has," called a clear voice from outside. "Look, Doctor! Somebody must have forced a knife blade through here."

Nurse Olive Smith demonstrated what she meant by jumping excitedly up and down outside the window.

"Look out!" called Miss Withers, but it was almost too late. The nurse's low-heeled shoes had wrought havoc with any traces that might have remained in the dust.

Miss Withers pushed the girl to one side and pointed out a single rough oval marked on the ground. It was very evidently the print of a rubber heel, and it bore in reverse an initial K, with the upper bar of the letter broken.

"I'm so sorry," breathed Nurse Smith. But nobody paid any attention to her. Chief Britt stared at the print and nodded slowly.

He lifted his own worn brown oxford and showed them all a similar heel. "Koch Shoe Hospital," he announced. "They got branches in every town on the mainland. This isn't going to be much help to us, I'm afraid."

He went out of doors and placed his heel next to the blurred mark which remained. The two were very similar, except that the K on his print was much less distinct. "I've worn these shoes two months since they was soled," he informed them all. "If only we had the whole footprint we could tell the size of the shoe that was worn here last night, but all heels are about the same size."

"I'm sorry," repeated Nurse Smith. "I didn't mean—"

"You didn't do much harm," the doctor comforted her. "The other prints were smeared all out of semblance to anything like the mark of a foot, or a heel either. I noticed that when I saw them."

Britt placed an empty pail over the mark and gave orders to Ruggles that it be photographed at such time during the day as the proprietor of the local art store could conveniently shut up shop and come over. His little porcine eyes were troubled, however, by deeper worries than footprints.

"Now why should anyone want to steal what you'd think they would want least in all the world?" he inquired of Miss Withers. That lady did not answer.

"Body snatchers most likely done it," insisted Ruggles, the octogenarian deputy.

"Looks more like a crazy practical joke," suggested O'Rourke. "Couldn't be body-snatching. There's no medical school where anybody could sell a body near here."

"Doesn't look at all practical, or like a joke either, stealing bodies like this," protested Chief Britt heavily. "This thing's getting to be too much of a mystery for my taste."

"That's where we differ," cut in Miss Withers brightly. "The more complicated a case is, the easier it is to break. Inspector Piper has told me that many a time. All the same, this stealing of the corpse looks simple enough."

"Huh?" Chief Britt scratched his neck, and his shoulders were sagging.

"The murderer returned to steal the body of his victim," insisted Miss Withers. "For a very good reason—he knew he could no longer hope for a certificate of natural death, and he dared not let Dr. O'Rourke make an autopsy for fear of what would be discovered!"

Chief Britt shook his head. "But this crazy business of substituting the skeleton—"

"That was an afterthought," Miss Withers decided. "When he—or she or they, for that matter—crept through the window last night, he didn't know if the doctor had come in yet. He couldn't risk having the alarm raised at once. Or perhaps he feared someone might look in and see that the body was gone. He needed something to make the sheet bulge up—went to the closet for a coat and saw the skeleton—and there you are!"

"There I am," repeated Britt sadly. He led the way out of the infirmary. But his attempt at making anything of the trampled prints outside the door was interrupted.

The voices that Dr. O'Rourke had heard early that morning raised in argument were still going on. "Ain't a-goin' to buy ye a new one and that's all there is to it," someone was insisting.

A man in faded blue denim caught sight of the chief. "Hey, Amos—here's a case of petty larceny for you! Somebody stole George's wheelbarrow."

"Go on and let me be," retorted Chief Britt, with an edge to his tone. "I got me more important worries than to hunt up lost tools for your ditch diggers."

"Perhaps you haven't," said Hildegarde Withers softly. With the tip of her umbrella she poked at that flat and wavering indentation in the dusty ground, which led along the side of the infirmary.

Britt stopped short and stared at her. "Perhaps hunting for that lost tool is your most important worry right now," she went on. "I don't know much about such implements, but couldn't this mark have been made by a wheelbarrow?"

Chief Britt squatted laboriously. "Looks like it could," he admitted. "And it runs where no wheelbarrow would naturally go—which means—"

"Say!" Deputy Ruggles brightened. "Then all we got to do is to follow this trail and find the body again!"

He set out hopefully and came back wreathed in clouds. "Lost the marks in the alley," he confessed.

He found Miss Withers and the chief walking slowly down the street in the bright sunlight, their oddly contrasting shadows slanting behind.

"But why—" Britt wanted to know.

"It isn't time to ask why," Miss Withers told him sharply. "You ought to be asking *how*—how anyone could have climbed through that window, stolen a corpse in the room underneath the one where the doctor was supposedly asleep, and taken it away on one of the noisiest conveyances ever invented. That's what you ought to be asking."

Britt pulled at his lower lip thoughtfully. "Does look funny. But O'Rourke is a heavy sleeper. There was a fire across the alley from his place a month or so ago, and both our engines and everybody in town turned out. He slept through it. This is a pretty sleepy town after sundown, ma'am. And when the Casino shuts down at twelve-thirty or so, then everybody is in bed."

They were standing in the doorway of the curio shop. "But don't you have policemen or patrolmen or something?" Miss Withers, used to Manhattan with its cop on every corner, was scandalized.

"There's only me and Ruggles," said the chief gently. "And most generally we have to sleep at night. Of course"—Britt held the screen door of his shop open—"Of course, there's Higgins. He's night watchman on the docks. We'll ask him if he heard anything."

Miss Withers followed the chief back into his office in the rear and heard him take down the telephone and request the immediate presence of Mr. Dan Higgins. There was some argument over the phone, but finally he replaced the receiver.

"Dan's just got to bed, his wife says," he told Miss Withers. "Seems sort of mean to wake him."

Mr. Higgins was even more decided about it when he arrived, in suspenders and carpet slippers. "Naw, I didn't see nothing and I didn't hear nothing," he insisted. "It was quiet as a tomb last night—and dark as pitch too, after the fog came in. I was on the dock all night, and no matter what anybody says, I never closed an eye."

"All right, Dan, you can go close one now," said the chief.

"Wait a moment, please," interrupted Miss Withers. "Aren't you going to ask Mr. Higgins if any ships left the harbor last night?"

The chief looked as if he regretted heartily having allowed her to remain. But he put the question. "Any boats sail, Dan?"

"Never a one," said Dan Higgins. "The two piers was dead as a doornail. Sometimes fellows go out fishing, but not this morning. Never a boat—wait a minute."

Higgins frowned with acute concentration. "There was one boat, Amos. But she didn't land. Dory come ashore from the *City of Saunders* that anchored offshore about midnight. Narveson, the Swede that owns the outfit, came down to the dock and yelled to the men that they'd have to wait for him another day, and they pulled off."

"And they didn't come back to shore?" Miss Withers asked.

"Not that I saw," grumbled Higgins. "They could have landed on the rocks somewhere, but I don't see why."

Miss Withers intimated that she did see. "One thing more—what time did you say the fog came in?"

Higgins scratched his head to stimulate memory. "I'd say about one o'clock it got real thick."

"And it lasted all night?"

Higgins shook his head. "Only till about an hour or so before sunrise. I'd say a little afore three."

He was given permission to return to his bed, and Miss Withers faced the chief.

"There you are," she said triumphantly. "Very simple. If the body didn't leave the island last night, it's still here. All you have to do is to search the place thoroughly."

Chief Britt nodded a little sadly. "Catalina Island is over twenty miles long and near on to seven miles wide," he explained. "A search party couldn't even get across some of those canyons in the back country."

"Amos, you don't need no search party," interrupted Deputy Ruggles, who had been an interested observer from the doorway. "If the body was dumped in any of them canyons, all we need to do is set out on a mountain top and watch where the gulls is thickest. They're worser'n vultures."

Miss Withers shivered slightly. Then she changed the subject. "It seems very unlikely to me that the body was carried very far when a wheelbarrow was the only means of transportation," she pointed out. "The body probably lies in a shallow grave somewhere near by."

She rose to her feet. "I'll leave you to your labors, Chief Britt. I did not imagine, when I came after my sketchbook this morning, that I'd be privileged to see such a whirl of excitement. May I have the book?"

Chief Britt looked blank.

"I lent it to you yesterday when you were making a list of Forrest's personal belongings," she reminded him. "I want it back, because there are some unfinished sketches of trees in it."

Britt pawed through the heap of litter on his desk and finally found the linen-bound book. Laboriously he tore out the sheet containing his notes. At that moment two letters slipped out from the pages.

"If those are the letters which were in Forrest's pocket, I think you have a right to open them," suggested Miss Withers. "What's more, I think you ought to."

Britt nodded. "I meant to, soon as I could get around to it." He took a heavy jackknife from his pocket, and slit the scented envelope.

As he read, Miss Withers shamelessly peered over his shoulder. The letter was short, but not disappointing. The writing was feminine and careful:

HELLO, MR. FORREST:

Just to let you know that a lawyer from Mr. Welch was to see me and he says Mr. Welch is going to Europe because it is not very healthy around here. He said he heard that you were thinking of coming back, but he said he didn't think it would be healthy for you because Mack wouldn't like it. I was up to your house Sunday like you said but Mae was there and wouldn't let me in. She said she was sending all your stuff to Acme storage and if you wanted your gun you could get it there. She said a lot more too.

Yrs. respectfully,
MABEL (BLUMBERG)

P.S. I have another job so don't worry about me.

"H'm," said the chief. "Mae's his wife. Wonder who Mabel is?"

"And I wonder who Mack is," said Miss Withers. "This was a warning letter, Mr. Britt. Too bad Forrest didn't stop to open it that morning."

The chief put it aside and took up the official-looking envelope with the letterhead of Fishbein, O'Hara & Fishbein. This was even shorter, and still more interesting. The envelope was addressed to "Mr. Roswell," but the letter to Roswell T. Forrest:

At your request we have communicated with our client, Mrs. Mae Timmons Forrest, and are sorry to announce that your wife refuses to consider changing her pending suit for absolute divorce to one of separation.

Yours very truly,
AARON FISHBEIN.

"Which explains why she was willing to bury him only if absolutely necessary," Miss Withers pointed out.

Ruggles's excited voice broke in upon them. "Say, Amos—I just saw the Kelsey guy who gave me the slip last night! He's going down the street talking to that La Fond woman!"

"Get him and bring him here," ordered Chief Britt. Ruggles leaped to obey. "That guy knows a lot of things he hasn't told us—and besides, he was on the loose last night."

"Which is in itself proof of guilt," sarcastically suggested Miss Withers. She relieved the chief by picking up her sketchbook and moving toward the door.

As she passed out through the crowded counters of the curio shop, she came face to face with Barney Kelsey, the young man with the gray hair. There was no sign of Phyllis, and Kelsey was in the tight grasp of Deputy Ruggles.

All the same he smiled a good-morning to Miss Withers. She paused a moment. "Mr. Kelsey, when and if the chief sets you at liberty, I'd like a chat with you." She noticed that the palm of his right hand bore a large blister.

Barney Kelsey studied her. "Any time at all," he said, without enthusiasm. Then he preceded Ruggles back into the office.

Miss Withers stared after him. "A tough nut to crack," she said to herself. "But I wonder if there isn't a way to crack him."

By way of a pleasant contrast to her adventures of the morning, Miss Withers while striding down the Main Street chanced upon the newlyweds. They were buying picture postcards at a candy stand, and Kay hailed her.

"Good-morning, Miss Withers!" The events of the preceding day had touched Kay Deving lightly. Only her voice was a little strained. "I was wondering—"

"We were wondering—" put in Marvin.

"Marvy and I were wondering—about this dreadful business and everything—"

"Don't let it spoil your honeymoon," advised Miss Withers cheerily. "Just think what a lot of excitement you're having. Not like most honeymoons, I can tell you. You can tell your children about all this."

"Yeah," said Kay doubtfully. But her words had brightened Marvin considerably.

"But we wanted to ask you," he continued. "Do you know if the doctor finished the autopsy and what he decided? I hope that poor guy wasn't murdered, as you seemed to think."

Miss Withers stared at him. It had not occurred to her that the news of the missing body was not already blazoned from the housetops.

"Didn't you know?" she said kindly. "There's been another accident. There was no autopsy this morning because while we were sleeping last night somebody stole the body and left a skeleton in its place!"

Miss Withers paused for dramatic effect—and received an effect that she had not bargained for. Marvin Deving took it rather well, though his face, which had been colorless, flushed as if he had found breath again. Kay was trembling and as shocked as if she herself had come face to face with the grim relic on the infirmary table. The brown eyes were luminous.

"It can't be true—why—" She shook her head, so that the red curls were loosened. She turned quickly toward Marvin and then back to Miss Withers. "It can't be true—such things don't happen—you're joking, aren't you?"

"I wish I were," said Hildegarde Withers. "Now you children run along and forget all this black trouble."

"I wish we could," said Kay. But gratefully they watched her out of sight.

Ten minutes later Miss Withers walked in upon James Michael O'Rourke, who was engaged at the moment in pacing up and down the infirmary floor. Nurse Smith obligingly disappeared, and Miss Withers surveyed the little doctor through cool blue eyes.

"Well," said O'Rourke uncomfortably. "I suppose you came to crow."

"Came to scoff and remained to pray," she quoted. "Doctor, I suppose that you agree with me now about the need for that autopsy?"

He shrugged his shoulders. "Need or no need, it can't be performed without a corpse. My midnight visitor left me a bag of bones, but whatever was to be discovered from the corpse is beyond our reach now."

"That's why I came," said Hildegarde Withers. "I'm not so sure. You see, yesterday afternoon the murderer struck again—"

"Good heavens, woman! Another corpse?"

She shook her head. "As it happened, no. And I think the whole thing was an accident. But a little dog named Mister Jones nearly died of whatever killed Roswell Forrest. I saved his life by giving him an emetic of sea water after we left the *Dragonfly*. He was very sick on a rock. I wondered—"

"But, Miss Withers, why should anyone want to kill a little dog?"

"I don't think anybody did," she explained. "But Forrest died in a certain seat on that plane. Miss La Fond's little dog was under that same seat, later that day, and came out deathly sick. Suppose there was a capsule of poison—and the dog picked it up? It might be there still, where he threw it up, mightn't it?"

"No capsule could do that," pointed out O'Rourke. "But—"

"But me no buts," Miss Withers told him. "Come on, we're going to hire the bus and go up there and see. I should have thought of it sooner."

She carried along the doctor by sheer weight of purpose. Still arguing, they caromed over the hills to the airport landing and hastened down to the beach. "We're in luck," Miss Withers called out. "The rock is well above high tide."

So it was, but there was no sign of anything that Mister Jones might have deposited there.

For a long time they searched, with O'Rourke increasingly skeptical and Miss Withers considerably nettled.

The clear blue-green waves rolled in from the open sea in a monotonous procession, splashing foam over her stout calfskin oxfords. Half a mile out from shore, a broken bundle of white feathers rose and fell on those same clear blue-green rollers, but Miss Withers and the doctor were looking for other evidence than the lifeless body of a murdered sea gull.

CHAPTER X

A SMOOTH-LIMBED, virginal young pepper tree dominated the view from Miss Withers's window at the hotel. It stood a few hundred feet away, on the very edge of the cliff overlooking roadway and beach, so that at noon its trailing foliage was silhouetted against the sun, and a long pale shadow ran down almost to the hotel balcony.

The vacationing schoolma'am had come to take a special interest in this little pepper tree. This was partly because it was the only *tree* in sight. Miss Withers considered palms only overgrown ferns and was firmly convinced that, like most of the rest of Southern California's greenery, they were rented from the florist and that one of these days the men would come to take them back.

But more intriguing than the little tree's resemblance to Eastern trees was the fact that, on the second day of her stay at Catalina, she had been privileged to witness a small landslide some distance along the shore. This accident had deposited the pepper tree in the surf, from which it had been salvaged by the hotel handyman and taken to its present resting place. There had been much ado about fertilizer and water, and Miss Withers gathered that it was a matter of touch and go whether the little pepper tree would survive the rude transplantation at this time of year.

"The ground's like dusty powder," Rogers, the ancient and garrulous handyman, had remarked, as she constituted herself unofficial supervisor of the tree-planting. "It's a poor chance she's got, set in this red clay. But they tells me to plant her in the rock garden and in the rock garden I'll plant her."

"You might have set the tree where it wouldn't be in danger of sliding down the cliff again," Miss Withers had pointed out. But by that time the planting was done.

Before the mystery of the demise of Roswell T. Forrest had usurped her time and her thoughts, Miss Withers had been in the habit of looking first thing each morning and last thing at night to see if the pepper tree was still there. But now all the pleasant routine of her vacation was pushed aside.

Today Miss Withers returned, hot and dusty and disgusted, from her fruitless trip to the airport beach in search of whatever it was that had caused Mister Jones such acute illness. She could hear the little dog whining in the next room, a sure sign that Phyllis was out.

The hotel was very still. In desperation, Hildegarde Withers washed her hair—a last resort. But today even that rite failed to dispel the sense of disappointment which filled her mind. She thoughtfully began to comb the wet locks.

It was a thoughtful hour. Miss Withers thought about the dog in the next room and what he could tell her if he would. The little dog Jones thought about the pepper tree, or any other tree. Even the pepper tree— if plants, as scientists say, can suffer, may they not be said to think?— was thinking thoughts shot with fear and foreboding.

Miss Withers was filled with unreasonable gloom. A thousand times she had noticed the plaque at the end of the hallway at Jefferson School— "It matters not who won or lost, but how you played the game!"—and a thousand times she had sniffed inwardly at the sentiment. It was not that Hildegarde Withers did not hold with sportsmanship, if by that one understands rigid adherence to a certain code. Her Boston background (all the more important to her because, through a call to a Unitarian pastorate in Des Moines, her father had moved the family from Back Bay to Iowa a few weeks before her birth) impelled her toward playing the game, provided the game was worth playing and against worthy opponents. But she was too intellectually honest to believe that it did not matter, matter terribly, whether you won or lost.

On her dresser lay a telegram from Inspector Oscar Piper of the New York police, written on the train and put on the wires at Toledo. "Wire me developments care Santa Fe," he instructed her. "Very important do nothing until I arrive."

Much as she respected her old friend and sparring partner, it was her farthest thought to obey the latter part of his message. All the same, that was exactly what she was doing.

She let her mind run over the events of the past twenty-four or -five hours. Roswell Forrest was dead, and everybody and nobody had a motive for killing him. There was no use to try to figure out who might have done it until she could decide what was done—and how. It was like playing a worn-out phonograph record over and over, with the needle scratching in its groove. Each time the tune ended on the same phrase, going round and round in her head.

Phyllis, the captain, Tate, Tompkins, and the newlyweds—yes, and Barney Kelsey—somewhere among them was the answer to the questions which fretted her. Not one of them was in evidence around the hotel, and Miss Withers had a furious itch to creep down the balcony, window by window, and search their rooms.

She shook her head. "Be yourself, Hildegarde," she said aloud. But she was not quite herself, in spite of the soothing effect of washing and combing her hair. Today nothing was quite itself on this ordinarily peaceful paradise, for the dark and bloody trail of murder crisscrossed everywhere.

She walked up and down the narrow balcony, quite oblivious of the eager, moist black button of pin-seal that was pressed against the window of Phyllis's room. There was an unwonted stillness about the place, and the white, vibrating sunlight reminded Miss Withers of the old Roman belief that the restless dead walk abroad, not at midnight, but at high noon.

Even the little pepper tree, which seemed to shimmer in the noonday glare, was somehow different. No longer could Miss Withers imagine it to be a wild and frightening thing, stretching leafy arms toward the little rock garden and leaning away from the cliff it feared, as if still dizzy and shocked from its former catastrophe. Now it was only a tree.

She had a sketchy luncheon in the empty dining room and then set out along the shore toward the village. It was one o'clock, and the chimes were sounding from the carillon ahead of her. Miss Withers sniffed and was suddenly homesick for the good honest striking of the clock in the tower at Jefferson School.

The red bus, piled three deep with sightseers, whirled past her in a cloud of dust, no doubt bound for the airport landing which had been made famous as the scene of the crime by the Los Angeles newspapers. Evidently the steamer *Avalon* had docked and for once had had a full passenger list.

As Miss Withers came past the Casino she met the ancient handyman, Rogers, loaded down with several pails and some complicated-looking contraptions of metal and rubber.

"You're not going to transplant our pepper tree again, are you?" she inquired. Rogers shook his head and looked up toward the cliff behind her.

"No, ma'am. Reckon she's a-goin' to make it, after all. Leaves look a little green." He nodded. "Today I had a different job, and one I don't like half so well."

Miss Withers took it that she was expected to inquire as to what the job was. Rogers grinned, showing an expanse of brown chewing tobacco with one surprisingly white tooth standing as a monument to his past prime.

"It was a plumbing job in the Casino," he told her. "I'm sorta a specialist in such. You'd be surprised what they throw in them bowls. Other day I took out two oranges, and last week a wedding ring and fifty foot of fishline. People ain't got no sense at all about what'll go through a two-inch pipe."

Miss Withers's nose had been steadily lifting itself in the air as the doddering old man rambled on. But his next sentence made her forget her squeamishness.

"Today was the queerest of all, ma'am," he was saying. "And as for me, I don't understand why anybody at the Casino last night would go to such a place to throw away such a thing. It does beat all!"

"It does, doesn't it?" agreed Miss Withers. "May I ask what—I mean— the nature of this object?"

" 'Twasn't an object." The old man grinned again. " 'Twas nine objects." And he told her what they were.

Miss Withers restrained herself with some difficulty from crying "Eureka!" After all, her wild guess might be wrong. Besides, it was something that could not be proved, unless—unless a small miracle had happened or would happen.

"I have a friend who makes a collection of objects which people throw into er—such places," she told the man. "I don't suppose that you kept what you found?" Her voice was extremely casual.

"As a matter of fact, mum, I did. They're right here in this pail, because I didn't want to risk having to take the plumbing apart on a deeper level. I was figuring on taking the whole mess and throwing it off the cliff into the ocean."

Miss Withers saw to it that he changed his plans, and was rewarded for her pains by the realization that this old man thought her a howling maniac.

"One more thing," she wanted to know, as he picked up his pails and gadgets again. "Were these thrown into the plumbing from the Men's or Ladies' Room?"

"Ain't no telling that," said Rogers amiably. "Found 'em below the V." He stared with some degree of pleased surprise at the silver dollar she placed in his palm.

"Say, mum—if your friend is interested in any more of such truck, I'll start saving whatever I find. Last year there was a pair of silk step-ins—"

But Miss Withers was already out of hearing.

She found Avalon town filled with tourists, as she strode vigorously down Main Street. Having little or no sympathy with the great American habit of rubbernecking, Miss Withers pushed impatiently through the mob. "The man who made the best mousetrap never got such a crowd as this," she reflected. She had read somewhere that in Los Angeles itself the officers of the law were often embarrassed to find, upon arriving at the scene of a crime in their patrol cars, that the room was filled with gawking spectators who had tuned in on the police calls!

The fact that, at least to the casual eye, her own actions during the past few hours placed her more or less in the same category never occurred to the good lady. She bustled into the curio store of Chief Amos Britt, to find that establishment under the management of a plump dame who turned out to be Mrs. Britt. What Miss Withers would have called "a land-office business" was going on in the less expensive gadgets, as here was the center of the crowd's interest. Outside the door at the rear were Ruggles and a little huddle of newspapermen, whom Miss Withers eluded with the ease of long practice. She knocked sharply on the door and was somewhat surprised, upon announcing herself, to hear the chief invite her to come in.

Amos Britt, red-faced and perspiring, was in close conclave with Barney Kelsey, also red-faced but not so damp as the chief.

"I'm sorry to interrupt," she apologized.

"You ain't interrupting anything," Chief Britt told her bitterly. "We been at it ever since you left, and we're getting nowhere, fast."

"Forrest hired me in Philly, and he didn't confide in me. I've told you all I know," said Barney Kelsey. If possible, his gray hair seemed a shade lighter than it had yesterday, and his voice was without conviction.

"You know very little, then," said Britt. "You don't know who sent Forrest money to stay out here, and you don't know who his friends are back East, and you don't know anybody who'd be likely to kill him, and you don't know how it might have been done, and—"

"I told you, I never saw him from Thursday afternoon when he left the Hotel Senator until I came on his body under the sheet in the infirmary."

"And I suppose you can't tell us why it didn't stay under the sheet at the infirmary?"

Kelsey insisted that he could not. "I was asleep in my room at the hotel."

"So was everybody else," said Britt, still bitter. "Forrest must have come to life and walked out on his own, I guess. Probably he'll come in here and give himself up one of these days."

Miss Withers noticed that Barney Kelsey gave an appreciable start at this grotesque fancy.

"All right, Mr. Kelsey, you can go. But you're not to go far, see? For two cents I'd clap you in jail right now as a material witness."

Kelsey wasted no time in getting out of the office, and Britt turned to Miss Withers. "I've changed my mind about that fellow," he complained. "He's too smooth and oily for my taste."

Miss Withers pointed out that the possession of aplomb was not a hanging offense.

"Yeah," nodded Chief Britt. "But what did he want to give the slip to Ruggles for last night if he'd nothing to conceal?"

Miss Withers gave it as her opinion that there was nothing morally or legally binding upon a person under police surveillance to keep within sight of his shadow.

"Well, I wisht I'd of arrested him anyhow, as a material witness," Britt told her. He rose from his chair and kicked the waste basket savagely. "This would have to happen just when the marlin are beginning to strike in the channel."

"You couldn't very well arrest as a material witness the one person involved who was farthest from the man when he died," Miss Withers continued. "There are eight people—and two pilots—who are ever so much more material to this investigation than Barney Kelsey."

The chief's little eyes widened. "You ain't suggesting that I put 'em all in the hoosegow?"

"I am," said Hildegarde Withers. "It would be the wisest move you ever made, but you won't do it." As a matter of fact, the chief didn't.

He shook his head slowly. "I dunno. We never had a murder, or a body-snatching either, here at Avalon. I wisht this New York detective would get here—mebbe he'd have some ideas."

"I doubt the value of his ideas," said Miss Withers acidly. "But Inspector Piper will be here soon enough. He's on a train somewhere between Toledo and Chicago."

Her voice died away, and her blue eyes narrowed as she stared at the door which led into the store. "Somebody is listening," she whispered.

"Somebody is *what?*" The chief turned toward her, blankly.

"I heard a rustle outside that door," she said. "If you'd been awake—" She crossed the room and tore the door open, but there was nobody there. In the street outside she could see Deputy Ruggles posing for the newspaper photographers, and across the store Barney Kelsey was admiring a table lamp made of clustered sea shells, which Miss Withers considered one of the most loathsome objects she had come upon in years. But Mr. Kelsey was far from alone in the place.

Mrs. Britt was in the act of wrapping up a mother-of-pearl jewel box which Marvin Deving had just purchased for Kay Deving. The young bride was all in white today, from shoes to beret, and with her pale skin and fiery hair she made a pretty picture of girlish innocence.

It was a picture that cast into the shade the plaid-clad voluptuousness of Phyllis La Fond, who was engaged at the moment in rescuing a sharkskin walking stick which had caught the fancy of Mister Jones. It was pulled from the eager jaws with considerable difficulty and replaced with the others.

She caught sight of Miss Withers. "Hullo, there! So this is where you spend your days." She jerked the leash and Mister Jones away from a pile of polished abalone shells. "How about joining us for a walk?"

"Sorry," said Hildegarde Withers, "but I'm out for a jaunt up the hill with the chief. Am I not, Mr. Britt?"

The chief blinked and, as Miss Withers kicked him sharply in the ankle, nodded. He followed her out of the store, after giving directions to his wife as to where he might be found. The scene between the couple was short, but there was a definite note of tension in the air. "My missus thinks she ought to be putting up watermelon pickles instead of tending store, but I told her that pickles keep and murders don't," Britt confided as Miss Withers led him out into the street.

"Well, this murder is keeping all to well so far," Miss Withers told him. "I wanted to come out here because we can't be overheard. The safest place, you know, isn't a hideaway—it's the middle of a public square, where you can see everybody a block away."

The chief admitted the wisdom of this. "But what you got on your mind, ma'am?" They were going up a street lined with flimsy wooden rooming houses, and the incline was steep. He was very much in low gear.

"Plenty," said Hildegarde Withers. But she would say no more until they came out upon a little dusty knoll, with the town spread out beneath them.

"There won't be anybody listening in on us now," pointed out the chief impatiently. "What's on your mind?"

Miss Withers seemed not to hear him. She was looking across the little valley toward a farther hill. "What are those men doing?"

The chief smiled proudly. "An idea of my own, ma'am. I took a map of the island, drew a circle a mile around the town—which is about as far as anybody could carry a corpse on a wheelbarrow—and divided the circle up into squares of about four or five acres each. Then I swore in seventy-five of the local unemployed as special deputies and set 'em to searching for the body of Roswell Forrest."

"A miracle," said Miss Withers fervently. "They've been trying to square the circle since Euclid died, and you did it without batting an eye. I take off my hat to you, Amos Britt."

"You can save that till my men find something," he told her.

Miss Withers had a flash of intuition which told her that she would be saving her congratulations for a long time, but she did not say so.

"Until we find the corpse," she said finally, "there is no way to discover what method the murderer used to kill Forrest, is there?"

To this the chief agreed. "If it is murder," he added—"and there isn't any reason why the body'd be stolen otherwise."

"Exactly. And since the Death Ray is still a myth, and there were no signs of violence upon the body, I have inclined since the beginning to a theory that poison was the method used. Particularly since the little dog Jones was very ill from something he ate in the *Dragonfly* plane."

The chief nodded. "So far so good," he said. "Mebbe the autopsy would have brought your poison to light. But if it was poison, then how did he take it? The hotel people over to Los Angeles maintain that he left that morning in a tearing hurry, without stopping for breakfast. We've traced him to the place where he rented the car—a block down the street—and most of the way down to Wilmington. And he never ate a mouthful. I never heard of a poison that would lay back that long and suddenly catch a man."

"Perhaps this is how it was done," said Miss Withers softly. She opened her bag and took from it a little newspaper-wrapped parcel. This she began to unfold.

"Through a stroke of pure and unadulterated luck, I got these from the plumber who found them clogging the sewage disposal pipes of the Casino," she explained. "Probably they're nothing at all, but I want them analyzed all the same."

She spread out before the surprised chief of police a damp exhibit consisting of nine green-wrapped sticks of a popular brand of chewing gum.

"Nine little steps to heaven," she said softly—"or steps to wherever it was that Roswell Forrest went."

CHAPTER XI

THE glass-bottomed *Mermaid*, world famous for the views of the ocean floor which it afforded its passengers, was paddling serenely out through the harbor. Beyond it, two speedboats were racing, cutting the green water into wide angles of foam. Sounds of a thousand voices raised in merriment along the sandy shore came faintly to Miss Withers's ear as she stood on the lonely hilltop and waited for the chief to speak.

Finally he broke the long silence. If Hildegarde Withers had been waiting for extravagant congratulations or praise, she was sadly disappointed. "Hmm," said Chief Britt. He took the bedraggled bits of evidence and stared at them as if he expected to see stamped thereon the skull and crossbones of a pharmacist's warning.

"Never heard of poisoned chewing gum," Britt continued. "Don't seem likely to me."

"This is not a likely murder," Miss Withers told him. "So far the murderer has had all the good fortune—what my pupils call 'the lucky breaks.' It's about time we had a stroke of luck. I do a lot of snooping around, and it only stands to reason that once in a while I run into something. The long arm of coincidence reaches both ways, you know."

The chief was still staring at the chewing gum. "But it don't make sense!"

"Of course it does! Why should anyone try to get rid of ordinary chewing gum by throwing it into a bowl? The murderer prepared two packages of gum and used only one stick. He—or she—was afraid to get rid of the unused gum in any ordinary way. He couldn't be seen burying it or throwing it into the sea, where it might turn up. He couldn't leave it around to be discovered or to be picked up by some unsuspecting person."

"Don't strike me that chewing gum could be poisoned," said Amos Britt.

"Then would you care to try a stick of this?" Miss Withers shook her finger in his face. "You mark my words, an analysis of these nine sticks of chewing gum will show traces of the poison that killed Roswell Forrest—the poison in which the missing stick was dipped."

Britt scuffed the toe of his wide shoe into the rocky hilltop. "It still seems to me that poisoning food or something he drank would be more reasonable."

"Exactly. Except that he ate nothing for fourteen hours before he died. And as for what he drank—I would be inclined to agree with you except for the fact that Ralph O. Tate, the playboy movie director, also took a deep gulp from his flask after Forrest drank. In spite of the proverb, what's one man's meat is not another man's poison."

Chief Britt eyed her cautiously. "How'd you imagine anybody could administer poisoned chewing gum anyway?"

"I don't imagine!" Miss Withers retorted sharply. "I'll leave the imagining to you. But tell me one thing: Isn't it the custom of the airline to supply passengers with a package of gum as a remedy for air sickness?"

"Yes and no," said Chief Britt. "You see—"

"That's how it was done, then," said Miss Withers triumphantly.

Britt still lacked enthusiasm. "What do you mean by your yessing and noing?" Miss Withers demanded.

"Yes, they hand out chewing gum," explained the chief. "But no, it ain't this kind. The airline uses candy gum, not thin sticks like this."

Miss Withers bit her lip. "I don't suppose Forrest would have known that, do you?"

She stopped to draw breath, and at that inauspicious moment an interruption offered itself in the person of a tall and brawny individual with a large Adam's apple and pale eyes behind thick, horn-rimmed glasses. The newcomer was approaching from the slope of the hill.

"Hey, Amos!"

"Now we get some results," said Chief Britt to Miss Withers. "George is bossing my search parties." He waved encouragingly toward George. "Come on up and tell us what you found."

"We didn't," said George, when he had his breath. "The boys have gone over every square that you marked out, and found nary a sign of a new grave or even of a wheelbarrow track. We went through every building in the town, too."

The chief's face fell. But this was no surprise to Miss Withers. "Would it be correct for me to inquire if a search was made on the golf course?" she suggested.

George swallowed, and his Adam's apple bobbed like a cork. "I'll say a search was made! We dug up every sand bunker on the course, but besides a lot of moldy balls, there was nothin'."

He turned and stalked down the hill again, leaving the two of them alone. "Well, if the body isn't here—and if it couldn't have been taken away—where is it?" Miss Withers wanted to know.

"Throwed in the sea or burned," suggested the chief. "Only if it is in the water, it would of turned up. Whoever stole that body had no chance to take it very far out without a boat, and the water is so clear here that you can see fifty feet down. Somebody in swimming or in a boat would have seen it by now. I guess it must of been burned."

"Cremating a body makes a great deal of smoke and a terrible odor," said Hildegarde Withers. She polished the handle of her umbrella. "My opinion is that the body is buried somewhere—and not at the other end of the island, either."

Chief Britt smiled and then spoke with a weary patience, as if to a very small child. "Look at this ground, ma'am. Hard as a rock. It would be a terrible job to dig a grave here at all, and impossible to hide the traces of the dirt."

"Suppose it wasn't buried in the dirt," Miss Withers hazarded. "What about that building excavation next door to the infirmary? Suppose the body was sunk in some soft concrete ..."

The chief stared at her for a moment. Then he wrapped up the chewing gum again and stuck it into his hip pocket.

"I'll be looking into that," he promised her. "Only I don't think the digging has got to the concrete stage yet, anyway. This chewing gum'll go to a Pasadena laboratory on this afternoon's boat. Let's be getting back."

"Let's," she agreed. "We've done enough for one day."

"More than the Los Angeles police would have done, anyway," the chief announced. "They're crazy to get in on this case, you know. Good thing for me that, with the mayor out fishing, my brother-in-law is chairman of the city council. He won't ask for outside help. I don't need outside help."

"I should say not," said Miss Withers, without the sign of a smile.

She left Britt at the door of his curio shop and lingered long enough to see Mrs. Britt hurrying away, no doubt to her watermelon pickles. It was evident that nothing was likely to happen during the rest of the afternoon, and Miss Withers spent a busy half-hour in composing a night letter to Inspector Piper, care of the Santa Fe, which ran to three hundred words and outlined rather clearly the case up to this point. She spent another half-hour in coding the message according to the one cipher which she was certain he would be able to read—a simple deletion of all the vowels and reversal of the remaining letters. "That ought to keep Oscar's attention off the haystacks and cornfields for an hour or two tomorrow morning," she announced triumphantly to herself, as she signed the message "DRGDLH."

Miss Withers walked slowly back toward the hotel, pausing a moment on the breakwater outside the Casino to stare at the crystal-clear depths and wonder what secrets they could be hiding. A little way out from shore she could see the *Mermaid* coming back from its voyage, her twin paddle wheels churning noisily and the passengers clustered along the glass windows set in her hold.

A trip aboard the trim little vessel had been Miss Withers's first excursion at Catalina, when with half a hundred others she had drifted lazily above the submarine gardens which lined the shore from Seal Rocks to Pirate's Cove—the entire lee side of the island. She remembered vividly those glimpses of another and more populous world than our own, where sleek and rainbow-colored fishes darted through forests of kelp and sea moss, where the dessert-like purple jellyfish floated dreamily, and now and again the horrible yet ridiculous octopus stretched a spotted tentacle from the deeper shadows of the crusted rocks.

Suppose, she was thinking—suppose that those gaping ones aboard the *Mermaid* should come upon a glimpse of an exhibit they were not meant to see—the pale and bloated face of the man in the cocoa-colored sport outfit, tangled among the slimy fronds of the giant kelp, now only bait for the nibbling perch and the scuttling green lobsters?

It was not a pleasant picture, and Miss Withers shivered a little as she turned away from the shore.

The placid balconies of the St. Lena were a welcome sight as she came around the cliff beneath the little pepper tree. But a shout which rang across the water from the deck of the glass-bottomed *Mermaid* drew her back to the shore again. She could see, even at that distance, a commotion on board. The little boat ceased to move, and there was a splashing as her paddle wheels went into reverse.

Miss Withers prayed vainly for a pair of opera glasses. But she could see that the crew of the excursion boat were preparing to use a boat hook. She watched as they caught hold of an object which seemed to be floating, just awash, alongside.

Her eyes strained until she had a headache, but she could not make out whether or not it was as she feared.

Then, with a shout, the sailors pulled together on their hooked poles and dragged from the sea—not the corpse of Roswell T. Forrest, but only a rusty wheelbarrow. Miss Withers nodded to herself, for she could see it very clearly—as well as some other details which had, until now, eluded her.

She could not see the adhesive tape which had been wound around the rim of the iron wheel, or the heavy grease which still glistened on the axle. But remembering that neither the doctor nor the night watchman had heard anything, she was almost certain that these aids were there.

The *Mermaid* got under way again, headed for the pier, and Miss Withers hastened onward toward the sanctity of her own chamber.

But even here she was to find echoings of the silent scream which had sounded when the man who had not wanted to die choked out his last breath aboard the red-and-gilt *Dragonfly*.

It was something of a fortunate accident for Miss Withers—her second in the eventful day. But it began casually enough.

There was a low rumble of voices inside her own room as she came up the stairs. She paused for a moment outside the half-open door and then realized that her first fear of prowlers was unfounded.

It was only the maid, standing in the middle of the room with an armful of towels. But the maid was not talking to herself.

"I tell you," she was saying, "you going to get yo'self a heap of trouble if you don't tell 'em."

The voice of Roscoe, the gray-headed bellhop, chimed in. "B-but he give me a dollah to forget about it."

"You git yo'self in some trouble that a dollah won't help yo' forget," the maid promised him. "Iffen I was you, black trash, I'd git to the policeman quick as ever I could."

Miss Withers chose this moment to enter, and Roscoe leaped to attention from his seat on the windowsill. The maid put down her towels and made for the door, and Roscoe started to follow.

"Wait a minute, young man," ordered Miss Withers.

Roscoe froze in his tracks.

"What's this you don't want to tell the police? Something about the murder?"

Roscoe rolled his eyes. "Murder? No, ma'am. It ain't nothing."

Miss Withers realized that she had taken the wrong tack. "I'm your friend, Roscoe," she said kindly. "I know something about this case.

Suppose you tell me what is on your mind. Then I'll decide whether or not you ought to go to the chief with it. Murder is serious business, you know."

"Yas'm," said Roscoe dubiously. "But this ain't got nothin' to do with this murder everybody's talkin' about. No, ma'am!"

"About the body, then?" Miss Withers knew that Chief Britt was endeavoring to keep the theft of the body a secret from the newspapers and the public alike, but perhaps it was a futile gesture.

Roscoe was still dubious.

"Well, who gave you the dollar not to tell?"

"Oh, that was Mistah George, the movie man." Roscoe brightened. "He give me a quarter to tote his bags upstairs yesterday when he come, too."

Miss Withers nodded. "Roscoe, you've nothing to fear. But if you keep silent you may find yourself under suspicion of being an accomplice, you know. Tell me what you know, or I'll have to go to the police and have them make you tell."

"Oh, Lawdy Jesus!" Roscoe eyed the door, but Miss Withers still blocked his way.

"Come, come!"

"I been worryin' about it all day," Roscoe admitted. "Ever since I heard what happened down in the town las' night. But it didn't have nothin' to do with the murder, no, ma'am. It was only—" Roscoe gulped—"it was only that Mistah George and Mistah Tony, the movie men, they got up awful early this mornin'. They had to meet a truck that was goin' to take them to the movie location at the Isthmus, they said. I toted down all their stuff, and then they sent me up the road to see if the bus was comin' from town."

"From the town?"

"Yas'm. It seemed funny to me, too, when the Isthmus was the other way. But I went up as far as the Casino, and then I heard a car over here and come back. The movie bus was outside the hotel, right at the carriage entrance, and I seen—"

"You saw!" corrected Miss Withers automatically.

"Yas'm, I saw Mistah George and Mistah Tony carrying it through the lobby. They was sort of hurrying and looking both ways to make sure nobody was watching, and then I saw 'em drag it into the back of the truck. The truck drove off sort of slow, but Mistah George seen me and he waited. 'You don't know anything about this, do you?' he asks me, and gives me a silver dollah. Then he runs on ahead and catches the truck."

Miss Withers was able to contain herself no longer. "I don't suppose you could come to the point and tell me just what you saw them carrying?"

"Yas'm." Roscoe lowered his voice. "It was a dead body!"

For a moment Miss Withers digested this somewhat amazing disclosure. "A dead body—could you see how it was dressed?"

Roscoe shook his head. "They had him in the closed truck before I got there, mum. But I saw a sort of dark overcoat throwed over him."

Miss Withers nodded. "Did you see who drove the truck?"

"No, mum."

"Was Mr. Tate in command of operations?" Miss Withers pressed onward. "In other words, do you think that his assistants were acting as accomplices in the carrying out of the disposal of the body?"

Roscoe blinked admiringly at her choice of words. Then he wagged his head. "I didn't see Mr. Tate around nowhere this mornin'. Now—you-all through with me, mum?"

"You may go," said Miss Withers. "But it may be necessary for you to repeat this testimony in the office of the chief of police."

"Yas'm," agreed Roscoe, evidently relishing, now that he had taken the plunge, the thrill of being the center of the stage.

"And Roscoe—I think that when you see Mr. George again, you should return the dollar."

"Yas'm," echoed Roscoe unhappily.

Miss Withers had thought that her day's labors as self-appointed criminal investigator were over, but this new evidence, contradictory as it seemed to be, was nothing which she could ignore.

It was manifestly her duty to inform Chief Britt of this latest development in the case at once. She hastened downstairs to the telephone booth in the lobby and was almost immediately connected with the chief's office.

Instead of Britt's lazy drawl she was disappointed to hear the querulous voice of Deputy Ruggles.

"Amos is busy," she was informed.

"I have no doubt about it," Miss Withers retorted. "But he must speak to me. I've got news of the missing body."

"Party? Amos can't go to no party, he's busy I tell you!" Like most persons afflicted with deafness, Deputy Ruggles raised his voice to a scream whenever he was having trouble in hearing.

"If Chief Britt is busy, I've got news that will make him twice as busy. You ask him to come to the phone. To the phone, understand?"

"Of course I understand," answered Ruggles testily. "I ain't deef. But he can't come to the phone. He's busy arresting Barney Kelsey!"

Miss Withers was completely flabbergasted. "Barney Kelsey? What for, in heaven's name?"

"For the murder of Roswell Forrest, that's what for," came back Ruggles happily. "Caught escaping red-handed, almost. They're bringing him back now—"

"Escaping? But how in the world—there's only the steamer and the plane—"

Ruggles laughed cacklingly. "He figured out another way. You see, there's a feller on the pier who rents outboard motorboats to the tourists for a run of the harbor, at two dollars an hour. Kelsey rented him one this afternoon and headed her out to sea. He run out of gas, like the dumb greenhorn he is, about halfway between here and Long Beach, in the middle of the channel, and Lew French in the *Dragonfly* sighted him. The chief went out in a launch to nab him—now do you understand?"

Miss Withers slowly replaced the receiver and came out of the booth. "No, I don't think I do understand," she remarked to nobody in particular.

CHAPTER XII

"THE Ancient Order of Dragonflies is in session," called out the effervescent Phyllis, as Miss Withers put in a tardy appearance at the dinner table that night. She waved toward a vacant chair, covering up a somewhat strained silence which had greeted the advent of the schoolteacher.

Miss Withers made a brief survey as she sat down between Phyllis and the male half of the newlyweds, at whom she smiled benevolently. There were several vacant chairs this evening, and the Ancient Order of the Dragonflies had hardly a quorum. Phyllis, Tompkins, the newlyweds, and herself made up the party. The three movie men, she imagined, were still up at the picture location on the Isthmus, busy with whatever mischief it was that Roscoe had unveiled to her. As for Captain Narveson, Phyllis went on to announce that she had glimpsed him entering the local pool and billiard emporium shortly before six.

Tompkins, pale-faced and shakily sober, received a distant nod from Miss Withers. He was having ham and eggs, the newlyweds shared a magnificent steak, but the newcomer followed Phyllis's lead and ordered an omelette.

She noticed that the young couple had surrounded themselves with a litter of travel pamphlets and guidebooks dealing with the island.

"I see you're bent on enjoying yourselves," Miss Withers remarked conversationally. "I suppose this island paradise is a pleasant change from your work."

Kay Deving looked blank.

"Miss La Fond tells me that she has seen you on the stage somewhere."

Still Kay looked blank. "Why," she smiled, "Marvy and I aren't on the stage! We met in a Charleston contest years ago, but that was in a Chicago ballroom."

"I've had about every job under the sun," Marvin Deving took up the explanation. "But I never got into show business, with or without Kay. It's always been a sort of ambition of mine, like it is of 'most everybody. Only I've been behind a soda fountain most of the time. Right now I'm not doing anything, as a matter of fact."

"Maybe it was a couple of other guys," said Phyllis La Fond. But she stared very thoughtfully at her fork.

Kay Deving turned to Miss Withers, her brown-flecked eyes alight with expectation. "Don't you think, now that they've got the guilty man in jail, it will be all right for us to leave tomorrow or the next day?"

Phyllis interrupted, rather heatedly, as Miss Withers was pondering the matter.

"What makes you think they have got the man who bumped Forrest off? Mr. Kelsey didn't do it, he's cute. His trying to get away doesn't prove he did the murder, does it, Miss Withers?"

The schoolteacher pursed her lips. "Not exactly, no. All the same, Mr. Kelsey has made things very difficult for himself. I'm afraid the police will feel his attempt was prima-facie evidence of guilt. Yet, as a matter of fact," she elaborated, "Kelsey may have had perfectly innocent reasons for disobeying the order to remain here."

Marvin Deving, he of the slick hair and the slightly fatuous smile, entered the conversation. "Yeah," he said. "And maybe a cop goes into the back door of a speakeasy to get a glass of ginger ale."

"Marvy means," translated Kay sweetly, "that Mr. Kelsey may have had a reason for trying to save his life before they hung him."

"You think of the nicest things at the dinner table," objected Phyllis. "Let's call a moratorium on the murder, shall we? How about playing Ghosts or Missing Words? I know a swell limerick about the old man from Peru who found he had nothing to do …"

Her efforts at turning the tide of the conversation were efficacious but unappreciated. Kay and Marvin Deving returned to their guidebooks.

Miss Withers peered across the table. "Are you children planning on doing the place thoroughly?"

Kay nodded. "As long as we have to stay here, we may as well see everything. Today we went to the bird park and out for a ride on the glass-bottomed boat, and tomorrow there's a Sunday excursion to the Isthmus."

T. Girard Tompkins, evidently intent upon eradicating any unfavorable impression he had made on the previous evening, was spreading himself to be affable and gentlemanly. He tugged at a pocket of his coat and finally brought forth a globular object of dull red, which appeared at first to be an apple.

He put it down carefully on the table in front of him and turned to the newlyweds. "While you are seeing the island," he explained, "you ought to visit the pottery plant down the beach where this ware is made."

He picked up a silver knife and tapped the odd-shaped bowl near the small opening at its top. The piece responded with a clear, resonant musical note—D flat above high C, Miss Withers thought it.

"I happen to handle the marketing of a good deal of this pottery," he announced somewhat pompously. "It is of a very superior quality, as you can see for yourself. Only in Devonshire, England, is a clay found which is anything like the product of the Catalina craters. Once upon a time, you know, this entire island was a range of active volcanic peaks, and the oxides, kaolins, and the acid minerals, united with silicas and aluminums, are responsible for the richness and sturdiness of this Catalina ware. Watch—"

He rolled the little round bowl off the table, and though it struck upon a hard tile floor, it did not shatter. Tompkins made a breathless and triumphant recovery and placed it on the table again.

Quite evidently Mr. Tompkins expected somebody to say something indicative of interest in his bowl. Miss Withers obligingly picked it up and stared into the little hole which gave access to its hollow center. "What is it used for?"

Tompkins shrugged his shoulders. "Small flowers, old razor blades, matches, used chewing gum—" there seemed another awkward silence after that word:—"oh, anything you like."

Miss Withers nodded. "And where do they get the clay to make these?"

Tompkins shrugged again. "Most of it from the quarry—" He stopped as he saw her face.

"Quarry!" she had forgotten that she was not alone. "That's where the murderer of Roswell Forrest might have got rid of the body!"

But her excitement was short-lived. "The quarry is away out beyond the Isthmus," Tompkins informed her. "They used to dig at the crater of Mount Orizaba and Mount Black Jack, but landslides wiped them out years ago. Now all the digging is done twenty miles away, at Silver Peak."

Miss Withers nodded slowly. Then she moved as if to replace the bowl in front of Tompkins across the table. Unfortunately, she overturned a centerpiece of fresh nasturtiums, and as the ensuing cascade of water poured across the cloth, she let the apple-colored bowl go rolling on the floor, with a clumsiness quite foreign to her nature.

"I'm so sorry," she gasped.

They were all standing up, and a waiter was mopping at the damage. "I'm afraid I've damaged your little bowl."

"Not at all," Tompkins was saying, as he peered beneath the cloths of neighboring tables. Miss Withers noticed that he was wearing canvas shoes with sponge-rubber soles. But it was Marvin Deving who spied the bowl first and who knelt to rescue it. "Here she is," he announced lightly. "And there's not a nick on it. Aren't you relieved, Miss Withers?"

Miss Withers was not relieved, for while the pleasant young man had been kneeling upon the floor, she had seen all too clearly that his worn buckskin sport shoes bore new rubber heels—heels with a large initial K in relief on them. The K on the right foot had a broken upper bar.

The newlyweds excused themselves, as they intended, they said, to take in the movie at the Casino. Phyllis refused to accompany them, on the grounds that she had seen the picture as a preview a year before. "But I might be interested in that Isthmus trip tomorrow," she added. Then she bribed a waiter to filch some bones from the kitchen and departed toward the stairs with Mister Jones's supper. Tompkins, with his bowl in his hand, went out ostensibly to smoke a cigar on the beach, and Miss Withers remained at the table alone, her brows frowning.

It was impossible for her to believe that on his wedding night Marvin Deving had slipped through the fog to the window of the infirmary and had been responsible for the macabre and grotesque shifting of human remains which had taken place there before sunrise.

For a while she silently debated whether or not to take this information to the chief. He would immediately arrest Marvin—or would he? Barney Kelsey was already looking at the world through prison bars, but Miss Withers had no idea of placing anyone else in that predicament unless she was certain.

Did the print of Marvin's heel outside the window mean that he had worn the shoes that made it—or, for that matter, that he had ever gone through that window, even if he had stood outside?

She remembered the blank amazement on his face—and on Kay's too—when they heard of the theft of the body. Evidence was all right but Miss Withers placed more faith in her intuition.

Finally she gave the whole matter up and began to concentrate again upon the whereabouts of the body. "If we find it first, then we can start to figure who put it there," she told herself.

As she rose from the table, she saw a pamphlet lying near Kay Deving's chair—evidently a bit of travel literature which had fallen to the floor and been forgotten. She idly picked it up—and immediately became engrossed in a map of Catalina.

It was a fanciful, grotesque piece of work, but the landmarks and roads were there. She could see the peaks mentioned by Tompkins— the Isthmus, where the island had very nearly been separated into two islands by the pushing Pacific, and the height where she had stood with the chief and surveyed the vain search for the body.

The chief had drawn a circle around the town, estimating the farthest distance that a wheelbarrow could have been pushed in the night. But suppose it had not been a wheelbarrow, after all—or suppose that the body had been transferred to an auto "borrowed" from the local bus garage for that purpose—or from the moving-picture location at the Isthmus!

As she stared at the map her eyes came upon a notation upon the southwestern shore of the island—the shore on the side opposite the town and facing the vast stretches of the Pacific. There were no roads or ranches marked here, but only a wild crisscrossing of deep lines labeled "canyons," and farther up the shore, not more than two miles or at the most three from the town, the words "Old Indian Village and Burial Caves."

One thin and winding line from the plateau to the town showed that some sort of a road existed. Perhaps it was a road that a wheelbarrow passed over in the night. Perhaps—perhaps the burial caves had been called into service again.

Miss Withers made an instantaneous decision.

She folded up the map and nodded. "Tomorrow I visit the Old Indian Village, if I have to walk," she said to herself. But she did not dream of the manner in which she was destined to make her entrance into that prehistoric waste, or of the nightmares that were to follow after.

She climbed to her room, but left it hurriedly in order to escape hearing the woebegone howls of Mister Jones, who, Phyllis called from her doorway, had had his bottom warmed for him due to the discovery of an accident sincerely regretted by everyone concerned.

"Accidents will happen," Miss Withers told the girl. "Maybe if you walked him oftener—"

"I've walked off five pounds in the few days I've had him," complained Phyllis. "Tell me honestly"—she came closer—"do you think Barney Kelsey did the murder?"

Miss Withers stared at the girl critically. "My private opinion is still private, young lady. What do you think?"

"I think he didn't!" insisted Phyllis warmly.

"You seem very positive about that," Miss Withers told her. "Has Mr. Kelsey taken you into his confidence?"

"Huh?" Phyllis looked startled. "Oh, you saw us talking this morning. No, he didn't mention the murder at all."

Miss Withers let her fingers play an imaginary tune on the stair railing. "I wonder if you would have any objection to telling me what you did talk about?"

Phyllis was thoughtful. "Oh, nothing much. I said something about the places to eat here not being very good, and he told me about some little restaurants in New York where he'd like to take me—the Parisien and the Blue Ribbon for German food and the Red Devil for rum cake." Phyllis looked wistful.

"I know," said Miss Withers. "Anything else?"

"He said I had nice ears," Phyllis announced. "Nobody else ever praised my ears."

Now it was Miss Withers's turn to be thoughtful. She looked up and down the hall, and then beckoned Phyllis a little closer.

"I've got an idea," she said. "You've been playing Dr. Watson since this business began. Wouldn't you like to be the detective for a change?"

Phyllis hesitated for the fraction of a second. "Sure I would," she answered.

"All right. You've struck up an acquaintance with Kelsey. Suppose you drop in at the jail where they've got him prisoner at the next visiting hour, and draw him out on a subject or two? He might talk more freely to you than to me or the chief."

Phyllis nodded. "He might, at that. But he won't. I mean, I won't do it."

"Scruples?" Miss Withers's stare was sharp. "Or are you remembering my warning to keep away from the man? Understand, I'm not insinuating that he committed the murder. His ironclad alibi is enough to prove his innocence to almost anybody except that dolt of a chief of police."

"Or to you," Phyllis sagely put in. "No, thanks, I don't want any piece of it. If Barney Kelsey puts his curly gray locks into a noose, it's going to be through no work of mine."

Miss Withers knew when she had struck defeat. "It was just an idea," she confessed. "Well—I'm going for a walk. I suppose you're anxious to start dressing for the dance?"

"I'm not going to the dance tonight," said Phyllis. "If the excursion for the Isthmus leaves at nine o'clock, I'll have to turn in early to make it."

Miss Withers bade the girl good-night and went on downstairs and out of the hotel. T. Girard Tompkins hailed her, no doubt anxious to add to her fund of information regarding Catalina pottery, but she passed him by with a polite word of greeting and headed along the shore toward the town.

The little pepper tree stood bleak and solitary in the moonlight, but Miss Withers had no eyes for it tonight. She strode past the Casino, meeting groups of stragglers hurrying to catch the last show at the moving-picture theater, and came along the boardwalk into Avalon itself.

Luckily, Chief Britt was in his office. She found him in a most expansive mood, with a cigar tilted from one corner of his mouth and his feet on the desk.

"I s'pose you came down to congratulate me," he hazarded. "Yes, ma'am—just thirty hours since the discovery of Forrest's body, and I've got the murderer in the hoosegow."

"You've got Barney Kelsey in the—the hoosegow, as you put it," corrected Miss Withers tartly. "What good do you suppose that is going to do?"

"Do?" The chief took his feet off the desk. "It'll do plenty. We're going to hold an inquest one of these days, and I'll bet you dollars to dimes that the jury will find Forrest met his death at the hand of the man who was hired to guard him—Barney Kelsey!"

"You can't have an inquest without a body," Miss Withers told him. "You haven't what they call the corpus delicti, which doesn't mean exactly the corpse, but the body of your case, the groundwork, so to speak."

Britt pursed his lips. "The body'll turn up," he informed her. "Maybe it's turned up already, for that matter. Didn't you phone in about somebody seeing it?"

Miss Withers patiently repeated the message she had given Ruggles, regarding Roscoe the bellhop's dark secret.

Britt nodded sagely. "Seems like the last link in the chain to me. The two assistants, and maybe Tate himself, are in on this with Kelsey. You know how them movie people are. Murder don't mean a thing to 'em. Their part of the job was to dispose of the body. Tomorrow morning first thing I'm going over to the Isthmus and start a search."

Miss Withers was inclined to the opinion that Chief Britt's searches were not likely to bring anything to light, but she did not tell him so.

"To come back to the man you have in jail," she went on. "How and why could he have killed Forrest?"

The chief shrugged. "How? Probably poisoned his food. Although the Los Angeles police've been checking up on the movements of both of the men on Thursday night and Friday, and they say that Forrest left Kelsey at the hotel and went skylarking out to this—this house on Sunset Boulevard before dinner time, and that's the last time the two of 'em was together. I don't know of any poison that works as slow as that, but there must be some. Kelsey probably figured it would kill his boss during the night, and he'd go innocently along on his trip over here in the morning. Only the poison was slow, and Forrest didn't feel it till he was on the plane."

Miss Withers shook her head dubiously. "Suppose all this is true, then why did Kelsey do it?"

The chief waggled a fat finger in the air, making a dollar sign. "Didn't you tell me you heard from this inspector fellow that somebody in New York was offering fifteen thousand bucks if Forrest didn't ever come back to testify against the big shots? I guess fifteen thousand would be enough to buy any bodyguard."

Miss Withers nodded. "It would buy other people, too," she pointed out. "I've heard of murder being committed for less than that by such persons as airplane pilots, or doctors and nurses, or businessmen—or, for that matter, by schoolteachers and policemen. The infamous Dr. Webster was a professor at Harvard, but he murdered for less than five hundred dollars. And times are bad, Mr. Britt."

Before the chief could answer, his desk telephone shrilled. He lifted the receiver and his face brightened. "It's long-distance calling from Pasadena," he informed his caller. Then: "Hello, hello. ..."

He jiggled the hook. "Ever since the last temblor our phone to the mainland has been woozy," he explained. "Guess the cable was injured—hello!"

He listened for perhaps five minutes, and Miss Withers saw the self-confidence drain from his face. Finally he hung up and turned toward her.

"If that was your analytical chemist, what did he say?" Miss Withers prompted. "Or did the messenger lose the specimen?"

Britt shook his head. "Dr. Lundstrom has had that chewing gum for only an hour or so. Just time enough to give it all the primary tests. No trace of any of the acid poisons, no arsenic or anything like that. He says—"

"The man doesn't know his job, then," Miss Withers cut in. "Because that gum simply has to be poisoned!"

"He's the best chemist in the West," Britt told her. "I was going on to say that he's found something stranger than poison, even. He's found that the chewing gum doesn't match the paper wrapper it came in. It's only sweetened boiled chicle—and that's why he's going on with every test he can think of."

Miss Withers digested this for a while. "Homemade gum, eh?"

The chief was tramping up and down his office. "Now if we only had a body to analyze, we could get somewhere. With the vital organs in Lundstrom's hands, we'd know inside of an hour what all this means."

"That's what I wanted to talk to you about," Miss Withers told him. "Let's forget the gum for a while and concentrate on the body. I have an idea, in spite of what Roscoe the bellhop says, that it wasn't taken to the Isthmus at all. Tell me—you know the island and I don't—how does one get to the Indian Burial Caves that are shown on the maps?"

Britt looked surprised. "Them? Why, you follow South Street out past the ball park and keep going alongside of the canyon. But—" He suddenly understood what she was driving at.

"You're thinking that maybe these two movie fellers drove the body over there instead of taking it to the Isthmus? Forget it. The road hasn't been traveled this season on account of its being in disrepair, and their truck wouldn't get halfway there."

"How about a wheelbarrow?" inquired Hildegarde Withers.

The chief looked dubious. "Maybe. But there ain't much over at that Indian camp. It's five or six hundred years old, and nothing's left but some mud huts and some broken dishes and stuff, covered up with cactus. Who'd want to go over there, anyways?"

"I, for one," Miss Withers told him. She moved toward the door and then stopped. "I've got something else on my mind," she began.

"Then get it off," Britt told her wearily.

"Somebody ought to check up on the movements of all the suspects on the day or so preceding the tragedy," she pointed out. "I'd particularly like to know what the license clerk and the newspaper records have to say about the newlyweds. And—one thing more—I think the two pilots ought to be included in the survey."

Chief Britt blinked. "Those boys? Why, they wouldn't hurt a flea."

"But Forrest wasn't a flea," retorted Miss Withers. "Will you send the wires?"

He nodded. "But I don't see—"

"You will," she promised him and passed out into the clear but humid night. Walking had often served her as a stimulant for thought, and she had much to think about as she strode back down the darkened Main Street of Avalon. Only the corner drugstore and the local pool hall showed lights. Through the open door of the latter she could see the thickset figure of Captain Thorwald Narveson, engaged in a stiff game of rotation with two young men whom she recognized with a shock as being the pilots of the *Dragonfly*, Lew French and his partner Chick.

The captain stood away from the table to chalk his cue, and Miss Withers saw the lights reflected in the shiny seat of his blue-serge trousers. What she had said a few moments before to the chief seemed to apply everywhere. Times were bad—even for the owners of whaling ships. Times were bad—and fifteen thousand dollars was a lot of money. She remembered that Narveson had sat very near the dying man and that he alone had failed to show surprise at the discovery of the death. It was admitted generally, she knew, that good poker players make good murderers. She found herself wondering if that would also apply to pocket billiards.

She was thinking in circles, ever and ever again bumping up against the same stone wall. The body of the dead man was missing. It had been stolen from the infirmary, or at least the window had been burgled, some time after Dr. O'Rourke returned from escorting her to the hotel. Allowing fifteen minutes or so to give the doctor time to stroll home, that made the hour of the corpse-stealing sometime between one or one-fifteen and the lifting of the fog blanket shortly before three in the morning, unless the job was risked by moonlight, which she seriously doubted.

Yes, it was safe to say that the body of Roswell Forrest had been stolen and disposed of sometime between one o'clock and three. That was little time enough, considering the magnitude of the task.

Yet every one of the prospects had a splendid alibi for that hour. She herself had been in Phyllis's room until at least two-thirty, and during that time she had seen or heard Tompkins, George and Tony, Narveson, and the newlyweds—or at least had heard the young wife begging for silence because "Marvy" was asleep, which was almost as good.

Tate's alibi had been established a few minutes later, it was true. But still there would not have been time for him to do all that was done that night and then to appear, half drunk, outside Phyllis's door.

That left only Barney Kelsey, among the persons implicated in the case, and he had accounted for himself by insisting that he gave the slip to Ruggles and went directly to the hotel and to his room on the upper floor. As she knew full well, the lack of an alibi was no proof of guilt—in fact, the most ironclad alibis are the manufactured ones.

All the way back to the hotel the bewildered lady tried to decide whether or not one of the alibis could have been manufactured. Phyllis's was clear enough. So was Tompkins's. Unless the two assistant directors and the captain had hired someone to stand behind their doors and mimic their voices, their alibis were equally good. She came at last to the sorry comfort of deciding that only Marvin Deving stood unaccounted for. And if the slick-haired young man had contemplated anything in the nature of body-snatching, she was sure he would have presented the best alibi of the lot. Besides, both he and Kay had been speechless with surprise when she told them of the disappearance of the body—and that sort of surprise is hard to fake.

Yet she remembered the print of the shoe outside the infirmary window—the shoe with the nicked initial in its rubber heel. Marvin Deving's shoes had made that mark—but when and why she found herself unable to decide.

Weary and worn, Miss Withers came into the hotel lobby resolved upon only one conclusion. The entire mechanism of this crime lacked an important cogwheel. She was sure that it existed somewhere—but until she found it she was handicapped.

Except for the clerk and a blue-jowled gentleman engaged in reading a sheaf of newspapers, she found the lobby of the St. Lena deserted. It was late, and Hildegarde Withers was very tired.

But in spite of the weariness in her angular body, the schoolteacher was still in the grip of an insatiable curiosity. Acting upon an impulse, she paused in the lobby to engage the clerk in conversation. He was a washed-out person of late middle age, who looked as if he had seen better days and never expected to see any more.

He readily swung the register around to show her the neatly written signature of Barney Kelsey. Yes, Mr. Kelsey had registered last night about the hour of twelve-thirty. He had been shown by Roscoe to a room on the third floor rear.

Miss Withers frowned. Unlike the rooms on the second floor, there could have been no balcony outside Kelsey's room to afford him a secret means of egress. "Then he didn't leave the hotel after he checked in, you're sure?"

"Of course I'm sure," insisted the clerk, restraining a yawn with evident difficulty. "Chief Britt was up here asking me the same thing."

"And you were on duty all night?"

"Till seven o'clock this morning, yes, ma'am."

Miss Withers looked down at the well-cushioned wicker chair which stood behind the counter. "You didn't drop off to sleep, not even once?"

The clerk maintained that never had sleep touched his eyelids. But his gaze was evasive, and Miss Withers, dimly remembering that he had not given her a good-evening last night when she returned from the Casino, pressed her point.

"Good heavens, man, you're not a sentry. Nobody is going to shoot you for going to sleep on your post."

Presented in that light, the clerk was willing to admit the barest possibility that she was right.

She nodded wearily. Then the lobby with its open door and snoring clerk would have been no check at all upon the movements of Kelsey— or any other guest. She was right back where she had started.

Idly she turned over the page of the register and glanced down a column of today's visitors. There were a good many, for the season was in full swing, and what the newspapers were calling "the Red *Dragonfly* Mystery" had lured a number of curiosity seekers into remaining over the weekend.

It was the last name in the column which caught Miss Withers's eye: "Patrick Mack, Bayonne, New Jersey." The writing was round and almost childish.

"Patrick Mack," she repeated thoughtfully. There was a spark of something glittering in the bottom of her mind, like a new penny in a swimming pool. But for the moment it eluded her.

The clerk lowered his voice to a religious hush and nodded over her shoulder. "That's him, ma'am," he indicated. "Ever since he registered he's been hanging around as if he was waiting for somebody. Friend of yours?"

Miss Withers turned and saw across the room the head and shoulders of a man who was as out of place among these breezy Westerners as was she herself.

He was looking up from his newspaper, and their glances met and passed on. Above the pages Miss Withers could see a plump, swarthy face and a pair of shoulders wide with the curved padding in which Seventh Avenue tailors delight. He belonged in a ringside seat in the Garden, or among the low-voiced crowd who haunt Lindyck:'s restaurant and mark the tablecloths with matchstubs.

"No, I don't know him," said Miss Withers. But all of a sudden the case which had hitherto been such a muddle began to clear—just the merest fraction. Here, she decided with a swift flash of the intuition which usually guided her—here was the missing balance wheel of the whole machine. For the key to the mystery, she was almost positive, lay not in the sprawling Western metropolis in which Forrest had chosen to hide himself, but in Manhattan—and this stranger, in spite of his "Bayonne" on the register, spelled Forty-second Street to her.

She was remembering the letter written to Forrest by his former secretary—and the terse understatement, "... because Mack wouldn't like it."

Without realizing it, Miss Withers stared at the only other guest in the lobby with so burning a gaze that he looked suddenly up from his newspaper, flushed a shade deeper, and then rose to his feet with a very real yawn and disappeared toward the stairs.

"Mr. Mack represents a big shipbuilding and wharfage firm in New York," vouchsafed the clerk garrulously. There was something in Hildegarde Withers's clear blue eyes and slightly equine visage which impelled people to talk to her—an unconscious attraction which had often stood her well during past ventures into the realm of Sherlockery.

"And he's here on big business," the clerk continued. "If you ask me, he's planning on building a big amusement pier here—or buying the Casino or something. Because he just gave me a blue envelope full of valuables to keep in the safe overnight. All them big business men use negotiable securities nowadays, with the banks like they are."

"Indeed!" Miss Withers had no particular interest in blue envelopes. She found herself cursed with a burning desire to be in two places at the same time tomorrow. She was determined to run down the missing body if it was anywhere to be found—and she was possessed of a very definite hunch that if she were ever to solve this mystery she ought to stick closer than a brother to Patrick Mack.

The two paths, at the moment, did not seem to converge. Miss Withers bade the clerk a polite good-evening. "I suppose I'm practically the last of the Old Guard to check in, am I not?"

The clerk was thoughtful. "Well, I wouldn't say that, ma'am. Mr. and Mrs. Deving went to the movie and haven't showed up yet—and Mr. Kelsey isn't in, either."

Miss Withers nodded. "Yes, ma'am" rambled on the clerk. "With a fine night and a moon and all, I can understand the newlyweds being out. But as for Mr. Kelsey—"

"I can understand Mr. Kelsey's lateness," said Miss Withers shortly and went up to bed.

CHAPTER XIII

A THOUSAND elephants stormed through Miss Withers's dreams that night, so that she awoke with a distinct feeling of relief to see the pale light of early dawn at her window. She drew the old-fashioned watch from beneath her pillow and saw that it was hardly four o'clock. Then she sat up straight in bed, pinching herself just to make sure that she was not even yet in the grip of the nightmare, for the elephants still thundered.

A vase of flowers crashed from her bureau to the floor, and a bad reproduction of Reynolds's "Age of Innocence," which Miss Withers had always loathed, swung wildly on the opposite wall and then hurtled down. Her bed rocked like a skiff in a gale, and it was with trembling knees that the good lady finally reached the floor.

She got to the wall telephone, and after much rattling of the hook she succeeded in arousing the clerk downstairs.

"I must insist that the people overhead stop that commotion," she announced. "If they don't wish to sleep, I do!"

Not without difficulty, the clerk finally managed to inform her, his voice strained but heavy with studied calm, that she was mistaken in thinking that the people overhead had anything to do with the vibration which still rocked her room. "It's a mild temblor," said the clerk.

"A *what?*" Miss Withers was far from patient. "A Knight Templar, did you say?"

"No, ma'am—a temblor! What Easterners call an *earthquake.*" He hesitated over the last word, as if it were vulgar and outside the usage of good society.

"There is absolutely no danger," the man continued. "It is best to stand in the doorway of your room until it subsides, so that if the walls give way you will not be crushed." He hung up, evidently besieged with other calls. Miss Withers stood there shivering for a moment. She could hear Mister Jones barking in the next room, and a woman down the hall was monotonously calling for "Fred." Somebody ran down the hall, but it was not Fred.

The shaking subsided and immediately took up again where it had left off. Miss Withers clutched the phone for support and watched her bureau drawers slide out and empty themselves neatly on the carpet.

Perhaps she screamed. She was not sure about it afterward, although she always maintained stoutly that she did not.

At any rate, she felt an inward surge of relief when her open window to the balcony was darkened, and in stepped Phyllis La Fond, in negligee and slippers, and with Mister Jones gripped in her arms.

"One for all and two for five," greeted Phyllis cheerily. "If I'm going to be buried alive I want company. Mind if we join you?"

"Do I mind!" said Miss Withers heartily.

The room was chilly, and Phyllis immediately planted herself in the bed, where Miss Withers and the dog shortly joined her. "I suppose the rest of them will go chasing outside and catch pneumonia on the lawn," said Phyllis optimistically. "We're as safe here—I've been through three of 'em before. The first shock is always the worst." The room rocked again, and Mister Jones whimpered. Miss Withers realized that the pounding of the surf had taken on a harsher, sharper note. The fat, bewildered little dog pushed a cold nose against her, and she stroked it comfortingly, not without a thought of possible fleas.

The tremors followed one another in diminishing ratio and finally died away completely.

"This was nothing compared to the Santa Barbara quake," Phyllis informed her hostess. "Well, it seems to be over. I guess I'll go back and get some sleep."

"Do you mind," requested Miss Withers a little quaveringly—"do you mind getting your sleep right here?"

Strangely enough, they both did sleep, while Mister Jones stole down from the bed and fell happily to chewing on Miss Withers's best pair of stockings.

Phyllis woke first, and her exclamation on noting the slender watch on her wrist awakened the schoolteacher.

"Quarter-past nine," she wailed. "I've missed the excursion bus to the Isthmus!"

Miss Withers blinked. "You mean they'll run the excursion bus just the same after what happened?"

"Of course, why not? Good heavens, a temblor isn't anything! Nobody pays any attention to them out here. Sometimes they shake down an old-fashioned building, but that's all. Business as usual."

Phyllis had arisen hurriedly, but Miss Withers detained her. "I have an idea," she suggested. "No matter how you hurry, you've missed the bus. But I'm going to rent transportation of some kind today for a little trip of my own, and if you'll go with me, I'll have the boy drive you over the Isthmus afterwards. Besides, I'd like company."

"You're on," said Phyllis. "Meet you downstairs for breakfast in half an hour." She went toward the window. "Come on, doggie."

"I wonder if you'd mind bringing Mister Jones along?" Miss Withers asked. "I've got an idea."

Miss Withers spent some time in straightening her room, replacing her belongings in the bureau and picking up the picture and the smashed bowl. When she was dressed she went to the window and looked out half expecting to see a ruined landscape.

A silver-gray haze hung over the morning, through which the sun had difficulty in penetrating. The waves broke against the shore with a sullen pounding, but that was the only tangible result of the earthquake as far as she could see. The lawns and beach were much as usual, and a few sun worshipers were already sprawled on the sands.

Still she stared critically around. Not a palm tree had fallen, not a flower seemed disturbed.

Even the little pepper tree was still in its place on the crest of the hill. Miss Withers looked at it, frowning for a moment. The little tree did appear differently than it had when last she had tried to catch its outlines in her sketchbook. She hurried crossed the room and fumbled through her belongings until she found the canvas-bound book, searching for the drawing that she had begun before sterner problems usurped her leisure. But the half-finished sketch was not there.

She went back to the window with a puzzled expression on her face. Sketch or no sketch, the tree had somehow changed. It now seemed to be pressing toward the declivity, its two armlike branches stretched out to sea!

"Well, we live and learn," she told herself. Closing the sketchbook, she hurried down to breakfast.

Somewhat to her surprise, she found Phyllis already attacking a plate of toast in the dining room, with Mister Jones tied to a leg of the table and munching a crust contentedly. Miss Withers ordered coffee, and a box lunch to take out.

"This must be a real expedition," Phyllis hazarded. "Maybe I'm lucky not to have gone with the others."

"You don't know the half of it," she was told. Then Miss Withers looked up suddenly to see the stranger of last evening coming into the dining room. Patrick Mack of Bayonne looked somewhat worn and sleepless, and he had cut a neat gash in his chin while shaving.

He passed by their table without a single appreciative glance at Phyllis's well-displayed figure. Miss Withers sensed that he was made uncomfortable by her fixed stare, and also that he was looking for somebody who wasn't here.

He went swiftly back into the lobby, asked the clerk a question to which a negative reply was given, and received into his own keeping again the fat blue envelope. Miss Withers, who had risen from the table as casually as she could manage, watched him from the door of the dining room. He put the envelope carefully into his inside pocket and set off toward the town.

Miss Withers turned and beckoned toward Phyllis.

"That man is suspicious of me," she explained hurriedly. "Be a good girl and do me a favor. Follow him, casually, and tell me where he goes. I'll pick up the lunch and meet you in half an hour at the bus stand on Main Street."

This time Phyllis did not balk at playing assistant sleuth. With Mister Jones lunging ahead, half choked against the restraining leash, she suffered herself to be drawn down the hotel steps and along the boardwalk.

It was something more than half an hour later when Miss Withers, who had stopped to make a purchase in a corner toy shop, appeared at the bus stop. Phyllis and Mister Jones were already waiting.

"Clear all wires," sang out Phyllis. "Secret service operative Five reporting. The quarry is now having breakfast in a lunchroom down the street."

Miss Withers was disappointed. "So that's all!"

Phyllis nodded. "He went to the post office first."

The schoolteacher brightened. "Did he get any mail?"

Phyllis shook her head. "He didn't even ask for any. He just went to the window and rented a lock box. I didn't want him to see me, so I didn't get close enough to tell which one. But it was down at the end of the line."

Miss Withers thanked Phyllis. She wasn't sure what this meant, but it certainly meant something. If Mr. Mack intended to stay at the hotel, his mail would be delivered there. Lock boxes were used only by natives living outside the narrow limits of free delivery. Why should a man pay for a service that the hotel supplied free?

"I'm going to snoop a little," she told Phyllis. "Wait here for me— you might find out what it will cost to have the fat boy drive us to the Indian Burial Caves if you can find him."

"Right-o," agreed Phyllis. She had entered wholeheartedly into the spirit of the thing.

Miss Withers found the post office deserted, except for the postmaster in his shirtsleeves who was sorting mail in the rear. She strolled idly down the row of lock boxes, without the slightest idea of what it was that she sought. All the same, she found it. Through the thick glass in one of the last tier of boxes she saw the blue envelope!

For a long time she stood and stared at it. Somehow, she had known, deep in her subconscious, that it would be there. Patrick Mack had mailed his own envelope to himself—and the reason was something she would have given anything in the world to discover.

A plan suggested itself—a plan so daring and so daring and so simple that it staggered her. This was no time to hesitate. Perhaps she should have called in the aid of Chief Amos Britt, but that would take time and persuasion. Hildegarde Withers was strictly an opportunist.

"Here's to crime," she told herself and went back to the stamp window. After a few minutes' wait, the postmaster appeared, and the usual discussion of "the temblor" occurred before she voiced her request. "It's the one I had last year and I'd like it again if it's vacant," she lied boldly.

"Sixty cents for two months," she was informed. She paid her money and was given a slip bearing a combination.

"I'll show you how to work it if you need me to," offered the postmaster. "But if you had the box last year you'll probably know."

"I do know," Miss Withers assured him.

The man returned to his sorting, and Miss Withers went back down the hall. She spent a difficult five minutes in working the dial of her new lock box back and forth, until she had solved the problem of opening it. The glass door swung outward, and with a quick glance back at the empty office, the schoolteacher inserted her arm to its fullest extent.

As she had guessed, the back of the box was open, to allow the sorter of mail to insert letters. She fumbled for what seemed an age, stretching her wrist until it ached. At last her long fingers triumphed—and she touched the open rear door of the next lock box but one. After that it was another ordeal of stretching and anxious glances up and down before she felt the booty. Her thumb and forefinger closed around it—and then, ever so carefully, she drew the blue envelope out of its owner's box, through her own, and tucked it swiftly in her handbag.

She heaved a deep sigh of relief. No one had seen her. Pictures of a lifetime at Fort Leavenworth, breaking rocks, flashed before her. But somehow, she knew that the risk was worth it.

She went over to the wall desk, took up a pen, and pretended to be addressing the envelope. But luckily, at this hour, the place was deserted, and the man in shirt sleeves still sorted letters.

Strangely enough, the blue envelope bore no address. It bore no stamp. Evidently it had not passed through Uncle Sam's hands, a fact which made Miss Withers hope that her offense was lightened thereby. Perhaps it would only mean twenty years on the rock pile if she were caught.

For a moment she hesitated, and then, realizing that at any moment the inexplicable Mr. Mack might return, she decided against opening it. That would have to wait. In the meantime ...

She spent a busy five minutes in the rear of a nearby stationery store, pretending to be writing a letter, and then reappeared in the post office. This time she had to wait while a woman mailed interminable postcards, but finally the coast was clear again.

She opened her box, with a deftness born of her recent practice, and reversed the laborious process of a few moments ago. She slammed the glass door again and left the building tingling with excitement. There was no sign of her having been engaged in robbery of the United States mails, for again a glint of blue envelope showed itself in the glass door of the next box but one to her own.

She had plans which were interrupted by a hail from Phyllis as she came down toward the Main Street again.

"Listen," cried that young lady. "We're up against a snag."

It developed that the fat youth who piloted the red bus had vetoed any suggestion of a trip to the Indian Burial Caves. The road was in ill repair at any time, but the recent quake had shaken the hills so severely that a dozen small landslides blocked the road which led from the ball park on over the hills.

"There's not a prayer in a whirlwind of getting through, even if we tried to walk," Phyllis informed her. "The road is built along the side of an impassable canyon. He says it will be opened in a week or two."

"A week or two isn't soon enough," said Miss Withers. "Not by a considerable sight. I wonder—"

She stopped short. Far down the street she saw the rotund yet erect figure of the freckled captain, enjoying his morning cigar. "I've got an idea," she told Phyllis. "We're not stuck yet."

She waved eagerly at Captain Narveson, who obligingly crossed the street. "Ahoy, ma'am," he called out. "Why the distress signals—afraid of the temblor?"

Miss Withers realized that the topic would have to be pursued to its bitter end before she could broach the subject which filled her mind.

The captain was in full swing. "That's what yu get for sticking on land," he pointed out. "Earth shaking every which way—houses maybe falling on yu. Ay tal yu, Ay'd rather be to sea in a full gale—"

"That's what I wanted to talk to you about," said Miss Withers quickly. "The quake has closed the road to the other side of the island. Can you tell me if it is possible to get there by water?"

Captain Narveson blinked his faded blue eyes. "Ay tank so. There's a landing at Middle Canyon, if you catch it at high tide. But why—"

"Is that near the Indian Burial Caves?"

Captain Narveson was of the opinion that it was very near indeed to the remains of the Indian village. In fact, historians explained that the prehistoric residents of the island had used Middle Canyon as a landing for their canoes.

"Will you take us there this morning?"

Here Miss Withers was snagged again. The captain explained that his only ship was the whaler which still lingered offshore. "The *City of Saunders* couldn't get within half a mile of that coast," he went on. "Yu go see Sven, down on the pier. He rents boats—he fix yu up."

Sven, it developed, was not at all eager to fix anybody up. He eyed his prospective customers with a fishy eye.

"I've got boats to rent, sure," he told them. "But they don't leave this bay. Yesterday some smart fellow tries to take one to the mainland on me."

Miss Withers explained that she had no idea of operating an outboard motor. "We want you to take us around the island and land us on the other side," she said.

Sven was still reluctant. Finally, upon pressure, he set a price. Very clearly he put it high enough, in his own mind, to discourage the idea. "Fifteen dollars," he said.

"Fifteen dollars," agreed Hildegarde Withers. She might as well be in this for a sheep as a lamb. Besides, the inspector was on his way out here, and if worse came to worst she could borrow her fare back to New York from her old friend.

Instead of one of the light, clean-lined speedboats, Sven led them to a twenty-foot launch, with an enclosed deck which smelled horribly of ancient fish.

Mister Jones leaped aboard eagerly, and the two women followed, gingerly holding their skirts away from the planking. Sven threw down oilskins for them to sit upon and busied himself in the depths of the craft for a long time. Then he reappeared.

"Tomorrow'd do just as well as today?" he suggested hopefully. But Miss Withers was firm.

"You've got your fifteen dollars," she told him. He disappeared again, and finally the shuddering rumble of a motor arose. Sven cast off a rope or two, lifted Mister Jones by the scruff of the neck out of a tangle of lines and fish hooks, and then headed the launch out across Avalon Bay.

"This is real fun," Phyllis decided. "I'm certainly glad that I didn't go to the Isthmus, after all."

The roar of the powerful motor drowned out her voice. They were skirting a shore which was made up of millions of smooth white rocks the size of ostrich eggs. The boardwalk ended in a clump of buildings which Miss Withers rightly took to be the pottery in which Tompkins was so much interested, and then the mountains began to press closer to the shore, looming higher and higher. They were covered with downy clumps of greenish brown, and from the water looked like pleasant hilly pastures.

Mister Jones put white forepaws on the thwart and growled defiantly at the flying fish which scurried ahead of them. Sven turned from the wheel only once, to shout back something about dirty weather after they rounded Seal Rocks. As far as Miss Withers could make out, the day promised to be fair enough, in spite of the queer gray haze which still hung between them and the sun.

They passed Seal Rocks, where a husky-voiced congregation barked hollowly and waved flippers of defiance. Mister Jones gave back the challenge with great excitement. "I didn't know there were that many seals," Phyllis observed.

"Properly speaking, they're not seals, but sea lions," Miss Withers corrected. And the launch swung in a half-circle toward the southwest.

Suddenly—so suddenly that Miss Withers caught her breath—the entire mood of the day was changed. Instead of a pebbled beach and rolling mountains of pleasant greenish brown, they were passing under cliffs frowning and forbidding, which ran straight up for two hundred feet. The very hills themselves were a dirty slate color, and instead of pleasant greenish-blue waves beneath them, the launch was bucking an angry sea of powerful and malevolent dishwater.

A big roller caught them, and only a frantic grasp by Miss Withers saved the little dog Jones from a watery grave. "He wants to be a dog-fish and chase catfish," sang out Phyllis merrily. But Miss Withers and the little dog were still sober and shaking.

"That one came all the way from China," observed Sven gloomily. "And there's more on the way."

The fairy-tale summer-resort island had suddenly become a barren and unfriendly place. Here on the windward side of Catalina was no yellow beach, no fluttering green palms, no sign of habitation or of life itself except for the sea birds who flew screaming overhead and the gleaming flying fishes skittering out of the water ahead of the bows.

Miss Withers felt as if the face of a pleasant acquaintance had suddenly relaxed in an unguarded moment to show violence and savagery underneath. This then was the real Santa Catalina, the desert island of song and story. This was the island where bloody Juan Cabrillo came in 1542 to wipe out the last of the sleepy natives by a series of tortures intended to make them divulge their hordes of nonexistent gold. This was the Santa Catalina where Sebastian Vizcaino dropped anchor a hundred years later, reputedly to bury treasure sacked from a score of ravished Inca cities. The schoolteacher shivered.

"It makes you feel the way you do when for the first time you walk behind a swell movie set and see the framework and the chicken wire," said Phyllis. "This looks like the back door to hell."

They rolled on in silence, until at last the launch was put about by Sven so that she roared straight at what appeared to be a rocky cliff. They were almost ashore before Miss Withers made out the narrow fissure which Captain Narveson had called Middle Canyon.

Sven cut the motor, and the launch poked her nose gingerly up a tiny estuary. "Get ready to jump for it," he shouted. "The surf is rolling in here too high for me to beach her."

He pointed at the cliff to the left. "Up there's your Indian caves," he informed them. "Path heads up the canyon. I'll be back for you in a couple of hours."

"But I want you to wait for us," Miss Withers protested.

Sven shook his head. "I don't like the taste of the weather. This' regular earthquake weather, sure enough. I ain't going to get caught if there's a tidal wave. You be back here by two o'clock, or the tide'll be too low for me to get in and pick you up. Ready—jump when her bows is rising."

Phyllis caught up Mister Jones, and Miss Withers grabbed the lunch. As Sven put the launch full speed astern to keep her from being smashed against the great rocks of the canyon mouth, the two women pressed forward, not without some temerity, and prepared to leap.

Miss Withers went first and surprised herself by landing dry-shod upon a rock. She hastily scrambled higher, out of reach of the clawing combers. Phyllis was less fortunate, in that the launch swung around beneath her feet as she took off, and girl and dog came down on all fours in a muddy wash of shells and rock fragments.

"I don't think I'm going to enjoy this party," Phyllis protested. Miss Withers gave her a sidewise look and nodded to herself. Phyllis was right, she wasn't going to enjoy this. But it was too late for any turning back now. Sven and the launch were already drawing back beyond the breakers, head down the shore.

Mister Jones was scurrying delightedly up the slope of the steep path which wound along the dry stream bed. The two women followed, more and more slowly as the steepness of the grade increased.

The monotony of the climb was broken only by the discovery on the part of Mister Jones of a placid desert turtle, the size of a soup tureen, which calmly pulled in its head and legs and waited for the vocal attack to subside.

The creature bore a deep, defaced carving upon its carapace, which weather had practically obliterated. Miss Withers imagined that she could make out the first two figures of a date, "18—" but she was not sure. As the little party pushed on, at least one member very unwillingly, the ancient tortoise watched them with evil, reptilian eyes, as if, Miss Withers fancied, it was the familiar spirit of some local Sycorax.

Then at last they came out on the top of the palisade and stood lonely and awed between crisscrossed canyons and the interminable sea. The wind was fresh and chill.

"We picked a great day to go hunting Indian burial grounds," Phyllis said at last. "I feel like the man who went out bear-hunting and came back in a hurry without his gun, saying that he guessed he hadn't lost any bears."

"Maybe you haven't lost any bodies," said Hildegarde Withers pointedly. "But somebody has lost one. And I'm here to find it."

The friendliness had gone from her voice, as if in key with the change which had come over sky and sea and island.

Phyllis turned toward her and then spoke sharply. "Look out—don't fool with that!"

Miss Hildegarde Withers had taken from her capacious handbag a small blue-steel automatic pistol, and was aiming it steadily at the pit of Phyllis's stomach.

"I'm not fooling," she said.

CHAPTER XIV

TWISTED cactus and thorn bushes made an unfriendly, alien circle around them. Far overhead a flotilla of slate-colored pelicans beat their wings against the sea wind, convoyed in perfect flying formation by a flock of Mother Carey's chickens. Monotonously the great combers pounded against the foot of the cliff, bringing a sense of desolation to the fat little dog, who huddled halfway between these two clashing divinities and whimpered unhappily.

"I didn't bring you here for companionship," explained Hildegarde Withers. "We are alone, where you can neither get away nor scream for help. You haven't been frank with me, young lady."

Phyllis squatted on her heels and pretended to be interested in a blade of grass. "Is that a crime?" she asked softly.

"It is not," said Miss Withers. "But the withholding of important evidence *is* a crime. And I've heard that the police frown upon blackmail, too." The schoolteacher's blue eyes were clouded. She was finding this sort of thing harder than she had thought.

"You'd better talk," she said. "I want to know what is between you and that movie director, and why you are shielding him."

Phyllis seemed unworried but grave. "I'm not shielding him, particularly," she said. "Only—nobody asked me."

"I'm asking now," Miss Withers pressed on.

"And I'm telling you now," said Phyllis. "There isn't anything between me and Tate. I tried to make him the first day, you know that. He is powerful enough to give me the chance that I've been praying for. I was lucky enough to get something on him, and I made a certain bargain with him which I changed my mind about when the time came. There were too many strings attached. All the same, I'm not a squealer, and I kept my mouth shut."

"I would not be likely to agree with your ethical considerations," Miss Withers said stiffly. "In my opinion this is no time for keeping mouths shut."

Phyllis nodded moodily. "You may be right. I don't know. I've always played the game according to the cards I was dealt. I told you about that the other night. But how you got to know about Tate—"

"I have my sources of information," said Miss Withers. "But never mind that. Go on with your speech—and don't think I am ignorant of the use of this weapon."

"It happened on the *Dragonfly*," began Phyllis. "You remember I told you that when Forrest got sick, Tate gave him a pull at his flask?"

Miss Withers nodded, and Phyllis plunged on: "Well, I happened to remember when I was talking to you at the Casino that there was something unusual about the whole thing. It wasn't much—just a little difference. I got to thinking, and I remembered what it was. So I tried it on Tate, and he looked so scared that I knew I had something. I didn't know and I didn't care whether or not it had anything to do with the man's being killed. I wanted a job in pictures, and I thought I might as well make use of my information. Only when it came down to it, I didn't."

"And what was it you saw?" Miss Withers had dropped down beside Phyllis on the cold earth, the automatic forgotten in her lap.

"I saw Tate turn the flask very carefully around before he drank himself," said Phyllis. "And that's, honest to God, the whole thing."

Miss Withers stroked the curly head of Mister Jones, who had snuggled between the two women to escape the chill wind, which was freshening. She was trying to digest this latest bit of information, but without success.

"I thought maybe he had the flask fixed so that it would pour only one way," Phyllis explained. "That maybe he was faking the drink he took."

Whatever Miss Withers had hoped to hear, it was not this. She stared at the gray sea, which showed distant whitecaps toward the horizon.

"And that's all?" she asked.

"That's all," said Phyllis.

"It isn't very much," said Miss Withers sadly. "I feel as if I'd gone hunting elephants and bagged a mouse." She sniffed and then took out her handkerchief and blew her nose.

She prepared to rise. "I may as well get on with my snooping into the Indian caves," she observed. Then, after a moment's hesitation: "I suppose you won't want to come with me any farther, after what's happened?"

"Why won't I?" came back Phyllis, cheerily.

"After I held you up at the point of a gun?"

Phyllis grinned. "Look at your gun now."

To Miss Withers's astonishment, she saw Mister Jones lying in the lee of a large clump of cactus, happily gnawing on the weapon which had been in her lap. She moved to retrieve it, but Phyllis was younger and quicker. She pulled the gun from Mister Jones's strong white teeth and leveled it at the little dog.

"Look out!" shouted Miss Withers. But Phyllis pulled the trigger. A little liquid stream spurted forth to splash on the dog's white forepaws.

"I've seen enough guns to know a water pistol when it's pointed at me," Phyllis explained. "You didn't fool me for a minute. I knew all along that you were bluffing, so there's no hard feelings. Here's the gun—let's shake and forget it."

Miss Withers shook hands and took back the weapon. Mister Jones was sneezing, inexplicably.

Phyllis was already leading the way along the path. "Come on, bloodhound," she called to the excited little dog. "Here is where we find the body and get a prize from teacher."

Miss Withers lingered behind long enough to toss the pistol over the cliff. It had been loaded with spirits of ammonia, guaranteed by its maker to cause instant discomfort to marauding tramps or unfriendly dogs. She had not been bluffing as much as Phyllis thought, but she wisely kept her own counsel. She had a vague feeling that the whole thing had been foolish—a feeling which was to become stronger and stronger as the day went on.

For if Phyllis's secret had been disappointing, the visit to the Indian remains was even more so. In the first place, the path led for more than a mile up and down the sides of such precipitous canyons that the two women had the utmost difficulty in progressing, and Mister Jones had to be lifted by the scruff of the neck across the worst obstacles. If the way from the town was anything like this, Miss Withers realized that, wheelbarrow or no wheelbarrow, no body could have been transported to these regions.

They came, finally, to a barren little plateau which hung between the sea cliffs and the canyon-slashed slopes of the mountains. To their left, a wide trail led away toward the town—a trail which they knew to be blocked in a dozen places by the slides of earth and rock. There was no mark of a wheelbarrow upon it.

The Indian remains themselves consisted of half a dozen circles of

fire-blackened stones which once outlined adobe huts. Three genera-
tions of tourists had trampled everything flat, and nothing but extensive
excavation could have brought any objects of interest to light.

Such excavation was immediately begun by Mister Jones, who started
digging a hole near the black stones. But the soil was hard-baked and
unfriendly, and the little dog soon gave it up.

"I don't see any caves," protested Phyllis. They pressed onward toward where the path disappeared in a tangle of chaparral. Mister Jones
led the way, now and then making swift but abortive forays in pursuit of
the jack rabbits which sprang up on every side.

The path led down into a canyon again, and by dint of much scram-
bling and tearing of skirts, Miss Withers and Phyllis came upon Mister
Jones in the mouth of a narrow cave. Here it was that the exploring
party made its first real find of the day—a blackened and ancient coin
which was removed from between the little dog's jaws by force.

"A Spanish doubloon!" cried Miss Withers, remembering the tales of
buried treasure supposed to be hidden somewhere on Catalina. But Phyllis spat upon the coin, rubbed it against her sleeve, and shook her head.

On its face, the coin bore in relief an elliptical Ferris wheel and the
date—"1893." The reverse read "Souvenir Chicago World's Fair!" Phyllis gave it back to the dog.

The cave was not more than twenty feet deep, and it was white with
interlaced webs of spider silk heavier than cotton. A dark and malevolent
blotch clung to the wall and surveyed them—a hairy black spider with the
deadly red hourglass upon its belly. A smaller spider scuttled away.

"No body's been hidden here," Miss Withers decided. She took out
her handkerchief and slapped at spider webs. Phyllis was forcibly restraining Mister Jones from making an attack upon the deadly Black
Widow. They turned and came out of the cave again—but not into the
sunlight.

They had spent perhaps ten minutes on the futile search of the cave—
but that ten minutes in the semidarkness had sufficed for the world to
change from a dim and windswept solitude to a raging hell.

The storm which had announced itself with warning whitecaps far
out at sea was now upon them, howling as only a Pacific gale can howl.
Scudding clouds raced by—not overhead, but along the surface of the
plateau, condensing upon their faces and shutting out even the rolling
crest of the mountains.

The little dog humped itself down hopelessly, shivering. Miss Withers made an instant decision.

"Bring the lunch," she commanded Phyllis. "I'll carry the dog. We've got to run for it."

They ran for it, covering in a few minutes the tortuous path that had taken so long to come over. At last they rushed down through the canyon again toward what the captain had called "the landing." But it was no landing now. They stood fifty feet above the rocks which had received them when they leaped from the launch, and saw thundering waves crash into the little inlet and swirl up the dry stream bed almost against their shoes. The canyon mouth was a splashing maelstrom.

Even Miss Withers did not need to be told that there was no thought of Sven the boatman's coming back for them while this kept up. And the Pacific showed every intention of keeping it up indefinitely.

The whitecaps were gone now, and the force of the gale flattened the waves down into a wild nightmare of scudding foam. Even the far horizon, where it could be seen to the northwest, was obscured by a thousand jagged wavetops which leaped madly up and down.

"I think we'd better not try to man the boats," said Miss Withers dryly. Still carrying the little dog, she led the way up the canyon wall again.

"This won't last long," she said cheerily. It was beginning to rain, great, hot drops which stung their faces. Mister Jones, who had never seen the phenomenon at first hand before, snapped at the raindrops savagely.

"Back to the cave?" queried Phyllis.

Miss Withers thought of the hairy, malignant spider whose domain it was and voted instantly in the negative.

"We can't expect the launch in this gale," she said calmly. "We can't make it overland to the town, with the road crumbled away. But look—" She took out her map and pointed toward their situation. "It can't be more than a few miles from here to the Isthmus. The map doesn't show such deep canyons that way, either. Shall we try it?"

Phyllis looked at her. The girl had been very quiet since the visit to the cave, as if she had something on her mind which she both wished, and did not wish, to mention. Miss Withers put it down at the time to a lingering feeling of resentment at the pistol episode.

"Sure, if you say so," agreed the girl. "This is your party. The Isthmus was where I planned to make my Sunday outing, anyway."

"Then it's settled." Miss Withers turned up the collar of her light coat and ruefully surveyed her stockings. "Don't throw away the lunchbox, we may need it."

"I won't throw anything away," said Phyllis grimly. And the trek began.

True enough, the map had shown few deep canyons between the plateau with the relics of Indian habitation and the distant Isthmus. But over and over again Miss Withers whispered anathemas upon the head of that unknown map maker, for they were there, hundreds of them.

Stumbling, sliding, climbing, through mazes of cactus that seemed like a landscape on Mars, they made their way. The storm reached its climax and then kept magnificently increasing in volume, so that they had to lean against the wind whenever they came out upon open ground. Ever the pounding of the surf at their left kept them on the right track.

Miss Withers had estimated the distance between the plateau and the Isthmus at no more than six miles. When later she was to trace out the route they took that mad afternoon, she realized that it was six miles straight ahead and twelve up and down.

There was no trail. Not even the brown Indians whose territory this had been before the Spaniards came to make the world safe for Catholicism had ever set their flat brown feet upon these barren reaches.

Mister Jones made valiant efforts to keep up, but had to be rescued from thorn and cactus so many times that Miss Withers picked the little dog up in her arms again. She began to be convinced that whatever might have happened to the road from town to plateau, it could have been no worse than this. Phyllis took her turn at leading the way, uncomplaining. Her blonde hair came uncurled and streaked across her forehead. Mascara shadows formed beneath her eyes and were washed clear again. "This is more fun than I've had since Father patted the polecat," she sang out flippantly.

"We must be nearly there," Miss Withers somewhat optimistically decided. "Don't you think the shore is bearing to the right?"

The shore bore to the right, and then left again, offering canyon after canyon to be crossed with infinite pains. They plodded on only because it was easier to keep moving than to remain in one place.

"And they call this Pleasure Island!" said Phyllis. Slowly a more intense darkness was adding itself to the obscurity of the storm. Miss Withers looked at her watch and saw that it was after six o'clock … almost sunset, and they seemed no farther toward their destination than they had been four hours before.

"We'd better get there soon, or else camp for the night under a cactus," Phyllis remarked. "Because we can't run this steeplechase in the dark."

"I have a pocket flashlight," Miss Withers told her. She put down the dog and fumbled at her handbag. Then she gasped. The catch was open, and the bag hung wide.

Hastily she fumbled in the depths. There was her purse—there the flashlight. But something more important than these was missing.

"Good heavens!" she said.

Phyllis stopped short. "What's wrong? Lose anything?"

Miss Withers hesitated and then shook her head. "Luckily, no," she said. "I thought for a minute ..."

She looked back, but the prospect of a search over that impossible trail was out of the question. "Let's hurry on," she said.

They hurried on, through the thickening darkness and the howling gale. The feeble glow of the flashlight served only to keep them from plunging off precipitous cliffs into the sea and to warn them when cactus barred the way. On and on they toiled, with Miss Withers frantically trying to remember where it was that she had had cause to open her bag.

She had taken out her handkerchief in the cave, she remembered that. Just after they had seen the spider ... was it there?

They were descending a rocky ledge into the depths of another of the interminable canyons, and Phyllis was leading the way.

Miss Withers was jarred out of her thoughts by a shrill scream from the girl. She ran forward with the light to see Phyllis leaning against the rocky wall, her handkerchief at her mouth.

"I saw it—in there!" She was pointing toward a little sheltered shelf under the canyon wall. Mister Jones leaped down from Miss Withers's arms with a tornado of barking, and something clattered away into the night.

"I saw it, I tell you!" insisted Phyllis. "Its face wasn't a foot from mine. I tell you it was the devil out of hell—horns and a horrible ghostly gray face. ..."

Miss Withers nodded. "You can rest assured of one thing," she said gently. "Old Nick wouldn't run from this yapping dog of yours." She sniffed. "Unless I'm very much mistaken, you were frightened by a very rank old billy goat. I've heard that they run wild here."

Above the howl of the storm they could hear the diminishing clatter of frightened hooves. Mister Jones returned, muddy and discouraged, from the chase.

"What's good enough for a goat ought to be good enough for us," Miss Withers pointed out. "It's dry in here, and the wind doesn't strike it. I'm too tired to take another step."

The two women huddled beneath the curve of the rock, with Mister Jones between them. Wet, miserable, they crouched as prehistoric savages would have crouched under similar circumstances. Not being prehistoric savages, they had a good deal to say about the whole situation.

Miss Withers could stay bottled up no longer. "I did lose something back there," she admitted. "I didn't want to say anything about it, but perhaps you can tell me where you saw me open my handbag. It was open during most of our hike."

"What did you lose?" Phyllis's voice was strained.

"I don't know, exactly," said Miss Withers. "I know it was important. It was a blue envelope, but I don't know what was in it."

There was a long pause. Then: "I do," said Phyllis La Fond.

"You *what?*" gasped Miss Withers.

Phyllis nodded. "I know what was in it," she repeated. "Thirty of the biggest bills I've ever seen in all my life—fifteen thousand dollars!"

CHAPTER XV

MUDDY water dropped the back of Miss Withers's neck, like some ancient oriental torture, but that lady paid no attention to it. She was staring in wonderment at the girl beside her. For once in her life, the schoolteacher was at a loss for words.

"How do you know?" she finally managed to ask, weakly.

"I know because I opened it," Phyllis told her calmly. She handed over a damp blue rectangle. Miss Withers took it, glanced at the sheaf of bright new currency, and replaced it in her handbag, which she closed with a snap.

"I suppose you're wondering why I didn't mention it to you," said Phyllis. "It wasn't because I was sore at you and wanted to make you worry. I picked the envelope up at the cave where you dropped it, and I've been trying to decide ever since whether to give it back or keep it. You see—I could use the fifteen thousand."

Miss Withers nodded slowly. "I see your point of view. Finders are keepers—isn't that the idea?"

"And losers are weepers," Phyllis concluded. "When I opened the envelope and saw all that money, I made up my mind to cling to it. And then I don't know what got into me—I went softie, I guess."

"For heaven's sake, don't apologize for an honorable action," Miss Withers chided her gently.

The wind was dying down, as if its sole purpose had been to whisk this ill-assorted pair into that lonely niche in the rocks. Phyllis found a crumpled package of cigarettes somewhere about her person and managed to light one. Miss Withers pondered the meaning of this latest development. So instead of securities, as the desk clerk at the hotel had suggested, the blue envelope contained a small fortune in currency!

Fifteen thousand dollars—this was the second time that such an amount of money had entered the case. What was it that Oscar Piper had wired her from his office at Police Headquarters in New York? Something about certain parties offering to spend fifteen "grand" if Forrest was unable to testify before the Brandstatter Committee. Well, Forrest was forever prevented from giving the testimony which would reveal graft among the public officials who had made him a cat's-paw ... and here was fifteen thousand dollars, as if waiting for a claimant.

Miss Withers was fond of putting two and two together and making considerably more than four out of it.

"I think," she told Phyllis, "that you've done not only the honest thing, but also the wise thing in handing back that blue envelope. Because unless I miss my guess, it contains money that is tainted. You didn't notice anything wrong with it, did you?"

"Me? Of course not. They were all new five-hundred-dollar bills."

"There is blood on them," said Hildegarde Withers.

Her attention was suddenly brought back to earth by Mister Jones. The little dog was wriggling in her arms, sniffing and barking with a black button of a nose pointed across the canyon.

"He must smell another goat," suggested Phyllis. But Miss Withers shook her head.

"Listen," she said. "And tell me if I've gone completely out of my head, or if you hear a radio somewhere. I've read of seeing mirages, but never of hearing them."

Phyllis listened. Somewhere in the distance, faint but distinct, she could hear a jazz singer appropriately intoning "Chloë"

"It's a search party!" she said excitedly.

"I never heard of a search party with a portable phonograph for entertainment," Miss Withers told her. "Look at Mister Jones—he wants to push on across the canyon. We've failed as pathfinders, let's follow him."

They plunged down the canyon slope and came upon a winding path which led up the other side. Here, strangely enough, was a grove of twisted eucalyptus trees—and beyond them, not half a mile away, the twinkling lights of what Miss Withers instantly recognized to be the settlement at the Isthmus!

They stopped short and looked at each other, wordlessly. The wind had gone down completely now, and though the sky was still overcast above them, far out at sea the last pale light of a sunset was showing through a break in the curtain.

Acting on an impulse which neither understood, the two women shook hands. "I'll make a bargain with you," Miss Withers suggested. "If you'll forget about the fiasco with the gun, I'll forget about the blue-envelope business."

"It's a go," said Phyllis. And then, arm in arm, the girl who had had too many men and the woman who had not had any hurried gratefully back toward civilization, at the muddy heels of an excited little black and white dog.

Theirs was a reception profoundly satisfying as they stumbled up the steps of Madame O'Grady's Come-On-Inn, the Isthmus boarding house.

That good and buxom lady took them at once to her motherly bosom. "Mither of God, it's the lost ladies!" She wrapped them in hot blankets and conversation, plied them with steaming food and drink, and set them before a roaring fireplace to dry. From the lighted dining room, inquisitive faces showed that their welcome did not depend upon their being the only guests. Kay and Marvin Deving brought their coffee cups companionably before the fireplace and plied them with questions. The newly-weds explained that the storm had delayed the return of the Sunday excursion, owing to the danger of crossing mountain slopes already loosened by the morning's quake, and that the entire party had decided to remain all night. T. Girard Tompkins, who confessed that he had come along only because he understood that Phyllis planned to be a member of the party, showed a new animation at her unexpected arrival.

His paunch jogged up and down as he trotted about with hot-water bottles, lights for Phyllis's cigarettes, and a square bottle from which he poured liquid fire into their coffee and into Mister Jones's dish of raw eggs and milk. Under Miss Withers's stern eye he nobly abstained from taking any himself, and tonight there was no mention of his favorite tune.

"With three hundred and sixty days of sunshine in the year, you had to come wandering over thim hills on a day like this one," Madame O'Grady complained as she fussed with the great eucalyptus logs in the fireplace. " 'Tis a fine introduction to the loveliest spot on the loveliest island but wan in God's universe."

She militantly swept the hearth clean again and then put her hands on her wide hips. "Now wasn't it like a pair of greenhorns to go gallivanting off and get lost—with poor Amos Britt coming in every half-hour or so to give orders to the search parties that's combing the hills for ye."

Miss Withers clattered the spoon in her saucer. "The chief—is he here?"

"He is and he ain't," admitted Madame O'Grady. "He's drove over here four or five times to use my telephone, because it's the only one at the Isthmus. But most of his time he's been spending over to Mike Price's place, a half a mile across the Neck. 'Tis there that the moving-picture folk are staying, though God Himself only knows why, with oleomargarine on the table instead of good butter. They say that it's closer to where they're making their moving picture, though I'm thinking that it's only because Mike Price isn't as particular about their heathenish goings on as some others. Women walking around half naked, and those noisy trucks roaring around at all hours of the day and night!"

Miss Withers edged in a question as to what the Madame might know of Chief Britt's purpose.

"He's looking for a cold, dead body, they do be saying," she was told. "And he's got better sense than to come looking for it here."

Miss Withers rose, a little shakily, to her feet. "If you don't mind, I think I'll step outdoors and get a breath of fresh air."

Madame O'Grady shook her head blankly as the schoolteacher departed. "A dozen miles over the hills already today—and now she wants fresh air!" Phyllis called out "Wait!" and half rose in her chair.

But Miss Withers was already moving resolutely down the road toward the flickering cluster of lights which she knew to be Mike Price's place. They seemed to be within a stone's throw, but no matter how fast she walked, they kept tantalizingly the same distance away.

The road led along a silver beach, and Miss Withers could see, a short distance upon her right, another equally silvered strip of sand, and beyond it another expanse of rolling ocean. Truly, the tireless attempt of the sea to make two islands out of one was nearing its successful culmination here. Miss Withers paused to illumine a roadside sign with her flashlight.

"Fifteen cents admission to the ancient Pirate Ship *Ning Po*—have lunch where more than a thousand Human Beings were tortured to death!"

Miss Withers sniffed. "A happy thought," she observed. As she turned away from the cheerful placard and the looming dark wreck which stood embedded in the sand beyond it, she heard the roar of a speeding automobile coming toward her. It rounded the curve and flashed by on two wheels, its lights momentarily blinding her.

All the same, for a moment she thought that she recognized the bulky man who sat behind the wheel. But it was too late to do anything about that, and she pushed on.

Weariness such as she had never imagined came over her, but she never faltered. The flickering lights of Mike Price's place became a symbol in her mind, a goal which could not be, and must be, reached.

All the same, she was never to get there. She plodded past a little city of tents, where a campfire or two still lingered, and then came upon a long pier which stretched out over the water. The moon was now shining as clearly as if the sky had never been overcast at all, and by its light she could see the figure of a man sitting disconsolately upon a piling.

For a moment she thought that her quest was successful and that it was the chief, after all. "Hello!" she called.

Then she noticed that the solitary man was smoking a cigarette, a vice which Chief Britt considered effeminate. "I beg your pardon," she said stiffly.

The man rose to his feet, and she saw that he was wearing riding boots. "Oh, it's Mr. Tate!"

"Hello," said the moving-picture director, unenthusiastically. "Yeah, it's me. What's left of me."

Miss Withers approached somewhat gingerly. She was not one to believe all that she had read about movie directors, but then, you can never tell, as she often remarked.

"I don't know what you want," Tate told her bitterly. "But whatever it is, you're too late." He threw his cigarette viciously into the water and turned to her. "Listen, have you got any influence with this comedy constable of a Britt?"

"Possibly," Miss Withers hedged. "Why?"

"Because the guy is nuts, that's why. He's plumb loco, or else he's hired by some other outfit to put the skids under this picture I was trying to make."

Miss Withers, never averse to securing information of any kind, asked what it was that the chief had done this time.

"Plenty," said Tate. "He comes up here about noon today. Lucky it was too thick weather to be shooting, but we had an interior set or two we could have taken. But he has to poke around all over the location. Wouldn't tell me what he was after. Wouldn't tell me anything. Just sniffed around through the props, through the wardrobe trunks, in and out of the sound equipment, like a hound dog that's looking for a bone he buried and forgot where.

"I've got troubles," said Tate. "I've got five ham actors on big salaries hanging around. I've got a sound crew and two cameramen and God knows what else. We lost Friday on account of your damn murder, and Saturday we only took eight scenes because everybody was talking and thinking of nothing but the killing, and now today—what does that hick cop think he is, anyway?"

"Whatever he was looking for—he didn't find it?"

Tate shook his head. "Find it? Of course not! There's nothing to find."

"In that case, I don't think he'll be staying much longer," Miss Withers said comfortingly.

"Much longer? He's gone back to town already, hellbent in that flivver of his." Miss Withers realized that her surmise in the darkness had been correct. But Tate was not through with his tale of woe.

"And he's taken both my assistants with him, under arrest! How anybody can expect me to make a picture with all this circus going on. ...."

Miss Withers smiled. Somehow, she had expected this. Chief Britt was growing desperate, evidently. And so he had added George and Tony to his roll call at the local jail. All because they had been seen carrying a body out of the hotel before sunrise Saturday morning.

She decided upon a bold stroke. "You know," she remarked conversationally, as she rested her weary frame against the piling of the pier, "you have no right to complain of Chief Amos Britt. Because you haven't been on the level with him yourself."

"What?" Tate was taken aback.

"Phyllis has told me all about your flask," Miss Withers announced.

The great Ralph O. Tate lit another cigarette. "Oh, she did, did she?"

"Under pressure," Miss Withers admitted. "Well?"

"You've told the chief that?" Tate did not seem particularly worried, but he was evidently thinking fast.

Miss Withers shook her head. "I'd like to see it first, and I'd like to have you tell me why you turned it around before you drank—or pretended to drink. Not that I have any official right to demand it—but it might be easier this way for everybody concerned."

"Here." Tate reached toward his hip and produced the silver vessel. Miss Withers took it and stared at it. Not being familiar with such objects, she was forced to confess that it looked like an ordinary flask to her.

"It's what they call a duplex," Tate explained. "I bought it at a jeweler's on Hollywood Boulevard where they have a lot of trick gadgets. There's two separate glass bottles inside. The necks cross, like an old-fashioned oil-and-vinegar cruet, so that when you tip it this way, one bottle empties itself." He demonstrated by removing the cap and letting a few precious drops splash to the planking. "And if you want to tap the other side, you turn it like this." Again the flask gurgled.

"You see?" Tate was forgetting his unhappiness in the demonstration of a pet toy. "It's simple as A B C. And convenient, too. In my business,

I have to have a drink handy for social purposes all the time. Myself, I drink the real McCoy. Costs me a hundred a case, and it's worth it. But I'm not wasting that stuff. So I fill up the other half of the flask with local Bourbon, aged overnight, and nobody knows the difference. It's handy, too, when you got a girl who's getting noisy at a party. You let her drink out of the side that you've filled up with ginger ale."

It was, Miss Withers realized, simple as A B C. Almost too simple, in fact. But if she was dubious, she hid it well.

"You've been very frank," she said. "And very helpful, too. I can easily understand why you let the sick man on the plane have a drink from the second-best, and then took one yourself from the other. But why, since it was all so easily explained, did you let Phyllis threaten you into giving her a job?"

Tate laughed hollowly. "That? Oh—that was just a gag. I like to let dames think they're putting one over on me. If she hadn't got cold feet that night, she'd have got the cold shoulder the next morning when she came to go to work. Her kind are two for a dime in Hollywood. You know—just bums."

"I know," agreed Hildegarde Withers. "You're quite a psychologist, Mr. Tate."

"You have to be, in my business," he told her. "I get so I can tell everything a woman is thinking."

"You can, can you?" Miss Withers murmured. But he did not hear her.

"Listen," Tate was saying. "You got a lot of drag with this local copper. Now that you understand about the flask and everything, there's no use letting him get all hot and bothered about it, is there? Can't you just bear down on him a little and get him to forget all about me and let the boys come back to work? If it's a question of dough—"

This time it was Miss Withers who did not seem to hear. "Put away your checkbook," she said. "You won't need it. Because I'm quite certain that George and Tony were arrested on a misunderstanding, and that as soon as I speak to the chief they will be released. You see, Chief Britt has never heard of dummies."

"What?" Tate looked blank.

"He doesn't know as much about the way moving pictures are made as I do," Miss Withers explained. "I've read about the dummies that you dress up like your characters and substitute in falls and accidents. As soon as I heard that George and Tony were seen carrying a dead body from the hotel, I realized that in spite of the suspicious circumstances surrounding the affair, it was only a dressed-up dummy that you intended to use in this picture you are making."

Tate gasped. "The chief knows about that? Oh—I see why he was poking all over the place today! Looking for the body of Forrest—"

"Because the bellhop saw your assistants carrying a dummy out of the hotel, very secretly," Miss Withers finished. The director was laughing, and she joined in. "What a joke on the chief this is!"

Tate paused and looked at her. "It's not so much of a joke on the chief as it is on somebody else," he admitted. "You see, we aren't using any dummies in this picture, and if we did they'd be brought out on the property truck with the wardrobe and all the rest of the junk."

"Then—" Miss Withers drew away from the man.

Tate pushed the beret back off his polished dome and grinned evilly.

"You see, I'd had something of a night of it after the rest of you turned in, and when morning came I wasn't in such good shape. So it wasn't a dummy and it wasn't a corpse that the boys were sneaking out of the hotel before sunrise—it was me!"

CHAPTER XVI

OUT of the shadows into the clear morning sunlight came the red bus, roaring down the canyon and drawing up beside the patio of the Hotel St. Lena with a jarring scream of its brakes. Miss Withers was already on her feet, ready to disembark. "I was never so glad to get back from anywhere in all my life," she observed heartily.

Phyllis, with Mister Jones cramped uncomfortably under her arm, was close behind her. "And to think that we had the whole chase for nothing but fisherman's luck," she complained, a little bitterly.

"Um," Miss Withers responded, without committing herself.

They were walking up the steps toward the hotel lobby, followed by Tompkins, who carried Phyllis's coat in his most gallant manner, and by the newlyweds, whose baggage consisted of a camera and a handkerchief full of shells and beach pebbles which they had spent yesterday in collecting along the Isthmus beaches, in spite of rain and wind.

The remainder of the belated Sunday excursion party rolled away toward the town, not without backward glances toward Miss Withers. They had heard whispers of this strange lady's unusual avocation, and she was beginning to grow used to being surrounded, at the most inconvenient times, by a circle of goggling eyes. No doubt the tourists expected her to pull the murderer, or the missing body of Roswell Forrest, out of a hat, along with a rabbit and some white mice. She ignored them with a completeness which, since such spectators played little or no part in the development of the case, this account shall faithfully follow.

She pushed past a little man in a dusty derby who was talking to the clerk, and got her mail. There were two wires from the inspector, whose steady progress westward was evidenced by the fact that the first had been filed in Topeka, Kansas, and the second in a small town somewhere in eastern New Mexico. "Read your wire and advise Britt hold Kelsey," read the former. The other wire was also under the ten-word limit in length. "Arrive Los Angeles Tuesday five pm meet me."

145

Miss Withers shrugged. Barney Kelsey was already held, as tight as the local jail could hold him. And as for the inspector's second request, she very much doubted if she would leave the island and its tangled complexity of intrigue unless she had made at least a beginning on solving the mystery. "Let Oscar Piper find his own way here," she decided. She was later to regret that decision.

Anxious as she was to arrange a meeting with Chief Britt, the good lady felt that she owed herself the luxury of a long steaming bath and a leisurely luncheon in the hotel dining room. Then, and not until then, did she set off down the shore.

She was almost in the town before she realized that she was being followed by the dogged little man in the derby hat who had been at the hotel desk. He was not taking any particular pains to conceal his presence and, when she turned angrily to face him, only sat calmly down on the boardwalk railing and waited for her to go on.

Miss Hildegarde Withers was not in the habit of sidestepping anything. She turned and strode back to where he sat.

"What do you want with me?" she demanded.

The little man smiled placatingly. "Nothing with you," he admitted.

"Then why are you snooping after me?"

"They said you're looking for Roswell T. Forrest," admitted the stranger. "So am I."

Miss Withers pondered this for a moment. There was something in the little man's bearing which precluded the possibility of his being merely another curiosity seeker. Nor did he look like any newspaper reporter that she had ever seen. "May I ask who you are, and why you take the liberty of tagging after me?"

The little man produced a printed card, bearing the inscription "Harry L. Hellen" and a Longacre telephone number. "Hellen Damnation, they call me," he informed her, not without pride. "I'm the best process server in the world. Y' hear about how I hung a paper on Slim Lindbergh just before he took off on his big hop? I got a summons in my pocket for Forrest, and not knowing my way around here, I figured I'd stick with you."

"Oh," said Miss Withers. She handed him back the card. "I'm afraid you haven't been keeping up on current events, Mr. Hellen. Don't you know that Forrest was murdered last Friday morning?"

"I do not," said the human bloodhound. "Where's the proof?"

"But the body was identified before it disappeared."

"By who?" asked Hellen disparagingly.

"By whom," Miss Withers corrected. "By his bodyguard, Mr. Kelsey."

"Yaaa." Hellen made a lower lip that outdid Chevalier's. "It's a phony. That guy never croaked. I been following Forrest for six weeks. Almost nabbed him in El Paso, but Kelsey strong-armed me, the dirty bum. Lost the two of 'em in Colorado, and just picked up the trail again. They never get away from Hellen Damnation."

"I'm afraid this one did," Miss Withers insisted. "Why, it was obvious that the man was dead."

"Yeah? Nobody but a doctor can tell a thing like that."

"But Dr. O'Rourke did pronounce him dead."

"Sawbones can be fixed, like anybody else. And with the heat on him, Forrest was good and ready to drop out of sight. I've had 'em try it before. He only took something to make him stiffen up, and then that night the doctor brought him to and turned him loose. Forrest is around somewhere, laying low. They tell me you're working this case undercover for Tammany. Well, I'm on the other side this time, but we're going the same direction. What do you say we play it together?"

Miss Withers thought that one over. "You mean—I'm to keep on looking for the man dead, and you for him alive—pooling our results?"

"You said a mouthful, lady!"

It has been pointed out by a hundred historians that the smallest accidents often decide events of the most tremendous significance. "For the want of a nail the shoe was lost"—and Napoleon's bad handwriting, according to the legend, is supposed to have resulted in Waterloo. So it chanced that at this crucial moment, as Miss Withers pondered an alliance, Mr. Harry L. Hellen chanced to blow his nose loudly and unpleasantly. Miss Withers winced.

"I'm afraid," decided the schoolteacher, "that, as you say, we are on opposite sides of the fence." She gripped her handbag, with its precious contents, a little more tightly. "Good-bye, Mr. Hellen."

The subpoena server grinned. "Don't say good-bye, lady. You'll be seeing me around."

"If I see you too closely, I'll have my friend Chief Britt ride you out of town," she snapped. The little man made no reply and did not this time follow her.

It was a minor incident, but enough to begin the afternoon on a jarring note. Miss Withers strode through Chief Britt's curio shop as if borne on a gale of wind and slammed the door behind her. The chief was actively engaged in whittling the arm of his chair.

Miss Withers cut short his heavy pleasantries on yesterday's excursion and its unexpected ending. "Have you got those two movie men in jail?" she demanded.

The chief shook his head. "I ain't having no luck with my prisoners," he complained. "I had to let them go when they found out what I was accusing 'em of. Proved pretty clearly that they was trying to cover up the fact that their boss was dead drunk. I guess it wasn't the first time. The guy who came over with the movie truck to get 'em said the same thing. But that ain't what I'm worried about. It's Barney Kelsey."

"What about Kelsey?" Miss Withers was excited. "Did he escape?"

"Escape? No, not exactly. Not yet, at any rate. But he's getting mighty restless. You see, I ain't got evidence enough against him to book him for the murder, and he knows it. Especially with the news I got from Pasadena yesterday—"

"What news?"

"Didn't I tell you that?" asked the chief leisurely, although he knew very well that he had not. "Oh, yes, it come in while you were chasing around with the wild goats. Doc Lundstrom turned in his report, and he finds that your chewing gum shows traces of being doctored. It had been melted up and then doped and dried again. Most of the stuff had been soaked out of it, because of its sol—solubility in water. But he found traces of aconitine, mixed with digitalis. Aconitine is one of the swiftest and most tasty poisons known, and the digitalis makes it work all the faster, because of the stimulation to the heart. So that's that."

"It certainly is," said Miss Withers. "And of course that clears Kelsey?"

Chief Britt shrugged. "Seems to. He never saw Forrest from Thursday afternoon until he come into the infirmary and saw him dead. I don't see how he could slip his boss any poisoned gum that long before the guy chewed it. The people at the hotel said that neither one of the two of them ever bought any chewing gum at the cigar stand, or was seen chewing. Looks like we've got the wrong man."

"You are probably right," Miss Withers told him thoughtfully. "But all the same, listen to me. I've got a wire here from the inspector, and you can see for yourself what he says. Isn't there some way you can hold Kelsey a little longer?"

"Mebbe," admitted the chief. "He ain't got any lawyer, and there ain't any phone at the jail he can use."

"Good! Keep him there till Inspector Piper gets here, at any rate. That ought to be early Wednesday, if the inspector catches the *Avalon* at Wilmington. And another thing"—Miss Withers was very serious about this. "I advise that you keep Kelsey from having any visitors."

"I have been keeping the newspaper boys and the photographers away," said the chief. "But it's funny you mentioned that. I just gave permission for that bouncing young lady friend of yours to go in and see him—Miss La Fond, or whatever her fancy name is. She wanted to take him some magazines and cigarettes, and I didn't see why not. She's up there now—I suppose it's too late to stop her."

"I wasn't referring to Phyllis," said Miss Withers thoughtfully. "I was thinking of a little man in a derby."

Chief Britt let this go by. He was completely subjugated by this determined amateur. But he was agreeable.

"It can be fixed. I'll give orders that no gents in derbies can get in."

"Or gentlemen without them," Miss Withers added, "I don't suppose he has another hat, but he may. Were there any other developments while I was chasing around with the goats, as you so aptly put it?"

"There were." The chief shuffled a wad of telegrams. "I got answers to all my queries, or all your queries, rather."

"Was there anything really—interesting?" she asked.

"Depends on how easy you're interested," said Britt. "Nothing in 'em to set me jumping up and down, but you may be different. I found out what you asked me to about the movements of most of the suspects for the day or so preceding the tragedy. Isn't much to it. Tate and his two assistants were at the Paradox film studios, casting for their picture. This Phyllis La Fond woman was trying to get her furniture out of an apartment where the rent was unpaid for four months back. She spent Thursday evening at Graumann's Chinese Theater with a girlfriend. The Hollywood police checked up on it."

"And Tompkins?" Miss Withers asked casually.

"Thursday afternoon he left his place on the outskirts of Pasadena and stayed all night with relatives in Los Angeles. They say he was trying to raise money to keep the sheriff from taking his house away from him. But he didn't succeed. We didn't get much of a check on Narveson. He says he spent Thursday night at home with his family. Seems sorta queer, nowadays, but maybe it could happen."

Miss Withers agreed that it was within the bounds of possibility. "Did you get a check on the newlyweds?"

Britt's piglike eyes were twinkling. "Yes, I should say we got something. They weren't newlyweds till Friday morning, just before the *Avalon* sailed, when they came into a Long Beach justice's office and got hitched, with two clerks for witnesses. The preceding night the girl spent at the Y.W.C.A., and young Marvin registered at a Long Beach hotel but didn't use his room. A last night with the boys, I reckon."

"I've heard of that, too," admitted Miss Withers. "An old custom—the last fling at freedom."

"Which in this case is very strange," Chief Britt told her. "Because while the county clerk's office there has no record of it, the newspaper files in Los Angeles show that Marvin Deving was married to Kay Denning a year ago in Frisco!"

"A year ago!" Miss Withers sat up very straight.

"You ain't heard nothing yet. The boys up at the *Herald-Express* morgue also claim they've got clippings showing that Marvin Deving got married to Kay Wenning—notice the change in the name—in Seattle two years ago, and some time before that he was married to a Katie Manning in Santa Monica!"

"Heavens and earth! This isn't bigamy, it's quadrogamy, if there is such a word."

But the chief shook his head. "It's the same couple, all the way through. And no divorces, either. They were married, as far as the newspapers go, four times. But the only time they bothered to get a license was last Friday. Figure that one out."

"I'll do my best," promised Miss Withers absently.

"It's clear enough that they've been putting on a show for us," the chief told her. "Playing lovey-dovey like they have—and married four times. But they ain't a-going to get by with it."

Miss Withers looked quickly up. "May I ask your plans?"

"Plans? Say, I'm going to make them young scamps talk and talk plenty. I sent Ruggles up to the hotel with instructions to stick outside their door and as soon as they had time to change their clothes and get some lunch to bring 'em both down here, telling 'em nothing and giving 'em no chance to talk to anybody."

"Bravo!" said Miss Withers. "Was that your idea, or did somebody coach you?"

Britt blinked.

"Because it's the stupidest possible move at this time," she concluded. "You'll frighten them out of their wits, or else warn them. And what have you got to hold them on? Even less than you have on Barney Kelsey. What if the newspapers do claim they got married several more times than they got licenses for? That isn't a criminal offense. Suppose they explain that they announced their intentions to marry, and then postponed the event each time? For heaven's sake, use your head." Miss Withers pointed to the telephone. "Call off your deputy, or you'll have two more prisoners in your jail that you'll have to let go the next day."

Reluctantly the chief was won over. "Watch them, watch the whole bunch of suspects, as much as you can," she told him. "But don't tip off your hand. I got some information last night by making the most of a fragment." She told him about the flask that poured two ways.

"That would've meant something if Doc Lundstrom hadn't found poison in your samples of chewing gum," Britt admitted.

"We don't know for sure that the chewing gum was the method of murder," he was reminded. "The liquor in one side of that flask could have been poisoned. I don't think, frankly, that it was. But it could have been. In that case, the gum could have been a second line of defense, a spare tire so to speak, to be used if the drink failed. Had that occurred to you?"

It had not. The chief was despondent again. "If I could only get my hands on that body," he moaned. "Then we'd have a starting point." He carefully gathered together the messages and placed them in a folder which already held Piper's telegrams and a litter of other official papers relative to the case. Miss Withers noticed a familiar-looking sheet of brown paper.

"May I see this a moment?" she asked and abstracted the list of Roswell Forrest's belongings which the chief had copied out upon a sheet of her sketchbook. For a long time she stared, not at Britt's painful handwriting, but at the reverse of the sheet.

She spoke, and her voice was hushed. "Tell me, Mr. Britt—just how severe would you judge yesterday's earthquake to be?"

Britt looked surprised and a little hurt. "Oh, the temblor? Why, it was very mild. They hardly felt it on the mainland. According to the Los Angeles newspapers, it was what the experts call a 'point-ought-one' shake. Rattled down a chimney or two and broke a bottle of my wife's preserves."

"It couldn't, for instance, have performed any miracles such as moving mountains or turning trees around, could it?"

"I don't see what you're driving at," Britt told her. "Of course it couldn't. Even a major shake doesn't affect a tree."

Methodically Miss Withers gathered together her gloves, her handbag, and her umbrella.

"If you will come with me, I'll show you where the stolen body was hidden," she said.

CHAPTER XVII

WIND in the pepper tree ruffled its trailing foliage and set the pale shadows to dancing across the hotel patio far below. Miss Withers steered the chief of police into a certain position facing the cliff and then placed the page torn from her sketchbook before his face.

"Look at that tree—and then at my drawing," she commanded. "I made that sketch when the tree was first set there by the handyman."

Chief Britt, puzzled and impatient, fumbled for his glasses. "Very pretty," he murmured.

"I'm not asking you for art criticism," she told him tartly. "Don't you notice anything else? Look again."

The chief looked again. "Oh," he said. "You drew it wrong. You've got the two biggest branches leaning toward the highlands, and the tree is faced the other way."

"It wasn't—when I made that sketch," said Hildegarde Withers. "That's why I asked you if an earthquake could turn a tree around. I noticed that it was wrong, but naturally I blamed everything on the quake."

"All right," said Britt impatiently. "But you said something about the missing body of Roswell Forrest."

"You had men searching this end of the island looking for a new grave," Miss Withers told him. "You said that with the ground as hard as it is at this season, any disturbing of the earth would be easily noticed. The base of that tree is the one place where it would not be noticed. Dig it up—and you'll find your missing body. If the person who buried it there hadn't made the mistake of putting the little tree back in a reversed position, the secret would have been safe until Doomsday and after."

Chief Britt took off his hat and slapped his fat thigh with it. "Jumping Jehoshaphat! You mean, the murderer picked that place to dispose of the body because it had just been dug up, and then set the tree over the grave again?"

"Must I draw you a diagram?" asked Hildegarde Withers acidly. But

152

the chief was already puffing up the slope. She had no desire to follow him, but passed into the hotel. Deputy Ruggles was still idling in the lobby, a fact which dissatisfied her extremely.

He approached her and then squinted curiously through the doorway. "Say, what's come over Amos? He's climbing around like a locoed billy goat."

"I suggest that you follow him," Miss Withers advised. "He may need your help."

"But he told me to keep an eye——"

"I am under the impression that he has changed his mind, or had it changed for him," she said.

Ruggles peered up toward the hillside, where Chief Amos Britt was already wrestling with the little pepper tree. Then he set off on an obedient jog.

Miss Withers crossed the lobby, edging her way past screaming children, invalids in wheelchairs, and a throng of otherwise assorted tourists. The hotel was usually crowded at this hour, since the one-day excursion tickets to Avalon included luncheon at the St. Lena. She was about to climb the stairs to her room when she noticed that one of the telephone booths disclosed the red and perspiring profile of the man who had registered at the desk as Patrick Mack of Bayonne.

He was engaged in a conversation which occupied his entire attention, and she stepped quickly back out of sight. She found herself possessed of a burning desire to hear that telephone conversation.

She stepped quickly into the adjoining booth.

She removed the receiver but did not drop a nickel. This was for the benefit of anyone who might notice her from outside. Then she pressed her ear against the partition.

She could hear a muffled voice, but the words were entirely lost. Although built of roughly finished pine lumber, the booths afforded more privacy than she had hoped.

She was about to give it up as a bad job when suddenly she noticed a loosened knot in a knot hole, about three feet from the floor. Whipping open her bag, she found a nail file. Then she leaned over and picked at the knot, taking infinite pains to prevent it from slipping through into the next booth, where Mack still argued with somebody.

Finally, as she had somehow known it would do, the knot came free, and she crouched with her ear to the hole.

Mack's voice came clearly now, though she got only one end of the conversation. "It's your own blasted fault," he was saying. "I tell you,

you're not coming to my room, not with a hick copper and that snoop of a schoolteacher hanging around spying. I've arranged the payoff, and you'll take it and like it."

He listened for a moment and then cut in on his unseen friend: "Well, it's too hot already for me. I tell you, I'm not welshing. It's there, and you know the combination. Take it, you punk, and shut up." He slammed the receiver, and Miss Withers heard the door close.

She waited for a moment and was about to rise when the door was suddenly thrown open and a fat woman in knickers started to enter.

"I beg your pardon!" she said. The schoolteacher, thinking fast, pretended to search on the floor for the nail file which she held in her hand. Then, hoping that the back of her neck did not betray a flush, she stepped out of the booth.

The man on whom she had been playing eavesdropper was crossing the lobby on his way toward the door. She was almost certain that he had not seen her—almost, but not quite.

Then she noticed that the lobby was almost bare, and that everyone was crowding toward the patio. There were excited murmurs, and she heard a woman gasp. A mother dragged two protesting children back into the lobby, and Miss Withers knew without being told that Chief Britt had found what he was looking for.

The rigid and profaned body of the little man in the cocoa-colored sport suit was being laboriously carried down the slope. Chief of Police Amos Britt had his corpus delicti.

"And," said Hildegarde Withers to herself, "the investigation is right back where it started."

The roar of the *Avalon's* siren sounded through her reverie. From the two buses lined up outside the driveway came a blast of horns which signified that it was time for the day's trippers to hurry back to the steamship for the homeward voyage, corpse or no corpse.

"The ship won't wait, folks," the fat-faced bus driver was declaiming. "All aboard. ..."

There was one person in the crowd who did not share the almost universal reluctance to leave this position of vantage from which to view the gruesome display on the hillside. Patrick Mack of Bayonne came rushing back into the hotel and pounded on the desk.

"Give me my bill," he ordered. "I'm catching this bus." He caught sight of the sepian Roscoe in a corridor. "Hey, boy! Here's my key. Get my bags out of 305, and if you get 'em on the bus there's five bucks in it for you."

Roscoe caught the key and departed up the stairs, while Mack impatiently waited at the desk. The talkative clerk seemed to feel it a reflection upon himself and the hotel that the guest was leaving.

"I'm sorry that this excitement had to spoil your stay, Mr. Mack," he said. "But it will all be over in a little while. Nothing like this ever happened before—"

"Never mind that," Mack told him. "Add up my bill, will you?"

Miss Withers, who had been shamelessly listening from the neighborhood of the telephone booth, took advantage of his perturbation to slip out of the lobby and climb the stairs.

She met Roscoe on the second landing, a bag in either hand. "Wait a moment," she said.

"Can't stop, ma'am. The gentleman's waiting—"

"Let him wait," said Hildegarde Withers. She barred the stairway.

"But he said he'd give me five dollahs if Ah got his bags on the bus."

Miss Withers hesitated. "I'll give you seven-fifty if you don't," she promised. She displayed the money. Roscoe also hesitated—and was lost.

"Ah could tell him the lock of the door was stuck," he suggested hopefully. Miss Withers condoned the deceit.

"Has that gentleman done somethin' wrong?" Roscoe queried. Miss Withers paused in the doorway of her own room.

"Not yet," she informed him cryptically and withdrew. She closed her door, locked it, and then drew the shades of her windows. During the next twenty minutes she made a survey of her room and of the bath, as minutely as if she had lost something of great value. Whatever it was, she finally came to light upon the fat Gideon Bible which lay upon her bedside table. Seated upon the edge of her bed, she busied herself with the volume for a long time, then put it down and, with a new feeling of security and hope, stretched out for a nap.

When she awakened, the daylight was no longer shining through the cracks in her window shades. The wall telephone was buzzing, and she lifted the receiver wearily.

"The chief of police is on his way up to see you," she was told.

Hurriedly she straightened the bed, raised the curtains, and adjusted her hair. In spite of her trouble, the chief when he arrived was in too much of a stew to notice anything.

"I thought you might like to know," he announced, "that Doc O'Rourke is making his autopsy right now. Though there's little enough to work on."

"Meaning?"

"Meaning that the corpse wasn't bettered by lying up on the hill since Friday night," Britt told her. "I don't mean decomposition, either. But the clay on this island is of a peculiar type. It's full of acids. Good thing Kelsey identified the body in the infirmary that day, because nobody could identify it now."

"I see," said Miss Withers. She was actually beginning to see, at that.

"And another thing," said Britt. "You asked me to get a report from the mainland on what Lew French and Chick Madden, the *Dragonfly* pilots, were doing the night before the murder. They did happen to be on shore Thursday night, though they usually stay here on the island between trips. The L.A. police have found that the boys was over at the Burbank airport, bargaining to buy a secondhand airplane that they were planning to use on a transpacific flight."

Miss Withers was thoughtful. "Planes like that cost a lot of money, don't they?"

Chief Britt was willing to agree to that. "And do you happen to know what salary the pilots on the airway draw every week?"

Britt didn't know, but he was willing to venture that Chick and Lew could not earn more than seventy-five dollars apiece.

"I suppose they make seventy-five a week and put four thousand of it in the bank," Miss Withers told him. "Like Commissioner Welch, who used to be Forrest's employer. That's all I wanted to know."

"They didn't actually buy the plane," Britt told her. But Miss Withers was thinking of something else.

"I wish you'd do something for me," she said casually. "I've got an idea, and I don't want to explain any more about it unless it comes to something. But have you got a man—I'd rather not have Ruggles do it because everybody knows him—a man who could loiter around the post office and make a list for me of every person connected with this case who goes in and out of there during the rest of today and tomorrow?"

The miraculous discovery of the body had made the chief firmly convinced of her omniscience. His was not to reason why.

"That's as easy as falling off a log," he assured her.

The discussion broke up on Miss Withers's admission that she had never fallen off any logs.

CHAPTER XVIII

THE watched pot was beginning to boil, Miss Withers felt. There was a tension in the air which permeated the wide and pleasant dining room of the St. Lena. Tonight there was no Phyllis to gather the curious members of the ill-fated party together in a conclave of what she called the Ancient Order of Dragonflies. T. Girard Tompkins likewise failed to put in an appearance. Captain Narveson sat at a table near the window, with his wistful eyes on the trim whaling vessel which still hung offshore, and his steak tonight went almost untasted.

Miss Withers sat alone at the big center table, watching the newlyweds in the corner having an argument. The course of true love was running true to form, she observed. Well, this enforced vacation was growing unendurable for all of them. Even the schoolteacher, fired as she was by the thrill of the chase, was wearier than she knew.

As she climbed back toward her room, she met Roscoe in the hall with a tray. "Ah just took Mistah Mack his dinner," he informed her. "Say, was that white man mad at me for making him miss the bus! Iffen I hadn't dodged, he'd like to killed me with the toe of his boot."

"So Mr. Mack was upset over the necessity of staying, was he?" Miss Withers pondered that for a moment.

"Yes, ma'am. And jus' now he had another tantrum because I come into his room without knocking, bringing his dinner. He shoves a letter he was writing under his blotter and calls me all the names he can think of."

Roscoe passed on, shaking his woolly poll, and Miss Withers gained the sanctity of her own chamber. She spent the next hour in making meaningless marks upon a piece of paper and in wishing that the inspector were here to tell her what to do with the blue envelope.

The course which she had outlined for herself was so reckless a one that she trembled internally. This was her first experience as a lone wolf—for she put little faith in Chief Amos Britt—and her maidenly heart thumped alarmingly.

Just before nine o'clock the telephone rang, and she leaped to answer. Instead of Britt's drawling voice, she heard the clipped tones of Dr. O'Rourke.

"Just by way of an apology, ma'am," he said. "I'm eating crow. Just finished the job that I didn't get a chance to do last Saturday morning, thanks to whoever burgled the infirmary. Well, you were right."

"I was right?"

"Yes, ma'am. I just came over to report to the chief. Forrest's insides show without any question that he was poisoned. Just to make sure, I made a couple of tests for the dope that Lundstrom found in your chewing gum, and got an instant positive. He had enough aconitine in his alimentary canal to kill a horse."

"Thank you, Doctor, for letting me know," Miss Withers told him. "I was practically on pins and needles. Would you mind asking the chief to step to the phone if he's near by?"

"Hello," boomed Chief Britt. "Well, we were right, weren't we? It was poison."

"Yes, *we* were," agreed Miss Withers, a little bitterly. "Tell me, have you got any report from the man you were going to put at the post office?"

"I sure have," said Britt. "I stationed George, the man who bossed the search for the body, outside the door and had him make a list of everybody implicated in this case who went in the place tonight."

Miss Withers held her breath. "And whom did he see?"

The chief hesitated.

"Hurry up, man. Don't you see that this is important? I can't tell you why, but I positively know that the murderer had a reason for going to the post office tonight. Which one was it?"

"It seems to have been one of several," said Britt succinctly. "I'll read you his list. Of course he didn't put down townspeople, or anybody who wasn't on the *Dragonfly*. But he lists Tompkins, the La Fond woman, Mrs. Deving and her husband, and Captain Narveson."

Miss Withers exhaled a deep breath. "Oh! Well, anyway, that excludes Tate and his assistants."

"Maybe it does and maybe it doesn't," said Chief Britt. "Because they sent one of their trucks over to get the mail for the whole crowd."

"A lot of help that is," Miss Withers exploded. "I suppose that Dr.

O'Rourke and the two pilots and Higgins the watchman all dropped in, too."

The chief shouted a question to someone at the other end of the line, and then told Miss Withers: "He says as a matter of fact that they did!" His voice became faintly apologetic. "You see, the post office here is quite a social center in the evenings."

"So I see," said Miss Withers. "But did your man put down what those people did there?"

"Nope," was Britt's answer. "I told him to stand across the street so as not to scare anybody away. You didn't say anything about that part of it."

The schoolteacher gave him a short good-bye and hung up. "I didn't think it was possible for a policeman to be stupider than Oscar Piper, but Amos Britt is changing my mind," she said to her mirror.

She flounced into a chair, but found the room suddenly stuffy. She was in the mood to do something, and there seemed nothing at hand to be done.

Crossing the room, she flung her window wide open. "Patrick Mack will sneak away on tomorrow's boat," she told herself. "And with him will go the secret of this whole mystery."

Suddenly she caught herself. The man whose name had just crossed her lips was sneaking away somewhere now. At least he was headed down the beach, hatless, and with a fresh cigar between his teeth. The moonlight was bright, and she could recognize those padded shoulders anywhere. From time to time the man stopped, looking searchingly behind him as if he were afraid of being followed.

"I wonder!" said Hildegarde Withers aloud. Fate had seemingly tossed into her lap an opportunity which was, if not golden, at least well gilded.

"It can do no harm to try," she told herself. "I'm already in this for a lamb, it might as well be a couple of sheep. After robbing the United States mails, this is naturally the second step."

She went hastily out into the hall, taking the key of her own room as she did so. At the head of the stairs she stopped long enough to make sure that nobody was noticing her, among the numerous comings and goings of the hotel. Then she slipped up the stairs to the third floor.

Room 305, Roscoe had been told when he went to get the bags. That was a large corner room. The locks of the St. Lena were of the type now obsolete except in summer hotels, consisting of the old-fashioned kind which could be opened with any skeleton key. Unfortunately, she had no T-shaped skeleton, and her own key failed to turn. But this was not the first time that Hildegarde Withers had picked a lock with a hairpin, and the operation took her less than a minute. She opened the door and stepped into the darkened room.

There was a strong odor of food, of whiskey, and of stale cigar smoke. It was evident that Patrick Mack had been brought up to distrust fresh air—another sign of his foreignness to this locale. All windows on both sides of the room were closed.

She calmly turned on the light and went straight to the desk in the corner. It was surmounted by the usual rack for stationery, and the gummy bottle of ink. But it was the blotter which interested Miss Withers most. She lifted it eagerly, but was instantly disappointed.

If Mack had concealed a letter here upon Roscoe's sudden entrance with his dinner tray, he had later removed it.

Perhaps, she thought, he had finished it and gone out to mail it. No, the post office closed at nine, and besides, he had been ambling along like a man without any particular destination.

His bags, still packed, stood beside the bed. They were locked and resisted Miss Withers's most crafty efforts with the hairpin. The bureau was empty, except for the usual matches, pins, and lining of old newspapers. Swiftly, for she had not much time for a margin of safety, she removed this lining, but there was no sign of whatever Mack had been writing.

The closet, which owing to some whim of the architects had been built against the outside wall and extended from the bathroom partition to the side window, was deep and roomy. In it hung a dark blue topcoat and a felt hat. The topcoat pockets contained a pair of gloves, three paper folders of matches, and a lot of fluff mixed with tobacco. The hat lining was empty.

"I don't know what I was looking for, but whatever it was I'm not finding it," she told herself. She came out in the middle of the room and stared at the two locked traveling bags.

Reluctantly she decided to give it up as a bad job and turned toward the door. Unfortunately it stood half open, and the padded shoulders of Patrick Mack filled the space.

He didn't look surprised, and he didn't look angry. There was no expression whatever on his pasty face with its blue jowls. He simply stood there and stared at her. Then he closed the door behind him.

Miss Withers thought faster than she had ever thought in all her life. "My mistake," she said, a little too loudly. "I seem to have wandered into the wrong room."

"The wrong room," repeated Mack woodenly. "Lady, you said a mouthful. You been in it going on ten minutes. Next time you try second-story work, don't turn on the lights. I could see that side window from 'way down the beach."

"Oh," was all Miss Withers could think of. She felt with trembling fingers for the bed and sat down on the railing. Her knees were strangely disposed to quiver.

"I'm going to call the cops and have you run in," said Mack. He reached for the telephone.

"I—I don't think you'll do that," Miss Withers told him quickly.

Mack looked up sharply. "And why the hell not?"

Miss Withers lowered her voice. "Because, you see, I happen to know why you came to Catalina Island. And the police do not, as yet."

Mack's face never changed in its set expression, but his hand slowly dropped from the telephone. His stubby fingers stretched toward his left armpit, and he casually drew out a thin automatic pistol. "Talk some more," he invited.

"You have a gun," Miss Withers said. "And I doubt very much if you can produce a California permit."

"Wrong," Mack advised her. He showed her his California permit. He also showed her a sheaf of permits, from half the states of the Union. "But don't worry," he said. "I've never used it yet." He locked the door and put the key in his pocket. Then he crossed the room and sat down in the chair beside the desk. "What was that crack about knowing why I came to Catalina?"

"I meant what I said," Miss Withers told him. Her self-assurance was rapidly returning. Perhaps this was the best and easiest way, after all. For this man knew what she must know, and perhaps he could be induced to tell.

She made herself slightly more comfortable. "Ever since you came here I've wanted a talk with you," she said. "As you probably know, I'm more or less interested in discovering the murderer of—of Roswell Forrest."

"And what has that got to do with me?" Mack took out a fresh cigar and lit it with a hand that did not shake. "If you give me a good song and dance, maybe I'll change my mind about turning you in, lady."

"My position here is a little more official than you seem to think," she said confidently. "And your position is a distinctly unpleasant one, Mr. Mack. You see, I happen to know that it is rumored about New York's sporting section that you, as one of the principal parties in danger from the Brandstatter Committee investigation, were so anxious to keep Roswell Forrest from returning to testify against you that you offered to spend fifteen thousand—I believe 'grand' was the term you used—to insure his continued absence."

Mack looked at her admiringly. "You talk like a mouthpiece, lady. But it don't mean nothing. What if I did say it? That doesn't pin anything on me. A lot of other boys are in the same spot and probably said the same thing. If they didn't, who's to testify that I did?"

"That isn't all," Miss Withers continued. "I have what you would probably call a deuce in the hole. Or is it a trey? Anyway—I am morally certain that you not only offered fifteen thousand dollars to anybody who would remove Roswell Forrest permanently, but that you were the direct instigator of the murder. You came here because you believed that the murderer had carried out his part of the bargain, and you intended to keep yours and pay him. Am I right?" She chatted casually—because it was the only thing to do.

"I'm letting you talk just to see how funny you can get," Mack told her. "You sound like a hophead. Been kicking the gong around lately? Go on with your song and dance."

"You are an intelligent man, Mr. Mack," Miss Withers told him.

He did not deny it. "I'm in business," he said. "A lot of different kinds of business. I may carry a gun to protect myself, but I'm no gangster. That stuff is out of date."

"And being an intelligent man," Miss Withers steamed ahead, "you must be clear-sighted enough to realize that this whole plot has gone to pieces. The murder was planned to look like a natural death. It was I who prevented the doctor from making out a certificate and insisted upon an autopsy. Then the body was stolen, but that only delayed matters. Today it was discovered, and the whole business is bound to come to light. Where will that leave you?"

Mack relit his cigar. "It'll leave me all right," he told her. "Go on with the fairy story."

"You feel secure because you had no actual part in the commission of the crime? No doubt a man of your experience knows how to protect himself against anything's being proved against him. Even if the murderer, when he is caught, denounces you I suppose you will trust to an absolute denial and the subsequent delay of the courts?"

Mack only smiled. "Hurry it up, the story's getting dull."

"It will grow more interesting for you when Inspector Piper of the New York police gets here tomorrow," she snapped at him. "The noose is around your neck, young man. Only one thing can save you. If you will go with me to the chief of police and make a confession implicating the party who actually committed the murder, you may secure a lighter sentence. Such things are arranged sometimes, I know. I am willing to promise you that I will use my influence to—"

Mack rose to his feet. "Nerts," he said tersely.

He came closer to the unwelcome visitor. "Listen to me," he said. "You've shot off your mouth long enough. I've got just one answer to the whole thing, and it's this. *So what?*"

Miss Withers raised her eyebrows. "I beg your pardon?"

"You heard me. I said 'So what?' Meaning, what if I have? Suppose this pipe dream of yours is true. Go ahead to your rube copper and spill the beans. Bring in all the inspectors that ever grew. They don't worry me. Because you've got nothing on me and you know it. Ask anybody to book me on any charge and see how far you get."

Miss Withers was more than a little nettled, or she would never have played what she called her "deuce in the hole." She regretted the words as soon as they had left her mouth, but it was not soon enough.

"You are not aware that I have the blue envelope," she said. Then she stopped short at the transformation which came over Mack's face. His nostrils widened, and the veins on either side of his forehead stood out like strange, branching worms. But he kept his voice calm by an effort.

"The blue envelope?" he repeated woodenly.

"The blue envelope," finished Miss Withers, nervous in her triumph—"the envelope with thirty five-hundred-dollar bills in it. It is possible to trace currency that big, I understand."

Mack put his cigar carefully in the ashtray and then rubbed the backs of his hands with stubby fingers.

"In that case," he told her evenly, "let's get going and call on your friend the chief of police. I'll talk."

Excitedly, the schoolteacher stood up. How easy those things were when you handled them in the right way! "Tell me the name of the murderer," she demanded.

"I'll talk when I get a promise of an easy out," Mack told her. "And not until then. What you say don't bind the cops. Wait a second, and I'll go with you."

Strangely enough, Miss Withers never thought of reaching for the wall telephone as he disappeared into the bathroom. If she had, there would not have been time to use it, for Patrick Mack reappeared almost instantly. He reached in the closet for his hat and then crossed the room to the door. Miss Withers was close behind him, eager to get out of this room in which she had been so uncomfortable.

Mack was smiling, almost genially. Miss Withers told herself that the man must be relieved to know that it was all over, and that the strain of his secret would soon be lifted. He was rattling the key in the lock. ...

Then the key no longer rattled, and though Miss Withers did not see him turn, she felt the world go black.

Something sticky and rubbery was pressed over her face from eyes to chin—a great square of adhesive tape. She fell backward, strangling— and felt herself caught roughly by the shoulders and eased to the floor.

She felt something wound tightly around her ankles, even as she began to kick them in a furious spasm. Her wrists were similarly bound, with a neatness and dispatch which she did not appreciate.

No more fiendish and diabolical scheme had ever been devised for reducing a human being to a quivering mass than this quick strangulation. Her arteries throbbed in neck and forehead, and white panic filled her being. Was death coming to her like this, then—all unexpected and unannounced?

Unconsciousness was unmercifully long in arriving, she thought. Then, as it seemed the horror could no longer endure, she felt herself seized by the neck and shoulders and lifted a little from the floor.

There was the click of an opening penknife, and then a stabbing pain at her nostril, followed by a meager inrush of the sweetest air that ever blew. The white inferno receded to a throbbing red and then paled.

"Lay still, or I'll put another one on without a hole in it!" promised Patrick Mack. "You goddam old hen."

She could neither see nor speak nor move. But the man still talked, as if he enjoyed the novelty.

"You'll tell me what to do, will you? You'll offer to get me a light sentence!" He let go her head, and it bumped on the carpet. She heard heavy footsteps.

"I wish I had you where I could take off the bandage and make you talk," said Mack wistfully. She heard a familiar click which told her that he was at her handbag. Well, he would find little enough in that. Except, of course, the key to her room. She sincerely regretted the habit which had made her bring it.

"Must be a novelty for you to listen," he went on. "This'll be good for you. Give your jaw a rest. It'll be a long rest, because I'm going to stick you in this closet. You'll still be there after I've caught tomorrow's boat, because I'm putting a 'Don't Disturb' sign on the hall door. I don't care whether they ever find you—but if they do, you'll have plenty to explain about why you butted in."

He punctuated his remarks by dragging her, a step at a time, across the room. She bumped ignominiously over the sill of the closet, and—

"I believe I like your face better this way," Mack told her. "You ought to wear adhesive all the time."

She writhed at that remark and thumped her heels weakly on the floor. "Go ahead and kick," Mack said. "The people in the room underneath moved out this morning, and nobody'll hear you. All the same, I don't think you'll get air enough through that slit to allow much kicking around. So long, auntie."

The closet door closed, and the furious, frightened schoolteacher found even greater difficulty in getting air enough into her tortured lungs. She heard Mack's heavy tread as he moved across the room, and then the hall door closed quietly.

There was a moment of silence, and then the sound of Mack's voice came to her, muffled and thick. His tone was one of surprise.

Then the indistinct words lost themselves in a high, almost feminine squeal, punctuated by the vicious and terribly final spat of a revolver. That was all.

CHAPTER XIX

TWELVE o'clock sounded from the distant carillon, coming thick and muffled to the ears of the helpless woman who lay intent only upon one purpose—the drawing of enough breath through the tiny slit in her face covering to keep it from being a death mask.

There was a ringing in her ears which continued and increased in intensity even after the twelve strokes had ceased to sound. Through it she heard, as one going under ether, the sound of running footsteps in the halls of the hotel. Doors were opening, and the high excited voices of women came meaningless and shrill.

Miss Withers had no idea how long this sort of thing continued, and then the clamor burst in upon her ears with a redoubled intensity. She realized that the hall door of the bedroom had been opened.

She heard the voice of the night clerk. "So help me God, he's blown the top of his head off!"

She thumped weakly with her heels, but even she could hardly hear the result. The effort almost strangled her, and she lay back and listened again.

"Bring him in—that's it. Lay him on the bed. Somebody get Dr. O'Rourke!" Another man's voice announced that the doctor had already been sent for. "But it's little good anybody can do for him," the unseen man went on. "His brains bane all over the hall."

"Captain Narveson!" Miss Withers screamed the name, but her sealed lips emitted not a sound.

Kay Deving's contralto rose above the din. "Oh, *why* doesn't somebody get the police?"

"Oh, why doesn't somebody get *me!*" Miss Withers moaned. But nobody did. She listened and prayed for the sound of Phyllis's voice among the crowd. Perhaps Mister Jones, the fat and excited little dog, would be with his mistress. And Mister Jones was the one living thing in that hotel who would be certain to know of her plight if he got within smelling distance.

Tears came to the schoolteacher's eyes as she thought of the little dog sniffing outside the closet and then scratching and marking to call the attention of the human beings to his discovery. She visioned the little terrier as a great dark St. Bernard, with a cask of oxygen instead of brandy at his collar.

But the miracle did not happen. It was only a fantasy, bred by the poisonous intoxication of carbon dioxide in her blood.

Nobody would dream of looking for her here. Not until tomorrow would she be missed, and perhaps not then. Perhaps the closet door would not be opened until the room was occupied by some other guest. And that would be too late. Tomorrow would be too late. Another hour would be too late.

She tried to kick against the floor again, but it was of no avail. The noise would not have frightened a mouse, and the effort left her swooning.

The voices in the room, shut away from her by the thin width of a partition, swelled to a cascade of sound, a nightmare in which she heard as in a dream the voices of everyone that she had ever known. Oscar Piper's dry, clipped speech came most clearly. Her eyes filled with tears again, tears which the tightly binding bandage forced back to smart and burn. Why hadn't she married Oscar Piper long ago? Why hadn't she done a thousand things that she would never do? Why—

The roaring in her ears increased to an unbearable thunder which lasted for twice a thousand years. Then—

"She's coming through," said a familiar voice. It was Oscar Piper's voice. Someone was speaking with his voice. Someone was looking down at her with his eyes. Contrary to the familiar fiction, Hildegarde Withers did not imagine for a moment that she was dead and in heaven. She was too conscious of a stinging tingling of her cheeks, of a dull ache through her whole body, to imagine that this was death. Death meant a release from that sort of thing. Besides, someone was waving a glass phial beneath her nose.

"I'm all right," she said weakly. Then she opened her eyes wide and realized that it was the inspector who held her, and not a creature out of her nightmares. He looked worried.

"Don't try to talk," he said. She saw Dr. O'Rourke over his shoulder, and even the piglike eyes of Chief Amos Britt.

"I'll talk if I want to," she managed. "What happened?"

She was breathing as if she had forgotten how the air could taste. With the soul-satisfying oxygen she drew in strength. After a moment she managed to sit up.

"Turn her the other way, so she won't see … it," came a feminine voice. It was Phyllis's.

Miss Withers shook her head. "I'm all right," she said. "What happened?"

"Steady, old girl," said Oscar Piper. He was without his usual cigar, and his lower lip protruded more than usual. He was all in dusty gray, and he smelled of tobacco and gasoline.

"I want to know what happened!" she insisted. She realized that the room was full of people and that she was sitting in the armchair by the writing desk.

"That's what we want to know," said the inspector quietly. "As soon as you feel able to tell us. I was waiting down in your room when I heard the shot."

"But," she protested, "you weren't due until tomorrow."

"You know how I hate airplanes," Piper told her. "But the desert was too much for me. It was 114 degrees in the dining car. So I left the train at Phoenix and caught the Transcontinental. It saved a day, and I talked the Long Beach harbor police into bringing me over in their patrol boat."

Miss Withers sensed that he was talking to keep her from using her voice. "I'm all right, really," she insisted. "But how did you ever find me in here?"

The inspector smiled. "Naturally I horned in when I heard the alarm," he said. "I helped them bring Mack's body in here. Then I happened to notice your handbag on the floor, with everything dumped helter-skelter. I knew there wasn't another handbag like that one left in America. So I started looking around—and there you were, trussed up like Rameses' mammy."

"You mean mummy," she corrected weakly.

Chief Britt horned in on the conversation. "Listen," he queried eagerly. "Who tied you up?"

She told them what had happened, or at least the events following her conversation with the man who now lay upon the bed, shielded from her by the crowd.

"But that can't be," objected Britt, when she told of the sound she had heard in the hall just before the shot. "Because nobody shot Mack. Less than a minute after the shot was fired, people come out into the hall. And there he laid, with the top of his head blown off, and his gun in his hand. Clear case of suicide— I guess you threw a scare into him. Appears to me that his suicide is a clear confession of guilt in the Forrest killing, eh, Inspector?"

Piper refused to commit himself.

"Nonsense," said Miss Withers. "A man doesn't go out into a hallway to kill himself. I know very well—"

She stopped short. Once already this evening she had blundered by letting her tongue run away with her. She was determined to avoid making the same mistake twice. "Could I see the weapon?" she asked.

Chief Britt produced a handkerchief-wrapped revolver, still warm to the touch. "There she is," he announced. "It's Mack's, all right. Just fits his shoulder holster. He's got a permit for it, too."

"I see," she remarked. Then she glanced significantly at the inspector. "I think I'd like to be helped to my room, if you don't mind."

Leaning on the inspector's arm, she looked down at the shapeless mound beneath the sheet which someone had drawn.

"He called me an old hen," she said softly and then suffered herself to be led through the door.

"Careful," said the inspector, leading her around a dark stain on the hall carpet. When they were on the stairs, she turned to him. It was characteristic of them both that they wasted no words in greetings or the usual chatter.

"I'm not as weak as you think," she said. "I can get back to my room. I wanted to tell you. It wasn't suicide, and that isn't Mack's gun that the chief has. I ought to know—I looked down the barrel of it tonight. He carried an automatic—one of those nasty little snubnosed things."

Piper nodded. "All this is pretty new to me," he said. "Your last wire gave me the lineup, but nothing of what's happened since Saturday. Mack's part in this thing I can guess. But who did the job on Forrest, and who killed Mack? I don't suppose he told you about the first murder when you were having your confab with him."

"He told me nothing," said Miss Withers. "But I'm pretty sure I know. I want to think, and rest. Let me sleep on it tonight while you go back and keep Chief Britt from making himself any more ridiculous than he must. We'll have breakfast together and talk this out."

The inspector frowned. "I hate to leave you alone. Suppose somebody takes a notion to bump you off in the night?"

"I'm as safe as you are," she assured him. "Besides, I'll push a bureau against my door. Good-night, old friend. And thank heavens you remembered my handbag when you saw it."

She gripped his hand and then turned suddenly away and closed the door of her room behind her.

Inspector Oscar Piper stood for a moment, staring at the door. "What a woman!" he said softly. "One in a million!"

He climbed the flight of steps to the third floor and then corrected himself. "One in two million," he said.

It was well along into the morning when Hildegarde Withers awoke. She sat up in bed and shook her head to clear it. Though she did not realize it, she was feeling an aftereffect of her last night's experience which closely paralleled a good thick hangover.

But the day was a momentous one—she knew it. The certainty gave her strength to climb under an icy shower. She dressed swiftly and then called the desk.

"Is Inspector Oscar Piper a guest here?"

"Room 360," she was told. "But he asked not to be disturbed."

"All the same," she told the clerk, "it's after ten o'clock and he's going to be disturbed."

A considerable time had elapsed before she got a sleepy response. "Meet you in the dining room in twenty minutes," he assured her.

He was there, washed and shaved and brushed, in a little more than fifteen. They sat down on opposite sides of a table which looked out on an expanse of lapis-lazuli ocean.

"Well!" said the inspector. Miss Withers looked back at him critically and repeated it. "Well," she said. They both smiled.

"What happened last night after I left?" she wanted to know.

"Plenty," said the inspector. "First of all, I got a sort of official standing in the community." He bared his vest and showed her a bright badge of shining nickel which bore the legend "Deputy Sheriff." It was pinned beside the massive shield of solid gold that his subordinates had given him on his twentieth anniversary as an officer.

"Chief Amos Britt plucked this from the breast of poor old Ruggles last night," he told her. "Neat, but not gaudy, don't you think?"

"What else?" Miss Withers was a woman of one idea. "What did you actually accomplish?"

"Nothing," admitted the inspector. "Which in itself may prove something. I was lucky to have my kit along with me. I tested the gun with fingerprint powder and found not a trace of a print. That means the murderer wore gloves or wiped it clean."

Miss Withers nodded. "Go on."

"Then I helped Britt dig the bullet out of the hall upstairs. It fits the gun that was in Mack's hand."

"That doesn't surprise me," Miss Withers told him.

"Then I made another test. You know that we can tell if a hand has fired a gun within twenty-four hours by microscopic powder burns that the naked eye doesn't see? It even applies to the new smokeless powder. Well, I tested the dead man's hand. It did not show any burns. With Britt's authority in back of me, I tested the hands—both hands—of every person who was in this hotel last night, whether they liked it or not. Excepting yourself, of course. And got a negative in every case."

"Then—that means the murderer came from outside?" Miss Withers was bewildered.

"Nobody came in from outside. As it happens, the desk clerk was awake, because I had just been escorted to the place by the boys from the Long Beach station house and had made him show me to your room."

"Then your test is no good—or else you missed somebody."

"The test is perfectly good," Piper told her. "And we missed nobody. I recognized a lot of the people you mentioned in your code wire. Tompkins and Narveson and those callow newlyweds and the gay girl in the next room who has the pup."

"What about a glove?"

Piper nodded. "It would have to be the thickest glove I ever struck," he admitted. "Those powder burns have been proved to go through leather and rubber. Maybe an iron glove would do it."

"Then it must have been an iron glove," insisted the schoolteacher. "Because the murderer could not have come in from outside. It doesn't fit!"

"If the glove fits, put it on," said Oscar Piper. "Well, you had the night to sleep on your idea. Suppose you tell me who is responsible for this circus."

Miss Withers smiled at him. "This is my murder," she pleaded. "It's the only case I've ever had all to myself. Let me have the glory. I earned it in that closet last night. You'll probably guess when I run over the events of the past four days. But don't make me spring the surprise until I'm ready."

"It's fun to be fooled, it's more fun to know," quoted the inspector. "But I don't mind playing Watson for a change."

"For a *change?*" Miss Withers inquired innocently. And it was at that moment that Piper realized that she was herself again.

As breakfast was placed before them, she began a résumé of the case, starting with the moment when she had noticed Hinch, the manager of the airport, running toward the plane. She told him of the autopsy that didn't come off, of the long search for the missing body. She painted a sadly revealing portrait of her venture to the Indian caves, and of the discovery of the pepper tree's odd behavior. Here and there, since she was a woman, she left a hiatus or two, but the inspector was none the wiser for it.

The luncheon menus were resting before them by the time Miss Withers had concluded her travelogue.

Piper shook his head. "You've certainly been over Niagara in a barrel with nails in it," he said. "I'm dizzy."

"Then you don't guess the murderer?"

"Sure," he told her. "I guess it's one of about eight or a dozen people."

"That's been my trouble, too," she said. "It wasn't until the other day that it suddenly occurred to me—it might be *two* of eight or a dozen people."

Piper rubbed his hands together. "You mean—that two of these supposed strangers are really acting in cahoots?"

"Figure it out for yourself," she advised. "I had to. She pushed back her chair as a distant siren sounded."

"Good heavens, there's the steamer," she said. "That means it's after twelve. Let's go down and call on Chief Britt. Perhaps he's solved both murders while we chatted here."

For all that, they had a good deal more to discuss as they ambled down the shore road, and Miss Withers was surprised to find that she tired more easily than usual. The chimes of the carillon had sounded for the first hour of the afternoon before they reached Chief Britt's curio shop.

The chief brightened as he saw them. "Well, it's about time," he boomed. "This is getting over my head."

Miss Withers asked him what the trouble was.

"Trouble? Ma'am, you don't know the half of it. First off this morning, I have to go over and separate two good friends of mine who are trying to mess up the ground with each other. Lew French and Chick Madden, the *Dragonfly* pilots, you know. Something about the nurse in O'Rourke's office. And then she threatens to walk out on the Doc, and sue him for back salary besides."

"How very interesting," Miss Withers observed. The inspector, feeling sadly out of place in an executive office not his own, bit the end off a cigar and lit it.

"That ain't all," Britt went on. "This second murder on top of the first starts hell humming on the mainland. They're threatening to shove the Los Angeles detective force or the state police into my lap. I stalled that by saying I had official assistance from New York, but it ain't going to stay stalled." He shook his head sadly. "But that ain't what worries me worst."

"What is?" Piper spoke without removing his cigar.

"It's Barney Kelsey," complained the chief. "He got himself sprung."

Piper now took the cigar from his mouth and threw it into the waste basket. "How in the—"

"I thought you weren't going to let him get to a phone or have a visitor, except for Phyllis with her magazines?" Miss Withers interposed.

"I didn't," admitted the chief. "If must have been that La Fond dame. Anyhow, somebody phoned to Los Angeles for a lawyer, and about half an hour ago a dapper gent gets off the *Avalon,* hands me a writ of habeas corpus issued by a Superior Court judge of this county, and that's that. I have to turn Kelsey loose, and he goes off with the lawyer and the girl."

Miss Withers thought it over for a moment. Then she spoke: "You really haven't lost much, have you? If Kelsey was in jail last night, he couldn't have killed Mack. Besides, there is no way for him to leave the island before the *Avalon* sails late this afternoon. A lot can happen in an afternoon."

A lot did happen in an afternoon—that same afternoon. The beginning of it all was when Miss Withers and the inspector, leaving Chief Britt's office, ran into a strange trio at the entrance to the local drugstore.

Phyllis La Fond, with a new self-confidence in her eyes, walked on the inside. Next to her, pale but smiling, was the young-old man with the gray streaks in his hair, breathing deeply of the air and sunshine. On the outside, carrying a briefcase, was a dapper gentleman whom Miss Withers rightly judged to be the lawyer.

"I'll introduce you," she said to Piper, forgetting that he had already met Phyllis via the acid test to her hands in search of powder burns. But that social event was to be postponed.

The trio swung abruptly and entered the drugstore. Miss Withers was nettled. "Whatever! Why should Phyllis act like that? Do you suppose that she blames me for your suspecting her last night, along with all the rest?"

The inspector wasn't paying any attention. He stood stock-still in the middle of the sidewalk, and the ash from his cigar fell unheeded down his vest.

"What's come over you?" Miss Withers demanded. "Are you having fits?"

"Yes," said Oscar Piper. "Fits or worse. Do you happen to know who that man is—the one in the middle who looks as if he'd been through seven hells?"

"I do," said Miss Withers casually. "I've known for some time that he's Roswell Forrest. But I hoped you wouldn't."

CHAPTER XX

"No more secrets," pleaded the inspector. "Come clean with me, woman. If you knew Forrest wasn't dead, why didn't you say so? And for the love of heaven, who is the corpse you've been chasing all over this island?"

"Come out on the pier and I'll tell you all," said Miss Withers amiably. "Or nearly all," she added under her breath.

They swung their legs from the very end of the smaller of the two piers and watched a fat, half-tame sea lion begging for fish scraps in the water beneath them. Plump, whiskered Charlie had rarely seen two humans more adamant in all his fifteen years as the harbor pet. They sat on the stringpiece for an hour and never once tossed him a morsel.

"Before I tell you anything, I'd like to know why you dropped everything in New York and came out here because you thought that Roswell T. Forrest was dead," Miss Withers demanded.

"Simple," said the inspector. "He was—or rather, is—an innocent pawn in a dirty game of chess. He never got a dime of the money that Welch and some of the others took out of the city treasury. But he knew about how it was done. Maybe he should have squealed on his boss. But again, maybe he shouldn't. Anyway, while Welch, the commissioner, is standing his ground and willing to take whatever is coming to him, some of the others aren't. Mack was the worse of the lot, a petty racketeer about halfway between a politician and a thug."

"Which is a bad place to be," put in Miss Withers.

"Anyway," went on Piper, "I was sent out here to find out what was what. If Forrest was bumped off to keep him from coming back and testifying—he had a good enough incentive to do it, with his property in jeopardy—then I intended to run down his killers. If he was bumped off for some personal reasons, I had instructions to hush the thing up as far as the Hall was concerned. But now—"

"But now that, by mistake, his bodyguard was killed instead of himself, you've lost interest?"

Piper slapped his thigh. "So that's it! *Kelsey* is the stiff!"

Miss Withers nodded. "Probably he was playing Forrest, to protect his boss, and the employer was pretending to be the bodyguard. It was a smart idea and kept the process servers from getting anywhere. At any rate, I first suspected it when I learned how the man who was killed in the plane hurried in an attempt to catch the boat. He hated planes worse than you do. Yet he took the *Dragonfly*—why? Because he was being paid to be with Forrest. If it had been the other way round, do you suppose Forrest would have tried so hard to be with his bodyguard? They thought they were safe—which is why Kelsey had a night off."

Piper nodded in agreement. "I should have known by your wire," she admitted. "You said in your description that Forrest had brown hair and dressed very well. It never occurred to me that trouble and worry could change the hair from brown to gray. So I let that fool me. I should have known that you would know better than to describe an overdressed sport like the dead man as well dressed. Anyway, even after I decided, I said nothing. Because at the time I was sure that Forrest did not kill his own bodyguard. ..."

"It wouldn't be so foolish," Piper pointed out. "After all, he hired a man who resembled himself slightly. Perhaps he planned to kill him in order to establish his own death and escape the hunt?"

"You're getting smart," said Miss Withers. "Anyway, after Forrest had gone to so much trouble to take advantage of the lucky break he had, and to switch identities, it occurred to me as a good idea to let him have all the rope he wanted. So I kept a deep silence."

"It must have been a great strain on you," said the inspector unsympathetically.

"It was. He walked into the infirmary that Friday morning and learned that because of those letters in Kelsey's pocket—letters that the dead man must have picked up at the hotel desk and forgotten to give his employer—he stood a chance of stepping out of his identity. He never hesitated, Oscar. I was there, and it was smooth as silk."

"That's clear enough," the inspector admitted. "But what's this about Mack's part in the case—the blue envelope, and all the rest of it? I told you that Mack, who had a reputation of being on the level in his own crooked way, let it be known around town that he'd put up fifteen grand to have Forrest out of the way. Did he come here to pay off without knowing that the murderer he thought doing his own errand was really working for another reason?"

"I have an idea," said Miss Withers suddenly. "Your questions will be answered in a better way than this. Come back to the chief's office with me."

To Chief Britt she outlined her plan, a suggestion of extreme simplicity and charm. "I don't see what harm it could do," that worthy admitted. "If you say so. ..."

He was completely at the mercy of this busy schoolteacher and had ceased to care. Events were moving too thick and fast for Amos Britt.

"Suppose you set the party for four o'clock," suggested Piper thoughtfully. "That will prevent any of them from leaving for the mainland until tomorrow." The chief nodded his agreement.

"I have a few errands to transact," Miss Withers explained. "I can do them better alone. If you want to be useful, try and find Forrest and the girl, and keep an eye on them."

The inspector somewhat reluctantly agreed and watched Miss Withers sail off in the direction of the post office. She passed straight through that valuable building, pausing only to notice that the box which she had burgled no longer contained the substitute blue envelope which she had so carefully prepared and stuffed with folded newspaper.

She had the last link but one in her chain. With a feeling of exultation unhindered by the realization that she had committed, or caused to be committed, at least two major crimes in the past few days, and had been an accessory after the fact in another, she set off toward the hotel.

Here she waylaid Roscoe. The ancient bellhop was without power to resist this importuning lady with the authoritative voice and the crisp five-dollar bills. She told him what she wanted him to find, and where he was to find it. Then she made him swear that he would appear faithfully at the appointed time.

With a sense of duty well done, Miss Withers lay down upon her bed and slept for an hour. She was still weakish from Patrick Mack's none too tender ministrations, and unless she was sadly mistaken she would need all her strength before the day was over.

She awakened at three-thirty, bathed her face, and figuratively girded her loins for conflict, which consisted of putting on her best dress, a navy crepe-de-chine with an ecru lace collar. This gave her a real but unreasonable sense of confidence and power.

She descended the stairs and found the Devings, Kay and Marvin, exulting in the lobby.

"Isn't it gorgeous?" the young bride demanded. "Haven't you heard? The police say that they *did* discover powder burns on Mr. Mack's right hand, and that he killed himself as a confession of the murder of Forrest. And after we all give depositions at Chief Britt's office we can go!"

" 'Gorgeous' would be putting it mildly," agreed Miss Withers. They passed joyously on out into the sunshine, while the aging schoolteacher watched them with a feeling of sadness tugging at her heart.

Roscoe winked at her from the stair landing, and she nodded and strolled slowly out and along the shore. Before she had gone a dozen steps she was hailed by loud hoots upon a motor horn.

She looked up in surprise to see Ralph O. Tate, the moving-picture director, waving at her from the front seat of one of the studio trucks. Beside him were George and Tony, also waving.

"Ride?" they chorused.

She was more than willing to ride, but she refused to answer their excited questions as to the tragedy of last night. "Well, thank God they're going to close the case and stop hindering me," said Tate. "That's why I didn't mind stopping work this afternoon and coming over when I got the call."

"I imagine that everyone will be glad when it's over," Miss Withers admitted.

They whizzed along the highway, passing the newlyweds in a cloud of dust and drawing up before the curio store with a shock that almost dislodged George and Tony from their perches on the running boards.

They went in together, to find that Ruggles stood sentinel at the door to keep out the idle public and possible inopportune customers for curios. He waved them toward the rear of the store, where counters had been moved aside to make a little clearing among the thousand and one curiosities of the stock.

The three movie men sat down obediently at one end of a row of vacant chairs, but Miss Withers passed triumphantly on into the chief's office. He looked up with an equal glint of triumph in his eye.

"Will they all be here?" she asked.

"Every mother's son of 'em." He laughed. "I had old Ruggles going near crazy for a while, but he ran 'em down," Britt admitted. "He says he found Tompkins down to the pottery, trying to talk them into giving him an advance on his commissions. Ruggles says the fellow put it over, too, which shows he's smoother than I figured he was. Ruggles also got hold of the movie fellers and the newlyweds by phone, and Cap

Narveson was down on the pier. The others were around, handy."

"Good," said Miss Withers. She found herself possessed of a pair of very cold feet. "I wonder if I'm wrong, after all?" she asked herself silently. Then she shook her head. She couldn't be wrong. This was the only way to trap the killer. She peeked through the door.

The guests were arriving thick and fast. It was five minutes to four, and already most of the chairs were filled. Narveson, freckled and complacent, puffed on his villainous corncob at one end of the row. Next to him sat Dr. O'Rourke and Nurse Smith, evidently reconciled for the moment. Beyond her were the two pilots, Lew French and Chick Madden, quite evidently far from reconciled.

The second row was filling up. Miss Withers saw the newlyweds enter, hand in hand. T. Girard Tompkins propelled his paunch carefully through the aisles and sank gently onto a chair. Last of all was Hinch, manager of the airport, and the man who Miss Withers knew to be Roswell Forrest, still in company with Phyllis.

The inspector showed his face in the doorway and came directly to the back room.

"I think our friend Forrest planned to make a getaway," he whispered. "He and the girl went down to the dock to see the lawyer off on the *Avalon,* and they looked mighty wistful. But they saw me and changed their minds."

"That's odd," came back Miss Withers. "Because not so long ago Forrest tried to make his getaway in a motorboat simply because he overheard me say that you were coming!"

"Let's go," said Britt, getting up from his desk. Miss Withers noticed that his clothes hung loosely upon him, and she realized with something of a shock that the affair had taken toll of others besides herself.

"All right, folks," Britt was saying. "This is just a little formality. We're doing it wholesale to save time, so you can all be sure of getting away first thing tomorrow. I'm going to ask questions, and this lady here"—he indicated Miss Withers with a nod—"is going to take down the answers. Then after they're typed out, you can sign 'em and go."

There was a rustling in the group, and the chief continued: "I'll take you in alphabetical order. A—there aren't any A's. First on the list is Deving. Mr. Deving, we'll take you."

Marvin Deving smoothed back his hair and prepared himself.

"Were you acquainted with Roswell T. Forrest?"

"No." Miss Withers drew a little circle on a pad of paper.

"Were you acquainted with Patrick Mack?"

Again the answer was in the negative.

Chief Britt glanced at the little list of questions which Miss Withers had given him. He asked half a dozen of them, rapid-fire. They were routine, simply establishing the first notice Deving had taken of the dying man in the plane.

"That will do," said the chief. Then: "Wait a moment. I want some personal data. What's your address?"

"Long Beach Y.M.C.A. will reach me," admitted the bridegroom. "We haven't picked a house yet."

Then the chief asked a question which Miss Withers was interested in hearing answered. "When were you two married?"

"At Justice Toole's office in Long Beach, early Friday morning," said Marvin Deving.

The chief peered at the young man. "That the first time?"

"Yes, sir, for both of us."

"Never gone through a ceremony before, eh?" The question was casual.

Marvin Deving shook his head. "Not a legal ceremony," he admitted. He hesitated for a moment and then plunged ahead. "We've had words said over us several times before. It's part of our business."

There was a sudden hush in the room. For the first time, a few of the brighter minds in the crowd sensed that there was something impending here beyond the glib explanation of why the gathering had been ordered.

"Will you explain that?" said Britt. "We got to get things straight."

"I didn't want to," admitted Deving. He was flushing. "You see, Kay and I have been partners for several years. We enter marathon dances together."

Miss Withers looked up from her pretense of making notes to see Phyllis give her a look which flashed "I told you so."

Deving continued. "We've been pretty lucky in several," he said. "Along towards the end of the marathon, it's a publicity stunt for a couple to get married on the floor. We did it three or four times. You get a lot of gifts from the crowd, the local stores give clothes and furniture and so forth—but the marriages aren't on the level, because there's a minister but no license. We were too sick of each other by that time to really get hitched. So we'd split the gifts and let it go at that."

"But you really did get married finally?"

"Yes, sir. You see, we've been out of work for a while. Marathons aren't what they used to be, and other jobs are scarce, too. Suddenly we realized that we cared about each other, now that we're through with the dance racket, and so we got married and came over here on our honeymoon. Which I wish we hadn't."

Miss Withers took a deep breath. One of the few gaps in the puzzle had been filled in with a surprising ease.

"That'll do," boomed Britt. "Mrs. Deving, you heard what your husband had to say. Any additions? If not, you can sign his deposition."

Kay Deving gratefully implied that she had no thought of changing a word of "Marvy's" testimony.

"Next is Lewis French," called out the chief. That young man ceased an attempt to start a whispered conversation with the nurse and sat up straight. "Yes, sir!"

James Michael O'Rourke shifted uneasily in his chair. He was totally uninterested in French's answer to the barrage of meaningless questions. He bent his head toward the nurse's.

"Listen," he argued. "Olive, you're a good kid and you're not a bad nurse. What you want to quit and marry either of those two scalawag flyers for I don't see."

"I'm not going to marry either of them," she whispered back. "I wouldn't marry either of them if he was the last man on earth, after the way they got into a fight over me. I'd as soon marry you!"

O'Rourke ran his finger around the inside of his collar.

"Well, why don't you?" he whispered back. "Marry me, I mean. It would solve your back salary anyway."

There was a short silence, and then Nurse Olive Smith leaned a little closer toward her employer. "I'll marry you and make you pay in suffering," she whispered. And so, as the subtitles would have it, two young souls plighted their troth in the shadow of a stuffed swordfish, while over their heads Lew French told his version of the death of his passenger, and then the man who hoped to be called Barney Kelsey answered questions cautiously.

Slowly Chief Britt worked his way through the list. From La Fond he went to Madden, the other pilot, and from Madden to Morgan—which, surprisingly, was Tony's last name. Miss Withers had never heard it mentioned, and the young man seemed unsure of it himself. Narveson followed shortly, and the old seaman's Scandinavian brogue thickened splendidly for the occasion. O'Rourke himself was next and told of the theft of the body.

"In your opinion could the body of Forrest"—the chief was still in the dark—"have been dragged through the window of your infirmary by a single person?"

"It could not," said the doctor.

"Have you got any idea of how it did disappear?"

"Not unless the fact that the nurse's key was stolen from the infirmary door on the day the body was brought in could have something to do with it," said O'Rourke. "If you remember, Amos, you turned the key in the door to keep the public out. Well, I didn't notice it at the time, as I had another key. But when the last of you left that night, the key was gone."

"Another piece in the puzzle," said Miss Withers. Her plan was working perfectly—so far.

Nurse Smith was passed over very lightly, and then Ralph O. Tate had a bad ten minutes in explaining about his two-way flask. "I knew something like that was the explanation when he handed out nickel cigars at the table and then lit a perfecto for himself," Miss Withers whispered to the inspector. "That's the way a movie director's mind works."

Miss Withers was watching the portly figure of T. Girard Tompkins, without doubt the most nervous person in the room. He knew that his turn came next—and the investigation was taking a personal and a caustic trend which he had not counted upon. George Weir, the second of the two assistant directors, was on the contrary as cool, Miss Withers noticed, as a cucumber.

Chief Britt, most of the boom gone from his voice, was just beginning upon the nervous Mr. Tompkins when Miss Withers saw a dusky brown face in the doorway. It was Roscoe, and his wide smile showed all too clearly that he had been successful.

Taking a deep breath, she rose to her feet. "Excuse me for one moment," she said, "but there's something in the previous testimony that I didn't get. Before we pass on, I should like to go back a little—" Every person in the room stiffened and looked wary. What sort of a game was this, anyway?

Miss Withers's glance swept the line and fell upon the young-old face of the man who she knew to be Roswell T. Forrest.

"Mr. Kelsey," she said softly, "perhaps I missed the question, and perhaps the chief forgot to ask it. But would you mind telling us, just for the record, why you had a blister on your hand on Saturday morning last?"

Forrest's face went gray as his hair, and he did not answer. Perhaps he prayed for a momentary respite. At any rate, one arrived.

In spite of the protests of Deputy Ruggles, who seemed to have lost his authority with his badge, the ancient and sepian Roscoe was noisily forcing his way into the group. Miss Withers frowned at him, but it was too late.

"Miss Withuhs tell me to bring her dis," he announced in a loud and militant voice. He carried a pillowcase in his outstretched hand, and without further ceremony he advanced and dropped it in that lady's lap.

"Don't go, Roscoe," she said. "I may need you." The bellhop sat down at the edge of the group, in the semidarkness.

"You needn't answer the question, Mr.—er—Kelsey," Miss Withers told him. "I know the answer."

Several of the group stood up, and there was a buzz of consternation. "The Angora is sure as hell out of the sack now," murmured the inspector. He was intensely relishing the whole affair, although his small part in it irked him considerably.

"Don't anybody try to leave!" shouted Chief Britt, who had mounted his chair. "Ruggles, get to the door."

Miss Withers went placidly on. "I have a little exhibit here in this pillowslip," she said. "In a moment I'm going to show it to you all."

There was a general craning of necks, and curiosity conquered alarm, as Miss Withers counted upon its doing. Only Roswell T. Forrest showed no interest in her great disclosure. He stared at the floor as if he hoped it would open to swallow him, and did not count too heavily upon it. Phyllis's hand clutched his arm, but he did not turn.

"I'll try to make it short," Miss Withers said, "so that most of you can breathe more easily. You have guessed by now that this is more than a taking of depositions. You have been brought here under false pretenses, because it was the only way in the world to get at the truth of two bloodthirsty murders.

"I said *murders,*" Miss Withers repeated. "There is someone in this group who isn't quite what he pretends to be. Someone who killed a man in the *Dragonfly* last Friday morning. Someone who, impossible as it may seem, killed another man in the hotel last night—without leaving a fingerprint on the murder weapon or bearing a mark of powder upon his own hand. Powder burns, I understand, go right through gloves. They go through cloth or leather. It only just occurred to me that they might not go through another substance which is found in every drugstore."

The inspector, who had not the slightest idea in the world of what the woman was driving at, saw the fixed stare in Roswell Forrest's eyes and prepared for trouble. He hadn't carried a gun since he had laid aside his uniform, but he wished for one now.

With a purposely dramatic gesture, Hildegarde Withers threw open the pillowslip and disclosed a small bottle with a familiar iodine label. She uncorked it, and the smell was not that of iodine.

"Collodion, ladies and gentlemen," she announced. "Common collodion, when spread over human fingers, wipes out all chance of leaving fingerprints. When extended to the rest of the hand, this quickly drying film is a sure protection against such things as powder burns. The only difficulty is in removing it afterward, but every druggist supplies the wood alcohol which instantly dissolves it. The person who shot Patrick Mack last night availed himself of this trick—"

There was a sudden commotion at the other end of the room, to which Miss Withers paid no heed. She turned to the waiting bellhop.

"Roscoe, tell the chief where you found this bottle."

Everything had gone wrong. The explosion which she was so fervently praying for still held fire. Perhaps this last desperate move would serve.

Roscoe rose to his feet. "Yas'm. I found it just where you told me— up in the bathroom of Mistah and ..."

"Can it!" came a clear soprano. "Anybody who makes a move gets this!"

The attention of the group swung from the schoolteacher to the slim figure of redhaired Kay Deving, who crouched against the wall, her teeth exposed in a catlike snarl. In her hand was a snub-nosed automatic which Miss Withers had seen before. Her young husband lay sprawled in a dead faint on the floor.

"Don't try to stop me!" she warned. "I've got all the guts that Marvy never had." She was swiftly making for the door to the rear office, with its wide-open windows. "You'll never get me alive!" She swung the gun toward Miss Withers. "And before I go, I'll—"

Nurse Smith giggled hideously. It was that sound, more than anything else, which made the scattered members of that little group realize that instead of melodrama this was real. There stood a girl, young, beautiful still, and in her hot brown eyes flamed the tawny lights that mark the killer.

Ralph O. Tate threw himself flat upon the floor, wisely and ignominiously. Miss Withers quivered like a leaf, but stood erect, paralyzed. Phyllis La Fond said, "Don't—oh, don't—"

But it was Inspector Oscar Piper who justified his last-minute importance in this history by going into action with the smoothness of a trip hammer.

He had already noticed that the only weapon within sight was that which bulged at Chief Britt's hip. That was out of reach, and also, police fashion, was probably chained to his holster to prevent its being used by the wrong person at the wrong time. Britt was too paralyzed to think of using it.

Piper stood up and took a step toward the blazing girl. "Put that gun down," he said softly.

She whirled on him. "Why you—"

"Put it down," he repeated. "You can't shoot. You can't do anything. You're through."

He was walking steadily toward her. His pleasant gray eyes, without a shade of the Svengali in them, were steady.

"Put it down," he said. The red-flecked eyes blinked twice. "I'm coming after you—and you can't shoot," he told her, as easily as if he had made a remark about the weather.

Then suddenly it happened. He made a lunge forward and caught Kay Deving's tense young body in the embrace of a lover combined with that of a football tackler. Her body went as limp as if every bone had turned to water.

Oscar Piper turned and faced the rest of them. "Many a cop is alive today because of that little trick," he observed. "Britt, have you got any handcuffs?"

CHAPTER XXI

PANDEMONIUM reigned in the curio shop and then miraculously abdicated. Chief Amos Britt, still bewildered, swore in O'Rourke and the two movie assistants as deputies and departed with the two profane and writhing prisoners under heavy guard. Inspector Piper, flushing to the roots of his hair at the shower of awed congratulations, slipped hastily after them.

Miss Withers wanted to cry for several reasons. Then she found Phyllis La Fond's arms around her neck.

"You old darling," cried that ecstatic young lady. "I was never so scared in all my life!"

The communion between the two was instantly reestablished. "And I thought you were after—*Him.*" She turned to look at Forrest, who was waiting restlessly near the chair which had held his rigid body for the past hour.

"So it's like that, is it?" Miss Withers asked. The others were going, some rapidly, led by movie director Tate, and some with backward, friendly looks, typified in Tompkins and the captain. But finally the three of them stood alone in the rear of the curio store. It was almost dark outside, and so restful were the shadows that Miss Withers felt that she could never bear sunlight again.

"It's like that," said Phyllis. "As soon as his wife's divorce decree is final we're going to get married. I decided to take the advice you gave me one night, remember?"

Miss Withers remembered. She remembered many things, including the little man in the derby who lurked about the steamer pier with a summons in his pocket.

"I wish you two all the luck in the world," she said. "Mr. and Mrs. Forrest." At the name, the two stiffened. "You know?" Phyllis was breathless.

"I've known for some time," said the schoolteacher. "But sometimes I don't tell all I know, in spite of my talkativeness."

Forrest approached, to take her outstretched hand. "I must explain," he said. "About the blister—"

She nodded. "You need not. I know about that, too. I'm not sure what the penalty is for obstructing justice by stealing one's own identified corpse. But your originality in burying your own body should be rewarded. It was a mad thing to do, but I'm willing to make allowances for the frenzy of a man who has been hunted until his hair turns gray. You thought that getting rid of the corpse would prevent a reversal of your identification and keep Roswell Forrest dead, didn't you? It's too bad you weren't used to wheelbarrows, Mr.—er—Kelsey. That blister was a mistake. I don't suppose you noticed that someone looked in through the window of the infirmary while you were there—and was frightened away? Someone who left a peculiar heel mark?"

"I notice the heel mark," admitted the young-old man. "That's why I smudged out the others and let it stand. A red herring, you know."

"I know," agreed Miss Withers. "Marvin Deving, the jack-of-all-trades who had been a drug clerk, had the same idea as you. Only you were there first, and you hid the evidence of the newlyweds' joint crime for them."

"I've acted like a fool," he said.

"Not like a fool. Panic is temporary insanity. Look at that girl today. She had not a chance in the world of getting away, but she tried." Miss Withers gathered her handbag and umbrella. "I must go find the inspector and tell him the things he's dying to hear," she said. "Good-bye, and good luck."

She stopped short. "Where are you two going?"

"We haven't any plans," Phyllis admitted. "But we'll get back to the mainland and trust to something."

"Have you any money?"

Forrest nodded, and Phyllis shook his arm. "Don't try to fool her, it can't be done. No, we're stony. The lawyer took our last pooled dollars. But what does that matter if we get away from here?"

Miss Withers frowned. "That may not be as easy as you think," she said. "There's a process server named Hellen Damnation waiting on the passenger pier."

Forrest grew perceptibly smaller. "I have an idea," Miss Withers told him. "I hope you don't mind my interference. But in Mexico, I understand, you can get a divorce almost instantly. I don't approve in most cases, but since your wife is divorcing you in New York on a charge of desertion, I don't see any reason why you shouldn't get one of your own."

Phyllis was alight, but Forrest shook his head. "How would we get to Mexico, and what would we live on?"

Miss Withers bit the tip of her thumbnail. "Captain Narveson has been waiting these many days to join his whaling ship and sail for Mexican waters," she suggested. "If I said a word or two he might take you with him. That would get rid of the little man in the derby, too. As for money—perhaps the captain would let you work for him on his ship. Something would turn up, I feel it. And I haven't been wrong recently, have I?"

"You have not," said Phyllis.

"We'll try it," said Forrest.

"Go and pack," Miss Withers told her. "I'll catch the captain and make him wait. For a day or so I'll have real authority around here. And another thing—" She called them back. "I have a sort of premature wedding present in mind. Here's the key to my room. Take it and go in and get your own present. It happens to be hidden in the Gideon Bible at the head of my bed. Take the book without opening it, or I'll never forgive you. I'll buy another Bible for the room. You can look when you get out of sight of the island. Promise?"

They promised, faithfully. Least of all did this couple dare to think of disobeying the all-powerful schoolteacher whose hour this was.

"Good-bye," she told them, a catch in her throat. "And listen to me, you idiots. You've both made a tangled mess of your lives, but you've got a new chance to use some common sense. Try and keep out of mischief. And may God help you both."

She kissed Phyllis and shook hands again with the man who used to be Roswell T. Forrest.

Then they were gone. Miss Withers wiped her eyes carefully, powdered her nose—a habit which she had recently adopted owing to the arid California climate—and stalked out of the empty building.

Luckily it was but a few steps to the pier, where she found Captain Narveson wigwagging out to sea with a pocket flash. An answer shone from the whaler.

"Ay am going!" he told her joyfully.

"Not for half an hour," she announced. It was easier to win him over than she had thought. She shook his horny palm and took a last admiring look at his freckles. "Good-bye," she said. Then she caught sight of the inspector, who was wandering about the streets with a worried look which vanished when he saw her.

"Oscar, let's leave this place," she cried. "You're not needed any longer to pin the crimes on those terrible juveniles, are you?"

He shook his head. "They've pinned them on each other," he admitted. "I was just beginning to appreciate the scenery here. But if you insist ... get packed, and I'll phone for the police boat. I guess a visiting fellow cop is entitled to some courtesies."

As they walked wearily along the shore toward the distant hotel, gay couples passed them, bound for the Casino and its gay evening of dancing. These joyful younglings had either not heard of the day's dramatic ending to a murder investigation or else they did not suffer it to affect their lives. The island was already taking up the pursuit of pleasure where it had left off, and Miss Withers was able to remember only with an effort the glimpse she had had of the older, sterner side of Santa Catalina.

As they walked, she enlightened the inspector upon the few remaining points which were not clear. "I can understand that the marathon dance couple probably met Mack through friends in even less savory rackets," Piper said. "As you say, he may have picked Marvin Deving because the boy had been a drug clerk and could probably gain access to poisons in some shop where he had worked. The marriage was an afterthought, to give them a splendid excuse to be on the plane, and it incidentally legalized a union of some standing. But I wish you'd go on from there."

"Listen," said Miss Withers. "It's very simple. Kelsey was posing as Forrest, and vice versa. Therefore the pleasant little team of murderers picked the wrong man. They learned of the trip which the two fugitives planned to Catalina, no doubt through the reservations Kelsey made. Then they melted the chewing gum with its deadly dose and rewrapped it. Probably Marvin Deving hovered around the Hotel Senator the evening before his wedding—remember, he was out all night. He may have planned to gain access to Forrest's room. Then he saw Kelsey— who had already been pointed out to him as Forrest—leaving the hotel. This was his victim. He followed the man out to a notorious amusement spot and seized his opportunity somehow to delay him in starting the next morning. He dared not strike then—he's the weak sister of the team. Follow me?"

"I'm not far behind," admitted Piper. "Go on."

"Well, how he accomplished it I won't try to guess. Perhaps he picked Kelsey's pocket during the night and set his watch back. Perhaps he bribed one of the girl entertainers to do it—or did something to the man's rented car. Anyway, he arranged that Kelsey, who he thought was Forrest, would arrive at the Catalina Terminal after the *Avalon* sailed.

"It would be human nature for the man to take the waiting plane, if only as a supreme gesture of defiance to the ship which had gone off and left him. The murderers were cunning, never fear. They provided for the possibility that Kelsey might wait for Forrest—or for the man they thought was Forrest—and both fly together. That is why the newlyweds sat on opposite sides of the plane, with a vacant seat in front of each of them. Wherever the victim sat, he was within easy reach. And then—"

"And then I stop," said Piper. "How did they administer the gum?"

"Air sickness is all too common," said Miss Withers. "And the first thing anybody does when airsick or seasick is to chew gum. I doubt if it helps, but the idea is universal. Well, when the plane made its first lurch, Kay Deving clutched the man in front of her. She was a honeymoon bride, mind you. But she grabbed Kelsey—thinking him Forrest—instead of her husband. That was what made me suspicious, when I heard it. While she was grasping him, she deftly withdrew the package of candy gum furnished by the airplane, and substituted one stick of the poisoned gum. The murderers counted on their victim's being in such a nervous state that he would not notice the difference, or the mildly pungent taste, when he reached for something to assuage his upset stomach. He didn't."

"I'm beginning to see," admitted Piper. "And then?"

"And then they went right on with the honeymoon, which was probably partly genuine. They got worried when the death wasn't certified as natural, and Marvin went out at night to do something about it. Probably he intended to burn the infirmary and destroy the evidence. Lucky for Dr. O'Rourke that Forrest was there and frightened the young fellow away. But Marvin left a heel mark. That puzzled me for a long time, because I was dead sure that the newlyweds could have had nothing to do with the disappearance of the corpse. Marvin Deving's heel print didn't fit. He couldn't have stolen the body. It was then that I got the idea of two separate parties on the same mission. One would be the murderer—the other could only be the one *other* person who would want the body to disappear. Quite evidently, the man who hoped it would stay identified as himself! The blister on Forrest's hand proved it for me. Ergo, if he was there, and if the second party who was there was the murderer, then Forrest was not the murderer of his double. See?"

"Whee!" protested the inspector. "Go slower."

"I'm nearly through," Miss Withers promised him. "Mack arrived to pay off his tame killers and got frightened at my interference. So he devised a method of paying them which could not involve himself. He was panicky about being seen near the real killers. He rented a lock box under an assumed name and phoned Deving the combination and number. He could then go away and let the blue envelope be picked up at Deving's convenience, when the chase cooled. Only I got there first and substituted a dummy envelope. That killed Mack."

"I don't see that," said the inspector dubiously.

"I foolishly told Mack I had the money. Intent upon getting it back, the man tied me up and hurried to search my room. Marvin Deving—or maybe the girl—had already got the dummy envelope, figured out that they were being double-crossed, as you call it, and set out on vengeance bent. It was a killing for money, and they wanted their fifteen thousand. Therefore, Marvin shot down Mack, as he so richly deserved, and hurried back to the second-floor room, where he removed the coating of collodion—and passed your test. The rest, as the books say, is history."

"There's more to it than that," Piper protested. "If Forrest stole that body and buried it under the pepper tree, he's in a bad way. It's a serious offense."

"Would they extradite a man from Mexico for it?"

Piper admitted that it was very doubtful if anybody would try. "All the same, you're going to do me a favor and say nothing about it," Miss Withers advised him. "Marvin Deving sneaked out of the hotel that night—which is why his bride had to get up and answer the drunken Tompkins' pounding—and left a footprint outside the infirmary window. Since he'll hang anyway, I don't see what harm it would do to have the body-snatching laid at his door."

"Nor I," agreed Oscar Piper. He was strangely meek this afternoon. They were coming underneath the cliff between the hotel and the Casino, and Miss Withers was overjoyed to see that the handyman had already laboriously replanted the pepper tree in its proper niche—with its branches again leaning toward the highlands.

A bus whirled past them in a cloud of dust—a bus evidently chartered for the occasion. In its wake followed a startled "Hello … Good-bye …" which told Miss Withers that Phyllis and her young man were headed full tilt for the boat in which Captain Narveson now sat so impatiently puffing at his corncob pipe.

"It's over—all over," she said to the inspector. Slowly they climbed the stairs and entered her room.

"All over but handing back the fifteen grand that you lifted from the mail box," Piper reminded her. "Or are you going to keep it?"

"It's gone," Miss Withers told him. "I was puzzled for days about what to do with it. I didn't want to have it go back to Mack's friends among the racketeers and politicians of our fair Manhattan. I didn't want it to go to the murderers who had earned it. After all, it was promised to whoever would arrange the complete and final disappearance of Roswell T. Forrest. Well, that gentleman has arranged it himself, forever and ever, so I gave it to him and Phyllis for a wedding present. She doesn't know it yet, but I cut away the concordance of the Gideon Bible and pasted the blue envelope there."

The inspector sat down hard in a chair. "You'll be the death of me," he said. "You've committed everything but arson this trip. Thank heaven it's all over. Now for a nice peaceful trip back East."

"I'd like some peace," Miss Withers agreed. "You know, it's all in my imagination. But I keep hearing little screams—very muffled and far away."

"Reaction," said the inspector wisely. "You need rest and freedom from responsibility." He went across the room to get her a glass of water and then stopped short. He cocked his head to listen.

"I'm getting it, too," he admitted. "And I'm not the type to have nerves."

He whirled toward the closet and whipped open the door as if to surprise the source of his annoyance, as he actually did. He slid weakly to his knees.

"Good grief," he muttered. Then he reappeared, holding a sheet of notepaper.

"It's for you," he said. "Evidently from that high-stepping Phyllis dame. She says—'We are both simply dying to open our wedding present but will follow your advice. Wanted to give you a remembrance, so here is Mister Jones. He likes you better than he does me anyhow. I put him in the closet because he doesn't feel so well. … Lovingly, Phyd.' "

"Now wasn't that nice of her to give me Mister Jones!" Miss Withers remarked. "Bless his heart!"

The inspector rose to his feet. "Bless *whose* heart?" He was choking with internal mirth. "When you get strength enough, come here and take a look." Miss Withers, bewildered, came and saw.

Mister Jones, quivering with pride and happiness, had just become the mother of four squirming puppies.

THE END

About the Rue Morgue Press

"Rue Morgue Press is the old-mystery lover's best friend,
reprinting high quality books from the 1930s and '40s."
—*Ellery Queen's Mystery Magazine*

Since 1997, the Rue Morgue Press has reprinted scores of traditional mysteries, the kind of books that were the hallmark of the Golden Age of detective fiction. Authors reprinted or to be reprinted by the Rue Morgue include Catherine Aird, Delano Ames, H. C. Bailey, Morris Bishop, Nicholas Blake, Dorothy Bowers, Pamela Branch, Joanna Cannan, John Dickson Carr, Glyn Carr, Torrey Chanslor, Clyde B. Clason, Joan Coggin, Manning Coles, Lucy Cores, Frances Crane, Norbert Davis, Elizabeth Dean, Carter Dickson, Michael Gilbert, Constance & Gwenyth Little, Marlys Millhiser, Gladys Mitchell, James Norman, Stuart Palmer, Craig Rice, Kelley Roos, Charlotte Murray Russell, Maureen Sarsfield, Margaret Scherf, Juanita Sheridan and Colin Watson..

To suggest titles or to receive a catalog of Rue Morgue Press books write 87 Lone Tree Lane, Lyons, Colorado 80540, telephone 800-699-6214, or check out our website, www.ruemorguepress.com, which lists complete descriptions of all of our titles, along with lengthy biographies of our writers.